Ivy

Ivy

E. R. (Flip) Flippen

iUniverse LLC
Bloomington

IVY

iUniverse books may be ordered through booksellers or by contacting:

iUniverse LLC
1663 Liberty Drive
Bloomington, IN 47403
www.iuniverse.com
1-800-Authors (1-800-288-4677)

ISBN: 978-1-4917-2844-4 (sc)
ISBN: 978-1-4917-2845-1 (e)

Printed in the United States of America.

iUniverse rev. date: 03/28/2014

Dedication

Ivy is dedicated to a man who drove a 1930 Dodge to college and, like modern medicines, has two names.

His generic name is J.E. McQueen, and his trade or marketing name, is L.Q. Jones. He has had great success as a character actor. I expected his success from those days when we collected coins to form a quarter that purchased a tad more than a gallon of gas so we could get to the midnight show on Saturday nights.

J.E. once told Louis L'Amour that Hondo was the only thing he wrote that was worth a damn. Louis' reply was that he had earned thirty-two million dollars with his writings; people must have liked some of his other works.

I have yet to earn thirty-two dollars with mine, but writing *IVY* has been a pleasure. Part of that pleasure is writing this dedication.

"Way to go, Mac!"

Author's Note

In 1876, A.W. Ormond and Mary Ormond, his daughter, visited a place in Florida Mary would later name Tarpon Springs.

Artists were among the first to settle there. Printing had been in existence for centuries, but newspapers, magazines, and posters depended on the work of artists to transfer images to the public. It was an age when artists were plentiful and popular.

When George Inness, a highly successful landscape artist of the Hudson River School, made Tarpon Springs his winter home, wealthy visitors began making it theirs also, but a shallow coral reef in the Gulf of Mexico gave the town its permanent wealth which was sponges.

In 1879, Margarite Doss, a tall Negro native of Jamaica arrived in Tarpon Springs with her mistress, a landscape artist, and their visit was business, not pleasure, so as soon as they settled in a hotel room, Margarite went directly to the sponge docks where Marley Simpson, a pearl diver from Key West eager to sell his wares since the area was attracting other divers, approached the lady as she walked passed each stall feeling sponges, and he politely asked if he could be of help.

She, liking his smile, returned his with one of her own, and asked, "Are there softer sponges to be found here?"

"You have found the right fellow," he replied. "The market is brisk, and in their haste for profit, the other divers do not squeeze out the gurry properly. I work twice as hard. I pound and squeeze every sponge until I am satisfied. Other divers do not spend so much time, half I am told. It is my nature, taught me by my loving mother, to do honest work. Come. Look on my boat."

They had addressed each other in English as precise and correct as the Lords and Ladies of the British Crown, yet they were not the white of royals, their dark skins rejecting the notion.

Recognizing the dialect meant they shared a similar island heritage, they became at ease as buyer and seller and walked through the market place and down the dock to a small wooden boat whose deck was laden with burlap bags filled with sponges.

Margarite Doss, after squeezing half a dozen sponges, said, "Mister Simpson, these are fine sponges, exactly what I have been seeking."

The lady had not asked a price, and, needing a number before he could suggest one, Marley Simpson said, "I am pleased. How many would you like?"

"First, can you cut them into smaller sizes?"

"Yes, madam. How small?"

"Very small. And thin. About two inches round."

"Madam, I am proud to say my sponges are as fine as any in the world, but cutting them so small will ruin them for bathing."

"Mister Simpson, they will not be used for bathing."

Marley Simpson's quick mind was puzzled. What, it asked, were the ladies going to use his sponges for if not for bathing? Mindful that he needed the money, he did not let his mouth ask the question.

"As for the amount," Margarite Doss continued, "we want you to fill a Jenny Lind trunk. Come and get the trunk. When it is full, come to our hotel, and we will gladly pay you two hundred dollars."

Marley Simpson would have done it for fifty.

Margarite Doss suspected that, but she was delighted her mistress could be overly generous.

Our days may come to seventy years, if our strength endures, yet the best of them are but trouble and sorrow, for they quickly pass, and we fly away.

Psalm 90

Chapter One

Foley, Texas

1880

Sam Ordway was a slender man, a little taller than average, his face the dark tan color of oiled leather made so by a never ending battle with cattle country sun. He was seventy years old but looked sixty, because he was still wiry lean with muscle and walked as straight as a bronze statue that moved.

He had been reflecting back on those years all morning, for he realized his courage, once fiery red, was turning yellow as time drew near for him to face what he judged would be his last big confrontation on earth. He found some satisfaction in knowing his courage had yet to fail completely; it was still brassy orange like the tint of the saffron powder Claire Winslow made when she baked.

For the last twenty years Sam Ordway had been town marshal of Foley, Texas. The earlier years had seen him as soldier, miner, cowhand, and rancher. His father was Sergeant John Ordway, one of the original members of President Thomas Jefferson's Corp of Discovery known to the world as the Lewis and Clark Expedition that traveled from Saint Louis to the Oregon Territory and back in the years 1803-06.

Sergeant John Ordway was chosen to keep the official journal of the Expedition because he was the most educated of the group, including Messrs. Lewis and Clark themselves. Sam had only a copy of his father's journal. The original was in the Smithsonian donated by Captain Lewis Meriwether and Lieutenant William Clark. The two leaders gave John Ordway three hundred dollars for it, and he spent the money on an apple and peach orchard located on the half section of land the government warranted him for making the expedition. The three hundred and twenty acres of land was at New Madrid, and the venture was highly successful until the orchid was lost to the New Madrid earthquake. The quake had been so violent it lifted sections of the Mississippi River high enough so the river actually began flowing backward in places.

The family escaped with only their lives making it necessary for the family to separate. It was then Sam began an odyssey that could be ending with the confrontation in Foley.

Sam had two hand-written letters his father had posted to his mother back in St. Louis, so they had some value. The letters, a few books, some gold nuggets, a small bank account, his clothes, boots, two horses, a saddle, Colt, Winchester, double-barreled shot-gun, and a small three-room house on one improved acre on Cedar Street one block north of Main Street in Foley, were the only things Sam Ordway owned. He wondered if those possessions were all his life had counted for.

"I have memories, by God; I have a history book full of them," Sam muttered with only himself listening. Realizing he had let his mouth speak private thoughts aloud, he chastised his inner self by adding, "Afternoon is a poor time to be daydreaming."

He looked out the window then, just in time to see young Jimbo Winslow running across Main Street as fast as his pudgy legs could carry him.

Sam, pulling his boots down off the battered old desk, got to his feet. There could be no mistake as to where the youngster was headed. The marshal's office with its four-cell jail sat in the center of the block, solitary as a leper, isolated from the homes and businesses of Foley. The citizenry and Old Bill Foley had taken great care to separate the jail from the rest of the town when they chose to begin building it along the banks of the narrow San Antonio River under the shade of its thick but humble trees; they loved law and order and despised the sight of drunks.

Sam, standing in the open door now, listened to the sound of Jimbo's boots thumping on the boardwalk racing toward him. He expected the widow Winslow needed her milk cow penned. The Jersey was like a magician at getting through the fence. Perhaps the widow needed some other manly task, for Sam afforded the lady the strength of his services from time to time since she had no other man around. He suspected, no, he was sure; the widow needed a masculine service he might be too old to provide, because on occasion she pressed her shapely bosom against him.

Sam felt sorry for her in that respect. Most of the men who worked on the two big ranches were Mexican. The others were young and shiftless, and the shopkeepers were all married; the widow deserved better.

"Marshal! Marshal!" the freckled-faced youngster yelled bouncing up the boardwalk, his voice high with excitement, "The stage is coming back. Somethin's wrong. A holdup, maybe!"

Sam turned back quickly and reached for his double-barreled shotgun in the gun rack. He wanted the weapon as a show of force for the citizenry and to please the impressionable young man. The stage had left Foley going south an hour ago; if it had been robbed, it would not be returning with robbers in it.

"Come on, Jimbo. Let's go see what the trouble is."

Main Street, following the pattern of western cow towns, was plenty wide, wide enough so that Twelve-team freight wagons could turn around without having to go past one end of town or the other to do it, and the pair took off at a trot with Jimbo Winslow leading, tugging the marshal's left hand. With their boots stirring up little dust devils, they angled across Main Street passing the Cattleman's Hotel heading for the stage office next to it where the pair stood waiting impatiently at the hitch rail outside the Butterfield office looking intently down the road at the stage rumbling into town toward them.

Moments later, the stage pulled to a stop in front of the Cattleman's Hotel before it got to the stage office where they were standing.

Mystified, Sam Ordway, tugging the child's hand now, hurried down the boardwalk to the parked stage then he pulled up suddenly when he realized this was not the regular stage; there was no Butterfield sign painted on the door, no marking at all, and the driver was not the Butterfield driver.

Sam, Jimbo in one hand, his shotgun cradled in his other arm, moved quickly passed the lathered team, and the two pulled up to the side of the coach just as the driver jumped down and was beginning to open the door of the stage.

"What's wrong?" Sam asked tapping the stranger's shoulder. "The team's spent. You runnin' from somthin'?"

"Nope," the man replied turning to face him. "It's Miss Ivy's orders. She likes to be off the road before dark, and we didn't know the exact distance," and he turned and opened the stagecoach door.

Adding to Sam's confusion, a rider appeared from behind the coach mounted on as fine an animal as Sam had ever seen, and he dismounted at the hitch rail forcing Sam and Jimbo to move aside.

"Sorry," the rider said.

Sam grabbed the rider's shirtsleeve as the man was turning to escort whoever was on the stage into the hotel. "I know your face," he said. "You look to be John Wesley Hardin. Are you?"

"His younger brother, Matthew," the rider replied. "I bother easy, but I'll be no bother unless I'm bothered. I'm the lady's bodyguard, not a desperado like John Wesley. Besides, your dodger's a bit outdated. John Wesley's not wanted. He petitioned the governor for a pardon and got one. He studied law in prison, and he's practicing in El Paso."

"Didn't know that," Sam replied apologetically.

Sam's next surprise was stepping down from the stage. She was a noble looking Negro woman. She was tall and wore a white turban wrapped around her head. When both feet were firmly on the ground, seeing Sam and the boy, she smiled to each one. The driver had said Miss Ivy. Was this Negro lady Ivy? Before his mind could find an answer, gracefully descending behind the black woman was the prettiest white woman Sam Ordway had ever seen. She was stunningly beautiful with a serenely innocent face and ringlets that let her hair fall gently to her waist as she made the descent. She had to be royalty from some far off land; there was no other explanation, for she descended from the step of the coach like a fairytale princess. Sam knew immediately she was Ivy.

Sam Ordway was mystified at her presence, and his face showed his consternation. It asked what's going on as plainly as if it had said the words aloud. Did this Ivy woman own a private stagecoach? And why in God's name had she come to Foley? Foley is nowhere. The nearest honest-to-goodness town is Granite Falls, the railroad stops there. The nearest honest-to-goodness city is San Antonio, a good forty miles north.

Just then the Ivy woman noticed Sam, and she, too, smiled. When their eyes met it was as if there was no one else in the world except the two of them. Her smile seemed for Sam and Sam only. She had that kind of magic about her.

Sam shied. His eyes quickly found the cracks between the planks in the boardwalk beneath his feet to look at, and the woman swept into the hotel.

"Where's the real stage?" Jimbo asked.

"Probably at the half-way station by now," Sam Ordway replied, but he was still thinking about the Ivy woman. Few women are rich enough to own their own stagecoach. And she has her own private driver, and a private bodyguard. Only two kinds of rich women travel on the frontier. Women who own fine whorehouses and ones married to rich cattlemen. He doubted the most popular madams in Fort Worth, Denver, New Orleans, or even San Francisco had that kind of money, and the Ivy woman, Sam judged from years past, seemed too young to be one of them. A rich madam might travel with a Negro servant. He was one hundred percent certain a millionaire Cattle Baron's wife would not. A Cattle Baron's wife would have a Mexican or a poor white servant, but never a Negro, so that left the Ivy lady a rich mystery. What, and the question became an echo in his mind, would such a rich woman be doing in Foley?

Made stationary by the mystery of the Ivy woman, Sam Ordway was caught flatfooted again when another man rushed passed him. This time the face was one he recognized. It was his grandson, Young Bill Foley. Sam knew immediately why he was here. Old Bill Foley owned the Cattleman's Hotel, and everything else in Foley. Foley was Old Bill's town, lock, stock and barrel, land and sky, and Young Bill was its guardian.

Guessing someone had alerted Young Bill about the Negro lady, Sam heard the hotel clerk say, "Ain't no colored lady allowed in *this hotel*. She'll have to stay in the livery stable with the horses."

Sam knew Young Bill had come to back up the clerk, but Young Bill's eyes found the Ivy woman's face, then his mouth hung open and words wouldn't come out.

"I'll gladly pay double," the Ivy lady said with a voice akin to an angel's as she was bringing out a sheaf of bills, a roll of twenty dollar certificates that could easily add up to four or five hundred dollars from the look of them; bait for any highwayman; no wonder she had a body guard, but why carry that much money?

The clerk's eyes eyed the money and got bigger but he managed, "I got my orders. No Coloreds in this Hotel!"

Young Bill never saw the money. His eyes didn't leave the Ivy woman's face. He finally found his voice, but his eyes never left her face when he said, "Homer, let the lady do as she wishes. I'll take responsibility."

"But, Mister Foley, you'll ruin the reputation of the Hotel. Once it's noted a Colored spent even one night under our roof, why no respectable white, man or woman, will want to stay here."

Young Bill Foley, grandson or not, was not one to miss an opportunity to show off his authority, and he slipped between the desk clerk and the lady, swept off his white Stetson hat exposing the same beautiful auburn hair all of his male Irish ancestors had been born with, and he murmured in his sweetest low Irish voice, "This is my town, Miss. I'll do my best to accommodate your wishes. Homer, give them however many rooms the lady wants."

The Ivy woman responded by extending her hand and saying to Young Bill, "I'm Ivy Vanderbilt. Thank you for being so kind."

"Bill Foley," Young Bill replied taking the lady's hand. "I'm fortunate enough to own the biggest ranch around here, *and* this town. I welcome you to stay as long as you like."

There was only one thing wrong with what Young Bill said, Sam Ordway mused; Old Bill ain't dead yet. Its true Old Bill never leaves the ranch anymore, so Young Bill has been running things for two years. Seems that Young Bill's mind has decided everything is his already.

The desk clerk, having lost a battle he fought with Southern passion, grudgingly turned the guest book around to Ivy Vanderbilt, and she registered for three rooms then changed her mind.

Turning to face Young Bill, she said, "You're being very kind to accept us. In return, to show I take exception to your desk clerk's fears, I'll have Margarite stay in my room and take two rooms for the three of us; my driver stays with our coach. If anything unkind is said after we leave, you may explain I respect her enough for us to stay together. She is my associate, and she is of Jamaican descent, not an American Negro."

Sam Ordway knew that some people would take great store in knowing the woman was from Jamaican stock, but the races were no different from one or another, like the Indian tribes. It made no difference to him. He had married a Chinese lady and, at times, lived with more Mexicans than Americans, and he knew Young Bill, who had lived four years in the North where he had been educated at the Irish University of Notre Dame, would know there was no difference in the two races except in speech.

"You'll find me most tolerant," Young Bill was telling her, "and so are our people. You'll find this true if you visit us for any length of time. Will you be staying long?"

"I'm not sure. We're looking for business property and ranchland if I see land that I like. I do portraits when I find someone interesting, but I paint landscapes primarily so any ranchland I purchase must have dramatic scenery. Maybe you can help."

"My pleasure. Since I own the town, the business part of your problem is taken care of, but land from the two big ranches is not for sale. I'll show you some mighty beautiful places that should catch your eye. Some of the small spreads are nice; especially when autumn visits us and turns the tree leaves rainbow colors. I haven't heard of any of them in trouble, but visiting them may keep you around a spell. It will be a pleasure to take you to a different one every day and make inquiries."

"Thank you very much, Mister Foley. I accept your offer. You have a lovely town. Quaint and clean. It's virtually unknown. I'm surprised more people haven't made it their home."

"Townsites are restricted. Only my father, my mother, or me decide on who lives here."

"Oh," Ivy said, plainly showing surprise. Deciding it was not something in her interest to pursue at the moment, she asked, "Can we begin the tour tomorrow?"

"Suits me," he answered. "Will you be rested enough for an early breakfast?"

"Is that an invitation?"

"It is. Is six too early?"

"No indeed. I love seeing a day begin. Do we meet here?"

"No. Next door. The Bluebonnet Café. Do you ride?"

"Well enough. I won't need a buggy if that's what you mean."

Young Bill shuffled his boots, then, encouraged that the lady had accepted his invitation, he chose to be even more forward, and he said, "You're the prettiest woman I've laid eyes on. Please accept that my intentions are honorable, but I cannot wait until tomorrow to find out if you are a married woman. Are you?"

"You are not bashful, Mister Foley," Ivy Vanderbilt answered.

"It is not my intent to be impolite, Miss Vanderbilt. Or is it Mrs. Vanderbilt?"

Ivy Vanderbilt's answer began with a smile, and she paused momentarily thinking about her answer then said pleasantly, "I'm pleased to say that it is *Miss* Vanderbilt."

Sam was close enough to hear Young Bill exhale gently, not surprised that he was taken with the woman's beauty.

"Now that I know its *Miss* Vanderbilt," Young Bill Foley said, "I will have difficulty sleeping tonight waiting to meet you for breakfast in the morning."

"Flattery is no longer one of my weaknesses, Mister Foley, because I've been spoiled by it all my life," the lady answered.

Her remark took some wind out of Young Bill's sails. "I'll remember that, Miss Vanderbilt, but I still look forward to tomorrow. We'll be gone all day, so I'll have the cook at The Bluebonnet Café make us a couple of lunches."

"Make it three. My bodyguard will go with me."

"Three lunches it will be," said Young Bill never showing a hint of disappointment to an unexpected chaperone.

Turning to the desk clerk, he said, "Homer, show them to their rooms. I'm sure they want to freshen up a bit before supper."

When Ivy and her group made their way up the stairs following the desk clerk, Young Bill turned and walked through the lobby to rejoin his regular poker game at the Rocking F's Town House across Main Street passing a stranger who had entered quietly moments before. The stranger had only one hand, a left hand, and with it he touched the tip of his hat as Young Bill passed. Young Bill must have had his imagination trying to surround the mysteriousness of Ivy Vanderbilt, because he failed to acknowledge the man or his gesture.

Sam Ordway had seen the man enter and remain by the door while the situation with the desk clerk was resolved. Now the stranger made his way to the desk passing Sam as he went. The man's range clothes were good ones but were ill fitting because of the shape of his body. The War, Sam thought. A lot of men lost limbs in the War. This one had lost his right arm, and Sam flinched inwardly understanding how much pain the artillery shrapnel must have caused when it hit him twisting his body grotesquely ultimately causing the loss of the arm as part of its damage.

The stranger slipped a furtive glance as he passed Sam then continued to the desk where he waited for the clerk to return.

Sam followed, and for the second time today caught himself tugging on a stranger's sleeve, a strange circumstance for it to happen twice, and he addressed the man. "It's strange to find you here," he said.

"Why, so?" he answered.

"I think you have family here. Why not stay with your mother?" Sam was still holding the sleeve of the stranger's lone useful hand.

"Have the child go away and we'll talk," the stranger whispered.

Jimbo Winslow had slipped inside the lobby and was standing by the big glass window, and Sam went to him and said, "Jimbo, wait outside for me. I'll be out in just a minute."

Dutifully, Jimbo trotted out and waited on the veranda.

When Sam returned, he faced the stranger eye-on-eye and said, "The Big War has been over a long time, so I could be wrong. When we got word on the other boy, knowing you two were together, we thought you were dead same as him. I take you to be Wyatt Winslow."

"It's true. I'm Wyatt."

"I don't see how you sat a horse long enough to get here, you're so twisted up. I knew you because of your eyes. They're the same color as your mother's. I'd know them anywhere."

"Don't tell her. You won't, will you?"

"That depends on why you're here.

Moving closer to Sam, Wyatt Winslow lowered his voice to a whisper, "I'm here to kill your grandson for what he did to Chastity. I'm fast enough to do it now."

"You had better know what you're asking for, Wyatt," Sam shot back. "Young Bill is fast with a Colt. His mother paid Lyle Sanford, the quick-draw artist in Buffalo Bill Cody's Wild West Show, to train him."

Sam realized, after he said it, that it was not the right thing to say. Wyatt Winslow would be a touchy man now. Reminding him that someone might be better would not sit well with him, but Young Bill could handle a Colt .45. Still, such a confrontation could be dicey for either man.

"It won't matter who taught him, Sam. I'm faster. And I doubt he's ever been under fire; I have. Plenty. I figured he'd be good. Figured he'd be well taught, because Young Bill has been given the best of everything. That includes my sister. I'll bet Chastity was the best of his virgins."

Sam knew the conversation was over. Wyatt Winslow was blind. Having his mother's eyes did not let him see with her compassion. Wyatt was going to challenge Young Bill come hell or high water, and Sam knew Wyatt Winslow, because of his hate and determination, had the edge.

Chapter Two

Sam Ordway spent a restless night. When daylight came, he dressed and made coffee. Sitting on his back porch watching the pale glow in the east become the sun, he was still meditating. When he finished his second cup, uncharacteristically because his natural bent was neatness, he left the cup on the table beside his rocker without washing it and walked to the barn and saddled his horse then rode downtown to the Bluebonnet Café to eat breakfast. He had decided to stir the stew that was brewing before it began to boil.

When he got there, Young Bill Foley and Ivy Vanderbilt had just entered with Matt Hardin following, and the three chose a table Sam had to pass on his way to a seat at the counter.

Young Bill and Ivy both smiled when he passed, and they said together, "Good morning, Sam," and Sam was flattered and secretly flustered learning that the Ivy woman had remembered his name. Matt Hardin, seated with them, acknowledged him with a nod only, no smile. Sam noticed Young Bill and Ivy quickly returned to their earlier conversation as if Hardin did not exist.

Just as Sam figured he would be, Wyatt Winslow was already there seated singly at a small table for two where he could watch Young Bill. Sam had already guessed Wyatt would continue to stalk his grandson until the two met with six guns deciding who would live and who would die.

Breakfast finished, Sam paid and waited outside for Wyatt Winslow. In a few moments, Young Bill and Ivy Vanderbilt passed him continuing their conversation totally unaware of a dour Matthew Hardin at their heels, and they waved to Sam as they mounted their waiting horses then turned west; Hardin following.

A moment later, Wyatt Winslow appeared, and Sam motioned him over with a head nod. "Wyatt," he said, "I've decided I need to tell your mother. I don't want to. Your mother's finally comfortable, and Chastity's gone somewhere to move on with her life. Why come back now?"

"Couldn't come any sooner. It took a long time for me to heal and learn to draw with only a pinched up left hand. That's my reason."

"Why don't you leave the past buried. Nothing good comes from digging it up. I'd like to spare your mother."

"Me too, Sam. I'm going to wait another day. I intend to think on it some more."

"Do that," Sam replied turning to go then turning back said, "Are you wanted anywhere, Wyatt?"

"No, Sam. I've shot up more men than I like to remember since the sacred War of Secession, but they've been clean fights. I won't say I didn't start most of them; I did. On purpose. Some for spite over the War. It was practice. Pure hate will do that to a man."

"I see," Sam replied thinking about Wyatt's hate. Morbid hate developed during the War of Secession had carried over into unnecessary peacetime hates by men of both sides.

Wyatt was one of those men. Sam had little hope he could undo Wyatt's hate at this late stage, so he said, "I'll give you until tomorrow. Change your mind, Wyatt. For your mother's sake."

"What about Daddy's sake, Sam?"

Wyatt Winslow was once a tall man. Even with his cramped body, he was somehow managing to stand straight enough to meet Sam's eyes, and his gaze was arrow straight and unblinking; he meant for the remark about his daddy to soak in.

Sam Ordway had no answer. His silence left Wyatt Winslow to justify his cause, "I should have done it when Dad had his stroke, but I was crippled and worried about Momma's grief. Daddy went to an early grave because of Young Bill's dallying with Chastity. Momma lived over it, and Chastity's well off. I'm here for Chastity but mostly for Dad. He was a respected minister in this town. There's no one to speak for him but me. After I meet Young Bill, my father, David Daniel Winslow, can lie in his grave like an honorable man."

The facts were true enough. Wyatt's dad had had an apoplectic fit when Chastity finally told the family she was pregnant and Young Bill Foley was the father but refused to marry her. Instead, he had given her and the expected child one thousand dollars to leave for an unknown big city where the disgrace would be bearable. The stroke made Dave Winslow a cripple that night; then he died. Chastity left town after the funeral and had not been heard from since, a sad circumstance for her mother who would have adored a grandchild, even an illegitimate one. After things calmed down, Sam had helped Claire Winslow sell their small ranch and move to town. Claire loved gardening and was just now finding some happiness growing flowers and raising herbs she made into fragrances, flavorings, and spices. Sam would not have known there was such a thing as saffron except Claire giggled and declared boldly she crushed male and female parts to make the powder she mixed with egg whites to color the icing on his birthday cake. Her smile showing pride in her handiwork as she cut the cake was proof that Claire Winslow was finally looking beyond the sadness of Dave's death.

Sam and Wyatt's conversation began outside the Bluebonnet Café door. As it progressed, they moved to one side as a few drovers and drummers passed. Separating with nothing settled, Wyatt Winslow turned and stepped down off the boardwalk ready to mount his horse.

Quickly following, Sam caught himself tugging on Wyatt's shirt sleeve again and he asked, "Wyatt, you know a lot about what happened to Chastity for someone who never came home from the War. How did you find out? Tell me."

"It ain't something' I like to talk about. Let it ride."

"Wyatt, as town marshal, it's true I can't stop a fair fight, but Dave Winslow, Old Bill Foley, and me drove the first herd up here together. With what you propose to do, one of my friend's sons will die; you or Young Bill. For God's sake, talk to me."

"Not here. Too many ears passin' by."

"The jail, then. Ride over to the jail. I'll be right behind you."

Sam headed for the jail taking long and hurried strides letting his mind sort out what he could about Wyatt Winslow's mood and plans. Wyatt was both right and wrong. The western code of honor made him right, but his mother's misery would come again and a new wound would open where the old one had healed, that made him wrong.

Wyatt Winslow waited on his horse at the hitch rail in front of the jail. He did not get down, and Sam had to look up at him.

"Anyone in your jail?" he asked.

"One prisoner. A Mexican vaquero. One of Waterman's crew."

"Most Mexicans understand English. In that case, we'll talk out here. Sam, I'm gonna tell you this up front. You won't stop me. I'm gonna face Young Bill on account he caused Chastity's disgrace and what that disgrace did to Dad. When it's done, Daddy will finally rest. Momma may hurt a little more, but her hair can't turn any grayer. She'll get over it."

"Maybe. Maybe not. That ain't open for debate just now. Tell me how you know what you know. You came home after the War, didn't you?"

"Yeah, Sam, I did. I wished a thousand times over I hadn't, but I did."

"Figured as much walkin' over here from the café. You gonna tell me?"

"It ain't something' I like to see in my mind let alone tell it out loud."

"I understand, Wyatt, but in a way, you owe me. I look after your mother and a kid brother you never had a chance to know. We ate a lot of meals at the same table."

"Understood. I'll make it short, Sam. No questions after. I'll tell it and be gone. I don't intend to dwell on it."

"Fair enough, Wyatt."

"We went through a lot of scrapes during the War without a scratch, but Douglas and me finally got it in sixty-three at Gettysburg when Pickett sent us marching across a half mile of open ground from Seminary Ridge up Cemetery Ridge like we were puppets in Napoleon's army instead of men in Robert E. Lee's. I lived, and I woke up a prisoner in one of those big ambulance wagons the North used to do portable butcherin' and found my body chewed up and a stub where my arm once was and wished I'd died and gone to hell. Hell would have been a lot less painful. When the war was over, like any kid, I wanted to go home, but what I could see of me was too pitiful. I lived by begging and relieving drunks of what money they had. I went to Saint Louis; thanks to farmer's kind enough to help me into their wagons. I finally had enough money, with petty stealing and begging, to buy a good horse, and I headed for home. With the war and healing, I was gone almost ten years.

"Well, Foley is far enough from the nearest town that a rider will not get here much before sundown unless he lathers his horse, so it was late when I neared our little ranch. From the road I thought I saw Chastity wanderin' along the path that runs through our little pear orchid. I recognized her, but she was a grown woman; when I left she was a young girl. I couldn't understand what she was doin' that far from the house that late and I called her name to make sure who she was then galloped to her when she called my name in wonderment. The sun was behind me, and she saw I had lost an arm when I jumped down, but she didn't see my face or the rest of me. When we hugged, she jumped back after feelin' my body, and she pulled my face around into what was left of the daylight. I should have turned around right then, because what I saw in her eyes I'd see again when Momma saw me. I tried to settle things down, so I asked Chastity why she was such a long way from home so late in the day, and she told me about her bein' pregnant with Young Bill Foley's child, and she was out walking tryin' to get enough courage to tell Momma and Daddy.

"She was grateful I showed up. Chastity thought God sent me. My showin' up was the distraction she needed to tell our folks about her condition. Then we met Daddy out lookin' for Chastity. He made light of my stub; said if I could learn to eat left handed I could learn to rope that-a-way. At the house, Momma came out to see about all the commotion and we went inside. That's when she saw what I was really like, and Daddy, too. Daddy seemed to get over it, Momma didn't. I went outside and washed up at the pump 'cause supper was already on the table, and she was setting a plate for me. I could hear them. Momma was cryin'. Daddy was tryin' to soothe her. All of a sudden, Chastity blurted out that she was pregnant and Young Bill refused to marry her. I guess the tension had been building up inside her so long it just exploded. There was a long silence, and the next second Momma screamed."

Wyatt was looking inside himself seeing the past, and to Sam it was as if the rider on the horse had turned into a stone statue. The man mounted on the animal was lost in eternity, his memory refusing to let go of events long since over. Sam respected the silence.

Finally Wyatt Winslow said, "Well, Sam, I don't believe in God no more. When you see the evil war does then come home and see your daddy like that, you don't believe in anything anymore."

"I understand, Wyatt."

"Sam, you knew the man my daddy was. Dave Winslow was strong, and something he couldn't see struck him. It brought him to his knees. When I got to him his face sagged on one side, and he kept tryin' to talk, but only blabber and drool came out. I tell you, Sam, I thought I had been roughed up so bad by the War nothing could touch me inside, but seein' Daddy droolin' cut me."

"Sad for me to even hear," Sam said making an effort to console Wyatt.

"Daddy kept tryin' to talk and couldn't. Best we could figure was he had a terrible headache because he kept holdin' his head in his hands and rockin' back and forth. Since the War most every ranch has laudanum, and Momma finally got some down him. Pretty soon, he was peaceful, so Momma didn't see any need to ride into town to get Doc Wedgewood at night. We were pretty sure there was not much a doctor could do. We were going to put him in the wagon and take him to town the next morning if he was still with us. The whole time Chastity was bawlin' like a calf without a mother, and she finally settled down, too. None of us slept that night."

"I suppose not," Sam said, then asked, "When did you decide to turn around and leave without so much as a word to anyone?"

"About daylight. After Daddy died. It was Momma's decision. She reasoned I wouldn't be able to work our four acres with one hand, so she'd have to sell it. Like Chastity, she said I was a godsend. I had been sent to take care of Chastity. I was to go with her to Saint Louis where she would have her child quietly. Sam, I didn't see where I was a godsend. Way I figured if God had made the plan, it was a poor one; Daddy would not have had the stroke if Young Bill had not got Chastity in a family way and left her."

"No use tryin' to figure out things like that, Wyatt. Is Chastity still in Saint Louis? Did she have a boy or girl?"

"Yeah, she's there, and she had a pretty girl. Most beautiful baby I ever saw. Has Bill's hair; you know, the color of the setting sun, soft auburn swirls. Young Bill has missed something' to make a man proud."

"Makes me wonder why Young Bill didn't want Chastity for a wife. Did she ever say?"

"I never asked. No use. I knew she wouldn't say."

"Well, I thought if I could get you to talk I might find something' that would ease up things between you and Young Bill. Looks to me that things are where they started. One last thing, Claire would love to see her grandchild."

"Chastity wants Momma to see her grandchild, too. She's in Saint Louis alright, but she won't come home. It won't work. We passed off as a married couple until the baby came. Even with my face as messed up as it is Cassie's hair color pretty much proved I wasn't her father. Chastity don't want the child to know anything about her real daddy. If she comes home everyone will know who the real father is. I tell you, Sam, Chastity's pretty hostile toward Young Bill, thinks he's not much of a human bein', don't want her daughter associating with such. She don't ever want to see Young Bill again or for him to know what a pretty daughter he sired."

"Claire could go to her. That would work."

"It would. I brought a letter from Chastity to Momma. The reason I brought it, it's got money in it. It's in my hotel room. We counted on you seein' that Momma gets it. Without tellin' her I brought it, of course. Let her think it came in the mail. She'll say only fools send money in the mail, but don't tell her otherwise."

"Be glad to."

"Chastity misses Momma and wants her to see Cassie. She's well off enough to send money for the trip. Like I said, it's in the envelope."

"I'm leavin' town in a few minutes. Here's a key to the jail. Leave the letter in my desk drawer and the key at the hotel desk."

"That's mighty good of you, Sam."

"Well, Wyatt, I said nothing had come of this conversation, but something' came of it after all. Claire will get to see a daughter she's missed greatly and her grandchild. I'd like to see her face when she sees Chastity and Cassie. I can't imagine a better gift, except you not tryin' to kill my grandson and maybe not getting yourself killed."

"Don't know about that yet, Sam. Like I promised you, I'm going out to the ranch and sit by Daddy's grave for a bit. Anyone livin' there?"

"Nope. House stands as it did along with four acres surrounding it. The ranchland around it belongs equally to Old Bill Foley a Whiskey Bill Waterman. They bought it."

"It figures. I won't run any of their cows. Don't want to be accused by them two rich men of running tallow off their stock. See you tomorrow, Sam. The letter with the money will be in your desk drawer."

Chapter Three

Walking briskly, passing business places places he normally stopped at on his morning round, Sam tipped his hat or gave a quick nod to bystanders while making straight for the livery stable where he waited impatiently for the day hostler to saddle his other horse. Part of Sam's pay was having one horse stabled, curried, fed and paid for by the City Father's who were, in reality, only Old Bill Foley. Bill Foley insisted on it. Old Bill also paid for the upkeep of a matched team for the surrey kept there for his and Abbey's town use even though the team was not used nowadays.

Sam had his pick of any horse or horses on the Rocking F range, but he preferred keeping his own mustang in his barn at home as his spare mount. It was his choice. It gave him another small measure of independence.

Martin O'Malley owned the stable, but rheumatism in his knees was so bad he rarely came around anymore hiring two young farm boys who took shifts and kept the place open until ten at night. Both boys excelled at laziness so the place was gradually running down. Leather was rarely oiled, and Martin's rent wagons, an old hay-hauling wagon, a buckboard, and Studebaker Surrey were neglected. The place needed a new owner, but the old barn and the corral out back had made a good living for Martin, and he refused to see the state of the building's disrepair and would not sell for a reasonable price.

When his saddled horse was finally brought around, Sam mounted and touched spurs to the animal's ribs with enough vigor to get him moving briskly to take advantage of his morning energy. To the Rocking F and back in one day took an early start, and it was two hours past daylight.

At the Frio River a mile above where the Hondo River joined it, Sam prepared to cross at a secluded spot. The two narrow rivers became one wide river below this crossing; the Frio pressed on and the Hondo lost its name.

Sam used the regular stage road for short stretches, but over the years he had made his own trail to the Rocking F. In doing so, he had discovered a crossing where the Frio ran shallow and had a sandy bottom. It was a narrow neck where a rider or two could cross, and it saved him more than a mile and led past a special place. The trail herds crossed below, because the land was open rolling hills, spacious enough to allow a large herd to scatter along the river's banks and water without undue jostling.

Sam and the horse settled into an easy rhythm once they crossed the river, and he allowed the animal to find its way along the big river's bank. The gelding chose a path that took advantage of the shade of the maple trees just as Sam knew he would.

At the serene place Sam had selected in his mind, he stopped his horse and dismounted holding the reins then dropped to one knee and removed his Stetson and began visiting with The Almighty. Sam always talked in a hushed tone to The Almighty making sure his words were low but unmistakably clear, and he said, "When a man reaches my age, he begins to think he might live forever. I've not made such a mistake. I'm ready to meet You and settle whatever scores need settling. You know what's on my mind. I've said it before. I don't want to end my time here on earth falling under Cecil Bill Waterman's heel. You and I know that as soon as Old Bill Foley goes to his reward, I'll have to face Waterman's Mexican bodyguard, Miguel Gomez. You saw what happened when Gomez came to the jail to get one of his drunks. He refused to pay the fine. I braced him, and he flashed that gun off his hip like it was a feather. He caught me flatfooted. Lordy, he was fast. He took his vaquero then said charge the fine to Meester Waterman and laughed when he left without paying. Well, I just put another of his drunken vaquero's in my jail. I'll test that bunch. Waterman purposely owes every merchant in town. For a rich man with all that land, he don't pay his bills. He's over his credit limit with every one of them. He's been sending Gomez and his men to town and they take whatever he needs for his ranch saying charge it. If Waterman intends to take over the town, and I think he does, I cannot win that confrontation when it comes, and it will come just as soon as Old Bill Foley passes on, and that could happen any day or any second now. I don't want my last memory to be of Waterman and that Mex grinning at me when I go down. God Almighty, don't let me die in front of those two sons-a-bitches. Sorry I said that, God."

Satisfied he had made himself perfectly clear he mounted and touched spurs to the big dun.

Chapter Four

Sam moved the animal at a brisk pace for a mile or so then walked him for short distances, and they soon left the river with its trees and shade for the rolling hills of cattle country grassland where they passed pod after pod of Rocking F cows grazing.

The miles had passed quickly, and Sam reined in the big horse atop a knoll of blackjack oaks that overlooked a flat plain. Down below, he could see the plush Spanish style hacienda built from Hill Country stone instead of the usual Mexican stucco. The house was fenced with stripped young saplings that had weathered to light powdery gray, and it was gated with cast iron gates painted black. The building inside the fences was spacious with a second story and a bell tower above that. Sam knew Old Bill could have had an even bigger home if he or Abbey, especially Abbey, had wanted it.

Abbey kept five Mexican servants, a cook, two maids, and two men hostlers. The two hostlers doubled as gardeners when they were not tending horses, and that was not often since nowadays Old Bill no longer rode, and Abbey never did. All five did their part on festive occasions which no longer took place.

Sam sat on his animal looking down at the stylish hacienda gathering his thoughts. He reminded himself he had opposed his daughter marrying his friend over twenty years ago, because she had been twenty, and Old Bill sixty and more. They married anyway, and it had been a success although Young Bill was their only child. How the years slip away, Sam's mind added.

His animal lowered its head wanting to crop grass, and the movement returned him to reality and the purpose of his trip. It was necessary to tell Abbey about Wyatt Winslow since she and Old Bill had always directed Young Bill's life. Wyatt's arrival was going to put her son's life in jeopardy, and Sam had no idea on how to deal with Wyatt's need for revenge, but he felt Abbey would know what came between Young Bill and Chastity, and it might be something to undo Wyatt's thinking.

Sam tickled the animal with his spurs and begin walking him down toward the hacienda. The mesquite trees surrounding it were making miniature shade umbrellas on the ground, their shadows slanting in the direction the early afternoon sun gave them. Beyond it, he could see Old Bill's original homestead cabin, its bunkhouse and barn. They were a good distance from the hacienda grounds, the distance being far enough away that flags were used to signal from the hacienda to the ranch hands that lived and worked there. The flag on the bell tower fluttering in the afternoon breeze was peaceful white. Sam knew the flag would be red for danger and all hands were needed above.

The scene sent Sam's mind drifting to his chance meeting with Bill Foley. Was it really a meeting of chance if Old Bill Foley had been waiting years to approach just the right man and decided Sam was that man? The year had been 1858; a year after Sam left California and ten years after Old Bill came to America. Over a drink at Irish Rose's Waterfront Saloon in Galveston, Sam had learned about a plan that would rival going for broke on a roulette wheel, except it was a game of chance where you could end up dead. What Old Bill Foley, who was young then, had proposed was a venture into Indian Territory to trade mirrors for land. No white man in his right mind would have gone for Old Bill's scheme, but Sam was not in his right mind; his wife had died of cholera and he had watched her, hopelessly and helplessly, letting bitterness make him a man who neglected his young daughter and reveled in hard whiskey. He changed, but he had been ready for something reckless. Only fools would attempt it, and they were the fools. Old Bill had let hate make him one kind of fool, and Sam had let self-pity make him another kind of fool, so as two different blind fools they became partners.

More memory was waiting to take place, but Sam was distracted when his eyes discovered a black stallion standing beneath one of two big cottonwood trees beside the hacienda. Sam was sure he knew the animal. He was just as sure it had no business being there. Adding to his concern was the black stallion was not at the tie-rail where it would be if the visit of the rider was to be a short one. No, the animal was left with reins hanging down loosely so he could crop grass at his leisure. It was enough for Sam to quickly spur his animal into a lope and hurry the rest of the way down to see what he was having trouble believing.

Chapter Five

Sam had just pulled up and was looping the reins from his animal over the tie-rail at the front entrance of the hacienda when the front door opened and Bill Waterman came through it.

Waterman, seeing Sam, hastened across the flagstone porch and met him on the steps where he offered his hand, and said in as friendly a voice as Sam had ever heard the man speak, "Good afternoon, Marshal. It's a pleasure to see you."

Sam did not take his offered hand. What Sam wanted to say was what the hell are you doing here? Instead, he said, "This meeting would be a lot more pleasant if you gave your Mexican *jefe* money to pay the fines for your vaquero drunks. I have another one in my jail now. I can promise you this one will not get out on credit like the last one did."

Waterman lowered his hand and pulled out his wallet. Handing Sam a twenty dollar certificate, he smiled, it was a small upturning of his mouth but seemed entirely sincere, and he replied, "Here, Sam. For this man and the last one. I don't need a receipt. Let the man go. Tell him not to return to my ranch. He's through. Beginning today, I'm going to change some things that may have been upsetting you."

Then, offering his hand again, Waterman said, "Sam, we need to be friends. For some reason, we haven't been."

Sam knew the reason. The reason Waterman didn't know the reason was because Sam had been just another face in the crowd at Waterman's trial almost twenty years ago. The place was San Francisco now. It was Yerba Buena then, and it belonged to Spain and Mexico. Catholic friars who established Mission San Francisco de Asis gave it the Spanish name, Yerba Buena, which is Spanish for good herb, because of the abundance of minty spearmint growing around it. Sir Francis Drake called the place Nova Albion back in 1579 when he came ashore during his circumnavigation of the world. He claimed the entire land for his Queen, and like Columbus who claimed the same continent for his Queen, and the others after them, LaSalle representing the French, and Hudson the Dutch, each claimed more land than they had people who wanted to settle it. The people who showed up in the New World of Columbus, Drake, Hudson, and LaSalle, were not elite citizens, they were men and women hungry for free land. Texas land was no longer free but it was cheap, cheap enough so Waterman showed up in Foley, and by accident or a strange quirk of fate, bought ranchland alongside Bill Foley's. Sam was shocked at the irony fate can put at any man's door when Waterman introduced himself after the purchase, because a year earlier, Indians would have roamed there. Waterman didn't know that.

At their formal introduction, Sam could see Waterman searching for what made his face familiar. Not finding an answer, every time they met after that, Waterman kept searching the past for Sam Ordway's face. Sam figured he was unfamiliar, because the Army uniform he was wearing as a guard at Waterman's trial was so different from his cowhand image.

Sam was permanent Army then, part of the contingent that came ashore in Monterey Bay when the United States declared war on Mexico to take California and all the land in between using what President Polk and the newspapers called Manifest Destiny. Manifest Destiny, Sam soon learned, was a grand phrase to cover a grand theft. The United States had just wrested big Texas from Mexico; now it wanted rich California.

William Tecumseh Sherman was only a lieutenant then, and he was quartermaster in charge of disbursing almost $30,000 in gold coin, and Sam was one of its guards. It was as close to combat as Sam would get, for none of Sherman's men saw action. Sherman voiced a lot of displeasure at his misfortune, and Sam had to listen to him on a daily basis. He moaned that other West Pointers were in Mexico gaining glory and combat experience, and he was stuck out here where he would get none.

Sam was forced to listen, but he listened with one ear closed. The marines and sailors from Commodore Robert Stockton's force in San Diego joined the remnants of General Stephen Kearny's Army of the West, and they defeated the Mexican dons. Kit Carson was responsible for uniting the two U.S. forces, and newspapers made it so dramatic he became more famous than president Polk who had joined the United States from ocean to ocean. It was Kit Carson who found glory; Sherman had to wait.

Sherman's misfortune was Sam's good fortune. Sam's good fortune was Waterman's trial let him meet Chan Li Wu. She was a laundress. As Sergeant of the Guard, Sam wore a clean uniform every day. Had it not been for the Waterman trial, he would not have stopped at the little shop to pick up one of his uniforms. Old Mister Chang Wu must have been busy ironing or otherwise indisposed, for it was she who came from behind the curtains with his freshly starched and pressed uniform. He would never forget her face. From that moment on, his mind would see the beauty of her face at least a million times.

He asked her name, and she pronounced it Shan Lee then spelled it for him, Chan Li. Madam Wu, her mother, explaining later, said Chan, in Chinese, meant beautiful and graceful, and she was. Her face was beautiful and the movement of her body had a graceful elegance other women did not have. Li, Madam Wu added, meant fragrance of Jasmine. The Jasmine flower is known to the Chinese as a gift from God. The white petals open only with the coolness of night, and Chan Li wore one in her hair every evening when the plants were flowering. The Wu family filled their garden with Jasmine plants using the dried leaves to make tea, and Chan Li dried Jasmine petals then made a fine powder so she could wear a light scent of her favorite fragrance year round.

But it was her eyes that completed his capture. They were the color of polished silver, almost blue, for her father had been a Russian seaman. The frost color of blue must have come from him.

Sam would never know, for Chan Li never met her father, and her mother would not talk about the encounter. It was not unusual for Russian sailing ships to work their way down the California coast from Alaska searching the Pacific for whales then trading whale oil and seal furs for American goods. On the other hand, it was most unusual for a Chinese settlement to be found along the California coast, for the Chinese were not colonists like the Spanish, French, and English.

The opium wars forced the Wu's to leave China. They were scholars who could not tolerate the depravity opium was doing to their people, so, reluctantly, they left choosing to shield their children from that moral corruption. Spain, the richest nation in the world, wanted to slow the flow of riches from its wealthy mines in South America and Mexico. Every year, Spain was forced to send two galleons from Acapulco to Manila loaded with silver and jewels to buy spices, silk, delicate clothes, art, and porcelain glassware that only the Chinese with their knowledge, skill, and patience could make. The outward flow of wealth was so great those ships received a title. They became known as the Manila Galleons. Spain began trading cheap opium, and the Chinese people were unaware of its addiction.

Chang Wu, his family and fellow stragglers from the opium wars, began the Chinese colony at Monterey by accident. They settled among the Mexicans when their ship was forced by strong winds and ocean currents up the coast from their original destination at Los Angeles. Exhausted by the long trip, they chose to remain where they landed.

Before Sam met Chan Li, when he saw Chinese people, they were nothing more than passing oddities. The Monterey Colony changed his vision. He quickly began to admire them for hard work and politeness. He discovered how intelligent the men of the Colony were, because as foreigners with a totally different language, they quickly learned American history. All this was unknown history to Sam Ordway when he first laid eyes on Chan Li Wu in 1849. The Chinese history of interest to Sam at that time came from his many visits to the laundry for a glimpse of Chan Li. The visits became so obvious old Chang Wu finally told him Chan Li was available for marriage. One day, he simply took Sam aside and explained there was a woman in the village that knew Suan Ming, adding Suan Ming was the ancient art of Chinese fortune telling, and a couple's fortune must be examined by such a fortuneteller for a Chinese girl to wed.

It was a matter of the couple's birth dates. If their birth dates did not conflict, the marriage could take place and have good fortune. Would he want him to ask the Suan Ming woman to match his birth date with Chan Li? He added quickly the Suan Ming woman was also a matchmaker so the expense would not be great. If Sam's desire was to marry Chan Li, he would summon the Suan Ming woman to begin the formalities.

In this way, Sam became the first Anglo to marry a Chinese girl from the Monterey colony. Chang Wu, realizing too few Chinese males had been born for the available females, chose Sam because he drank sparingly, displayed good character, and was suitable financially. As for Chan Li, she had no choice in the matter.

Sam's desire for the young Chan Li brought him this dilemma. Before her eyes made him her prisoner, Sam viewed his life as permanent army. His father had had a successful army career, and Sam, although he had no prospect or desire to enter West Point, thought the army would serve as a career for him also. He was one of a very few enlisted men who had been schooled, and it served him well so that his promotions came steadily from his ability to read, write, and understand numbers. He made sergeant quickly. He did not gamble, and he drank sparingly. His only spending vice was women. Life in the army meant a successful marriage was a meager prospect. Those men who tried it found them leaving wives at home while they were out on patrol for months at a time or being transferred to another post having to leave the family behind. The marriages never lasted. Sam answered the problem before he enlisted. He would remain a bachelor and become an authority on whores and whorehouses, and twice a year, he took a furlough and visited the best whorehouse, sometimes whorehouses, in the area where he was stationed, always careful to spend his money on such entertainment wisely.

He had a sizable nest egg. The ship that brought his detachment to California, taking almost six months, sailed from New York around the tip of Argentina to Monterey Bay, so there was no place to spend his pay. With almost ten years in an army uniform, he had saved money, even with his whorehouse adventures, so the expense of the marriage was not a problem. He knew he was no longer a fuzzy faced youngster, so he chose Chan Li then asked for a furlough and discharge.

Chapter Six

Sam, facing Waterman seeing that experience in his mind, tried to recover from the blank expression he knew must be on his face, and he reluctantly extended his hand to the ranchman. It was a lukewarm handshake, and Sam examined why. The Court of Inquiry had acquitted Waterman who had acted within the confines of maritime law. The law had changed two years later in 1850 when the United States Navy also banned flogging, but Waterman had been acquitted, so he, Sam, must treat him accordingly. With his facts in order, Sam asked, "Is my daughter home?"

"Yes, Sam. She's upstairs," Waterman replied.

An uncertain feeling began in the pit of Sam's stomach. It was unsettling to know Abbey was upstairs. All the rooms upstairs were bedrooms.

Without another word, Sam turned his back on Waterman, and hurried through the front door passing Old Bill Foley covered with a buffalo robe asleep in his Adirondack chair.

Skipping stairs on his way up the curving staircase to the second floor, he wondered where all the servants were as he walked briskly down the hall then through the open door of the master bedroom.

"Hello, Abbey," he said.

She was standing at the window looking out. Turning quickly at the sound of his voice, she asked, "Dad?"

She was wearing a beautiful Chinese kimono elaborately embroidered with flying cranes, white creatures against the red silk of the garment. Seeing her in the robe made him acutely aware it was mid-afternoon. The uncertain feeling in the pit of his stomach grew, and wordlessly and slowly he walked to her.

Looking for her eyes, eyes that were the same color as her mother's, he found them as hers found his, and they held for the moment with hers wavering asking questions.

Without leaving her eyes, Sam loosened the sash of her kimono and the garment fell open slightly. Without looking down yet seeing enough to understand, he said, "So that's the way it is."

Her eyes began flashing with anger. Reaching down, she grabbed the sash and angrily pulled on it pulling the kimono together again. Then she turned on Sam. "Yes! Yes, that's the way it is. What did you expect? You had to pass Old Bill on the way upstairs. You saw how it is. He's been asleep like that for two years. Two years!"

When Sam did not answer, her anger continued, "What did you expect? For me to be a nun? Well, I'm not."

Sam did not know where to go next with his daughter, so he said nothing.

Abbey's anger seemed to be washing away, and in a voice much calmer she said, "Dad, don't be so shocked."

"Abbey," Sam began to explain, "I'm sorry I had to do that."

"I'm sorry you felt you had to," she interrupted. "You had no reason. It is none of your business."

"You don't know the man, Abbey. I do."

"Oh, but Daddy, I do know him. He's a real gentleman. He's from a wealthy upper class family in Boston."

Sam knew when Abbey said he was a real gentleman from Boston it was hopeless trying to change her mind.

"I'm going to marry him after Old Bill passes on," she added. "He's asked several times. Last week he gave me his ring. I told him I'd give him my answer today. I said yes."

I can see that, Sam thought. The kimono in the afternoon meant a bargain had been sealed. What Waterman will get when he marries my beautiful young daughter is Old Bill Foley's ranch was the thought racing through Sam's mind. The son-of-a-bitch is too lucky to suit me.

Shrugging his shoulders, he knew he had to let the matter rest for a better time, so he said, "Abbey, I'm sorry you've already made your choice. I know him from way back, but it's foolish to explain where and when after today's fact. I hope you know what you're doing."

She understood what Sam meant when he said after today's fact, but she replied gently rather than gruffly, "That's okay, Dad. I understand you had to do it. You're protecting a daughter you love, and I love you for it. As for Mister Waterman, he's proved to be a gentleman. Three years ago, he came asking Old Bill to sell or lease him some water rights so he could increase his herd. Old Bill refused. When word got around Old Bill was down, he came to call. He came as a gentleman offering condolences and whatever help he could give not asking about water rights. After that, he came to visit Old Bill occasionally always inquiring about his health not for favors. Then his visits came weekly, and I knew it was me he came to see. Not once, did I encourage him, but I liked his manner. He's handsome and mature like Old Bill once was, so I didn't discourage him. Two weeks ago he asked me to marry him a suitable time after Old Bill is gone. He gave me a beautiful ring. Today, I accepted his proposal. Please understand, Dad. I'm young and still have desires."

Sam, helpless, let the matter go. It didn't seem a wise time to tell Abbey a gunman was in town eager to kill her son. His mission to find out if she knew anything that would lessen her son's responsibility in Chastity's disgrace had been a straw worth trying. There was doubt in his mind she could tell him anything about the affair that would persuade Wyatt Winslow to stop his revenge pursuit anyway.

Turning away, he walked downstairs to where Old Bill Foley was sleeping, bent over the old man, and gently shook him, and the old one came awake slowly like a bear from hibernation.

"Bill," he said twice. "It's me. Sam. Sam Ordway. Remember me?"

Old Bill's watery eyes blinked then opened fully and focused dimly on Sam's. Sam had to listen carefully, but he heard his friend's reply. Old Bill's gravel-like voice said feebly, "I remember you, Sam. Why?"

"There's a gunfighter in town. He's looking to kill your son."

His old friend's eyes opened wide and focused sharply on Sam's eyes. Sam knew he had penetrated Old Bill's senility. Penetrating that mist was a wistful hope gathered descending the stairs. That hope was alive now. The question to be answered was would it amount to anything.

Chapter Seven

Claire Winslow heard the wagon before she learned who was driving it. When she looked out her kitchen window and saw Molly Gibbs climbing down after it stopped at the front gate, she was surprised but delighted. Cass Gibbs and Molly lived almost a day's ride from Foley, so the young woman would need to spend the night, and that was welcome but a bit unexpected.

Recalling Cass and Molly's wedding almost a year ago Claire remembered Elder Gibbs had given Cass fifty acres and fifty cows to begin married life. An acre to feed a cow would not allow the herd to increase, but his son could sell off enough calves and older steers to make a living if they farmed land around the cabin. Molly's folks were farmers, dirt poor at their best, so Molly came to Cass with only the clothes on her back, but she knew how to farm. Molly was a worker, so they would make a decent living, but, just now, Claire knew the couple was probably penniless. If the couple needed something from town bad enough to spend a night, the question in Claire's mind was why Molly was making the trip and Cass had not. If Cass was hurt Molly would head straight for doctor Wedgewood's office, but she had not done that.

Wiping flour from her hands on a dish towel, Claire hurried from the kitchen to the front door to greet her.

"Molly," Claire exclaimed, "it's so good to see you. Come in this house. I'm in the middle of supper. You're just in time. It's hard to cook for just me and Jimbo, so I usually fix a little extra in case Sam Ordway comes by, but he's off somewhere. You can have his share."

They embraced, and Claire felt unease in the young woman.

"Miz Winslow, can I spend the night with you?" Molly asked.

"Why, yes, Molly, you can. Come on in. Is Cass hurt?"

"No, ma'am. It's me that's hurt."

"You?"

Tears came then. Trying to explain and stop crying while she did it made Molly stumble as she stepped inside, and she grabbed Claire and held on like a small child as her tattered old Lady Stetson fell from her head to the floor. Distraught, she had no knowledge of its falling.

Claire let her cling for a moment then reached down and picked up the hat admiring the brilliant auburn color of the young woman's hair before she did it. She had only seen it from a distance at the wedding. Up close, the hair color Claire Winslow was seeing with her own eyes proved that rumors she had listened to over the years with disbelief were now, beyond a doubt, true.

Claire, overcoming the momentary distraction of the young woman's hair, hung the hat on one of the hat pegs next to the door and quickly took the young woman's hand and gently led her into the kitchen to a chair where she had her sit. Then she said, "Tell me where you hurt, child."

"Inside," she answered pointing to her chest. "My heart hurts. Cass went off to a whorehouse in San Antonio."

"Did you quarrel?"

"No, ma'am. Sid and Everett come by huntin' Cass. They said they needed Cass to help them brand some calves, but they was drinkin'. I seen a bottle in Sid's saddlebag. Everett probably had one, but his horse was on the other side of Sid's, so I couldn't tell for sure. Cass saw them ride up and he came in from the back pasture. He said he'd be back before dark, but he didn't come home at all last night."

"What makes you think he went to a whorehouse?"

"'Cause he done it before. Maybe three or four months ago. Left with the same two who come visitin' Cass with a bottle, an' Cass didn't come home that night. Next evenin' he come slinkin' home all red eyed lookin' like a whipped dog after me worrin' myself sick, and promised he'd never do it agin. But he did. He's done it agin."

"And now you're leaving Cass?"

"Yes, ma'am. For now, anyways. I love him, but I ain't sure what to do. Is Jimbo home?"

Claire thought it was a strange thing to ask, but she answered, "He's still at the schoolhouse. He plays on the school ground after school. He'll be home in a little while. He won't miss supper. Why?"

Rising from the chair Molly said, "'Cause I want to know if somthin's wrong with me," and with the innocence of a child Molly Gibbs quickly removed her shirt and dropped it on the chair then slipped her chemise over her head, and she was bare to the midriff.

The act happened so quickly its surprise had Claire so fascinated she was unable to react until the younger woman was standing in front of her totally bare bosomed. When she found her voice, all she could manage was, "Oh, my."

"I knew it! I knew it! Somethin's wrong with my tits. They ain't pretty enough. That's why Cass goes to the whorehouse."

Molly was just before crying again. Her face said so. Claire could see the young woman's turmoil, but she could not help from giggling at the dilemma. "Molly," she said, "Your breasts are beautiful. They are so perfect, when I saw them, it caught me off guard. I was so surprised, all I could say was oh my, because I was thinking what a fool Cass is. The man is a pure fool."

"Maybe it's the rest of me. Let me git these pants off so you can see before Jimbo gits home. It's gotta be somethin'."

"I'm sure the bottom of you is as pretty as the top, Molly. The trouble is not with you. It's Cass. I can tell you what Cass's problem is. I had a problem like yours when the mysterious complexities of David Winslow's inner self surfaced in my own marriage."

"You, ma'am? You and the Reverend?"

"It was before he became a Reverend."

"Golly. It's hard to believe Reverend Winslow went to a whorehouse before he was a Reverend, but what's that got to do with Cass? He ain't about to become no Reverend. Least not the Cass I know."

"It wasn't a whorehouse visit, Molly. It was a private conflict between us about sex. Kind of like what's happening with you and Cass."

It was not a confession Claire intended to make, but the child's need was so sincere she was bound to help. Since that awkward time in her life Claire had examined males with the curiosity of a baby kitten. By using her feminine instincts like a scholar, she had come to an astounding conclusion; understanding males is amazingly simple.

Absolutely sure of herself, she consoled the grown child, "Most men are just boys who don't mature until they're about thirty. You have to forgive their stupidity. Young men like Cass stumble with two problems, the female body and whiskey. Both those things confuse them, especially the sex part."

"Cass don't have no trouble with sex. Seems to me if he gits me as much as he does then goes to a whorehouse after more, he don't have no trouble that-a-way."

"Young men are curious about a woman's body, Molly. They're born that way. After you've shown them everything, they're curious to know if the next woman is different. They can't help themselves. Liquor makes them more curious and eases their conscience when they cheat. Cass hasn't figured out how to hold his liquor yet, and Sid and Everett take advantage of him. Both those boys are a shade before pure ugly. Sid has a front tooth missing or never had one to begin with, and Everett has teeth almost as green as grass. They're so ugly they can't get into a nice whorehouse, so they use a fine looking man like Cass to get them in by plying him with whiskey, so Cass is a fool."

"I know. But I gotta do somethin'. I gotta break him of leavin' me. I just gotta. I can't stand knowin' he's lovin' some other girl. I figured on tryin' to get a job in town. Maybe live on my own for a month or two, long enough so he's broke to my bridle or I lose him once and for all."

"Honey, he'll come running after you. He'll get down on his knees. If I was a man, I would. I don't know about a job in town, though. The Emporium has only kin working there, so you can skip them. You're not educated enough for the bank. That leaves them out. There's Martha's Bakery, but it's just her and her girl, and I judge there's not enough business for them to take on another hand. The Bluebonnet Café might use another waitress. You might try there. Sam Ordway said there was a lady, new in town, considering starting her own business. You might try her. No one has any idea of what kind of business she has in mind. She's at the hotel. Her name is Ivy."

Chapter Eight

Sam Ordway was not happy with God Almighty. The Almighty had handled his coming confrontation with Waterman and Gomez just like Sam had asked. God had answered his prayer, alright, because Sam knew now he wouldn't die from either man's gun since Abbey was entertaining the rancher. What had him huffy was God had out-foxed him like he was a child. Sam was not sure he didn't prefer a showdown with Waterman rather than having him as a son-in-law.

Yessir, God had fooled him. Until he could feel better about the new turn of things, he was not going to speak to The Almighty. What Sam wanted was time to figure God out.

Abbey was easier to understand, even if Sam disapproved of her conduct, but it was Waterman coming into, then out, then into, Sam's life again that kept him perplexed, so, on the ride home, he decided to sort out Waterman's trial, and he figured the long ride was as good a time as any to do it.

Waterman first entered the picture when word of the California gold fields found its way back to Boston. People clamoring to join the California Gold Rush could use three routes to the gold fields. Around The Horn by ship just as Sam's army unit had done at an average of more than six months; it was the shortest route. The intermediate route was by ship to Panama, cross the Isthmus of Panama to the Pacific by land then by ship again sailing to California. Since railroads existed only in the East, and stagecoach lines stopped at the foot of the mountain ranges; using the land route meant crossing the Sierra or Rocky mountains by wagon fighting Indians and outlaws all the way. That route took over a year. By sea was the best choice, and a fast new Clipper Ship, Flying Cloud, had just been launched bound for California, and in command was Captain Josiah Perkins Cressy with his wife as navigator.

A week after Flying Cloud left Boston, Captain Cecil William Waterman, also left Boston. He was in command of the Clipper Ship, Flying Albatross, which was delayed from leaving the same day as Flying Cloud because she was being refitted with newer sails meant to give her more speed. It was to be a race with the later departure noted and accepted. Captain Cecil Waterman was the youngest son of Captain Samuel Fenton Waterman who had become wealthy exporting lumber to and importing pepper and other spices from the Orient. The expectation of father and son was Flying Albatross would overtake Flying Cloud. Several thousands of dollars was offered by different entities for the fastest recorded time, and young Captain Waterman pushed his crew to the limit.

A sailing vessel rounding Cape Horn, where the Atlantic and Pacific oceans meet, must navigate through a group of barren volcanic islands, Tierra del Fuego. Water where the currents meet is the most treacherous sailing water in the world. Gales are a constant menace. The temperature hovers around freezing. With howling winds and monstrous waves forty and fifty feet high, the lifeless islands are a graveyard for countless ships and thousands of sailors. Both, Captain Cressy and Captain Waterman had to navigate their ships through this passage. As his ship, Flying Albatross, picked her way between the rocky islands of Tierra del Fuego, Captain Cecil William Waterman shot and killed two seamen although he was charged with the death of only one.

A trial witness testified he thought he saw, but did not hear, Waterman give ordinary seaman, Jed Semple, an order to climb the ship's rigging to right a jammed topsail. Semple looked up the mast of the tossing Clipper ship and made his decision then faced his captain and was judged to say, "Nay, skipper. I'll not do that."

"You refuse my order?" Waterman was seen screaming at him through the howling wind, his words judged by facial expression.

The seaman, knowing he could be shot, of the two choices, the other falling into freezing water with death by drowning, Jed Semple probably chose to chance his fate to the captain's forgiveness, expecting time in the brig, and he answered, "Yes, Cap'n. I do."

Without a moment's hesitation, Waterman was seen to draw his .45 Colt pistol and shoot the man.

With weather constantly pressuring them, every man was bound to his job, so only one seaman saw Waterman shoot Jed Semple, and there were only guesses as to what happened next. The most logical was Waterman then yelled, "Up the rigging!" to the nearest man which was the helmsman.

The helmsman was not obligated to climb into the loft. It was the job of an ordinary seaman, and he was thought to say, "It's not my job, Captain."

It was speculated Waterman then shot the helmsman and shoved his body into the swirling sea. Without a helmsman, the ship was in danger of running aground, so Waterman took the helm.

The only known fact was Waterman was seen pointing to the topsail, and Semple shaking his head no. With howling wind, Waterman's pistol shots went unheard, so none of the crew could tell if one or two shots had been fired, so Waterman's explanation was the helmsman had been washed overboard by a gigantic wave, and there was no one to dispute it. Later, as the crew was questioned privately, all speculated the helmsman had been shot like Jed Semple. Unlike the helmsman, Jed Semple's body had fallen to the main deck, and there was no way for Waterman to be rid of it, so when the ship was clear of running aground, he addressed the crew and stated Semple had disobeyed a direct order, and by his right as captain of the vessel, he had shot him. The crew was to bury him at sea, which they did.

At the Court of Inquiry, where Sam Ordway stood guard each day of the three day affair, Captain Waterman, after he was found not guilty of a murder that was justified by the Code of the High Seas, was asked if he had any regret at having killed his crewman. Sam remembered Waterman saying, "Not in the slightest. Every man has his duty, and he must abide by the rules that duty entail. I did my duty. Jed Semple did not do his. He got what he deserved."

Sadly for Waterman, Captain Cressy's ship, Flying Cloud, made the passage in eighty-nine days. The time was spectacular. Eleanor Cressy had studied ocean currents under Matthew Fontaine Maury, a brilliant oceanographer in the U.S. Navy, and she navigated her husband's ship safely and quickly through the rough passage. Her husband gave her credit for the record passage, and newspapers made her a female hero. Eighty-nine days to the gold fields was front page news. Waterman's trial went almost unnoticed.

Chapter Nine

Sam, his mind frazzled from thinking about Waterman, began to doze in the saddle, and darkness set in to the point where he had to let his animal find the trail home.

He finally made out the lights of Foley as he was approaching Claire Winslow's house. When he passed it, he noticed the lamp was still burning and wondered if Jimbo or Claire was sick. He considered stopping but noticed an unfamiliar wagon pulled around back and an unfamiliar horse stabled inside her barnyard. That Claire had a visitor caused him to become fully awake, and his curiosity as to who it was almost had him turn back. Thinking Claire might have a male visitor gave his mind a twinge. Knowing it would not be polite to disturb them at such a late hour, he decided against it, but after he passed the house, he caught himself looking back one last time to be sure a stranger was there, and he saw the light go out, and his mind went back to Old Bill, Young Bill, Waterman, Abbey, Wyatt Winslow, and God Almighty.

His animal automatically made the left turn from Cedar Street onto Main Street without any rein guidance on his part, and he muttered angrily, "To damned many Bill's to think about. One too many, anyway. I sure could have done without Waterman showing up here. And now Wyatt Winslow shows up. I could have done without that, too."

Instead of going to the livery stable, he reined up in front of Irish Rose's Saloon. After looping the reins over the tie-rail, he walked up to the batwing doors thinking someone else had just showed up in Foley; the Ivy woman. "Wonder what she's up to?" he muttered as he entered.

Chapter Ten

Irish Rose's Saloon was not particularly large, the hotel and Catholic Church were bigger. The saloon was square at one hundred by one hundred, but twenty feet had been added at the rear for a stage. A piano sitting at the right corner facing the stage was used for special occasions; locals knew it was never meant to entertain bar patrons, and it would never been used by cancan dancers, not that Irish Rose was a prude, she wasn't, Kerry O'Shea could swear to that.

The place was not crowded. It was quiet tonight just as it was on most nights of the week. Walking to the bar, Sam recognized the normal scattering of mid-week patrons. Men seated at saloon-type round tables were smoking, chatting, and drinking peacefully, chatting and drinking being forms of entertainment used to ease boredom since sinful females were not available in Catholic Foley.

Irish Rose O'Grady was standing at her usual place in the center of a semi-round table dealing Black Jack to four seated patrons, one a farmer Sam did not recognize. That meant he was overdue a visit around the hillside to get acquainted with any new faces on the local farms.

Rose was the same Irish Rose who owned Irish Rose's Waterfront Saloon in Galveston where he and Bill Foley met and had their first drink together. Like most of the other business and professional people in Foley, Bill Foley had sought her out and offered her land and exclusive saloon rights to come to Foley when he decided to begin his town after he had become a successful rancher. Irish Rose accepted Bill Foley's word that she would be the only saloon allowed in town as long as she played by his rules, but she insisted on paying for the land and built her saloon without a dime from Bill. She admired independence.

The same cannot be said for the Kirkpatrick's at the Emporium, the Fitzgerald's at the bank, Daniel O'Connell and his daughter at the Foley Sentinel, even the blacksmith, Patrick Riley. Bill gave all of them the land where there businesses sat, loaned them money without interest to build, and quietly purchased forty-nine percent of each business to furnish business capital then let each of them run their businesses without interference. He personally funded the bank, along with another cattleman from San Antonio and one from Fort Worth.

The rail at the bar was empty when Sam hung one of his boots over it. Kerry O'Shea, alone behind the bar, finally noticed Sam, and he walked down the counter to meet him. Irish Rose's bartender was pure Irish, as Irish pure as Old Bill himself. Kerry O'Shea was rarely at a loss for words, and his ears were available to every drummer and visitor who entered the establishment. When Sam wanted conversation, or information, he visited Kerry O'Shea, who, it was rumored, removed Rose's garters frequently. Both were strong Catholics. Why they never married was everyone's guess.

Sam said, "Nighttime is a poor time to be daydreaming."

"T'was a fine one you caught me in."

"Rose?"

"Yep. You look tired tonight, Marshal. Long day?"

"Long enough. I'll take a bottle of Jack Daniels."

Sam knew the clear glass bottle behind the bar was a bottle for show only. Kerry refilled it from a ceramic clay jug below the counter.

"I'll take one drink here then take the jug home so your pretty bottle will be safe." Sam added, "A jug will be more than I need. I'll return it tomorrow."

"Suits me. Not too many likely to ask for Black Jack tonight. Strong drink, Sam. Not like you, Marshal. Bad things about?"

"Don't know yet."

"If you need help, I have free time for a few more days. There are only a few drovers coming by. Roundup is a few days off yet. There'll be lots more starting next week is my bet. Rose will tend bar for me as long as it's on a slow night."

"Thanks, Kerry. Find out anything about the Ivy lady yet?"

"Nothing. Ask Young Bill. If anyone knows anything, it would be him. He's with her every minute. Why?"

"No reason. Just curious. Young Bill's on my schedule first thing tomorrow. Any loose talk?"

"None."

Kerry uncorked the clear glass bottle and poured Sam a shot. Looking Sam straight in the eye with the whiskey bottle poised over the glass, he said, "It's not like you to do heavy drinking. I know better than to ask a tight mouth old man like you why. Just remember. I'll be around tomorrow morning to treat your hangover if Doc Wedgewood is out on call. My services have a standard charge of one dollar for a serious drunk. Depends on how much medication you need for the treatment before you get my final bill."

"Thanks, Kerry. It's a medicinal drunk. I don't think I need a big dose. I'll let you know if I need hangover help."

Sam sipped whiskey from the rim of the glass, and Kerry eased back down to the end of the bar. Sam's mind, having scratched every scab about Abbey and Bill Waterman on the ride home, rebelled at more scratching.

Looking around for diversion to delay going home, he examined the saloon with the eye of someone familiar with its history. Irish Rose's Saloon was not a saloon for rowdies or a place to look for lewd women. It was not whorehouse with a saloon to front it, because furnishings inside were not ornate and gaudy, just tasteful. Paintings behind the bar and those hanging on the walls were not of nudes.

It was a unique saloon by Western standards because of its lighting. It had Pintsch gaslights. Bill Foley was responsible for them. Bill worked for the Erie Railroad before he left Detroit and headed south down the Mississippi determined to get rich. He took three important things on the journey; scanty savings, a wealth of knowledge gained from French trappers he lived and worked with on the Canadian border, and the friendship of an Irish Erie Railroad superintendant, Mike Callahan.

When Rose complained about lighting the stage in her new establishment with coal oil lamps that could easily set the place on fire, especially if she used velvet curtains as she wished to do, Old Bill remembered that Erie Railroad coaches and cabooses used Pintsch gaslights. Pintsch lights are not flammable. The Erie Road was first to use them, replacing candles that frequently caused fires when rolling and jousting of the cars toppled them. Bill Foley sent a wire to Super Mike Callahan, and Rose got her special fireproof lamps that filled the saloon, and her stage, with limelight.

It was not all brotherly love for Bill to supply Rose. He bought lamps for the front and rear of his bank. A lamp's light will last all night, and that made The Foley National

Bank the safest bank for miles around. It also made Main Street safer, for neighbors were constantly on the lookout if the lights suddenly went out, so new depositors came. Fuel for the lamps was not readily available. It was made especially for two roads; the Erie and the New York and New Haven & Hartford. The fuel had to come from Mike Callahan, but each lamp burned for a year on the fuel stored in its cylinder.

Interrupting Sam's thought, the young farmer he had not recognized left Rose's table and nodded as he passed Sam on the way out, and Sam acknowledged his greeting with a nod of his own. The farms were small, as were the number of people who lived and worked them. The town and ranches needed fresh produce, and Old Bill made sure the farmers were all Irish. This young farmer was still wearing his bib overalls, so he must have come over to the saloon after selling his green goods to the Bluebonnet Café. This time of year, farmers made good money.

Sam then found his mind escaping his surroundings going back to the dilemma about Abbey and Waterman. It was not a pleasant feeling, so he downed the hard whiskey in a fiery gulp and left.

Chapter Eleven

Sam did not do his normal Main Street walk. The whiskey had been a jolt, so he rode home instead. At his barn, he unsaddled a tired animal, saw that it had feed and water then led it into a stall next to his other animal. With slow steps, he walked across the yard then up the two steps of his back porch and unlocked the door and entered the kitchen then lit the coal oil lamp on the table.

"Well," he continued the conversation between his voice and himself, "I'm going to be visiting with Jack Daniels. It's been years since I did it. Old Chang Wu called it getting sorry. Tonight, I'm gonna get sorry."

He found a small glass in the cupboard, set the two items on the table, and sat down and began to drink so he could wade through old and new memories and get sorry enough to walk the tightrope of circumstance that fate or The Almighty had led him into with Abbey, Bill Waterman, and Wyatt Winslow.

Before his first sip, Sam knew the answer to the question he was looking for most, he would not find. The discovery that happened when he loosened Abbey's kimono posed a question his mind could not sort out.

The memory of Chan Li, the young wife he had lost entirely too soon, reawakened at that moment, and her memory became part of the question. His mind saw it this way: Chan Li had never refused him. Any indication he wanted her, and she would prepare her body to receive his. In all other things, she had been submissive to him. The question, with the answer he feared, is Abbey like her mother?

His only child had chosen to live with two men who had achieved power and used it. She must be drawn to such men. Her first man had wrested power with brains and might. Her next one had inherited his without a struggle, exactly as the kings who handed down kingdoms from generation to generation did. The soul of each man was as different as night against day. There was no dawn or dusk for them, just black and white. If she married Bill Waterman, he would own half of all Old Bill Foley had built. Would she be as submissive to Bill Waterman as her mother had been to him? If the answer was yes, what would the future of Foley, Sam, Young Bill, and even Abbey, become?

It was not a question a man could answer.

Chapter Twelve

Sam Ordway opened his eyes then closed them. He had a headache, and his mind told him his tongue was coated with fur, but common sense told him that couldn't be, so he opened his eyes again.

Sam Ordway was mighty sorry he got sorry the moment he opened swollen eyes that he was sure were streaked red. His dilemma had not been solved with a little drinking, so he drank more. It came to this: there was nothing he could tell Abbey that she would listen to. And, he could not, not at this point at least, tell Young Bill about his mother's infatuation with Bill Waterman, yet his grandson could lose control of Old Bill's hard won ranching empire if he remained unaware of that threat. Then there was Wyatt Winslow. It was still possible Wyatt would change his mind about the whole idea. Should he tell his grandson who his adversary was and risk word would get out and hurt Claire Winslow? It would be safer for Claire if he said nothing until after she left for Saint Louis, so he would wait and tell Young Bill about Wyatt after the stage left.

Sam's mind changed when he remembered Young Bill would be out with Ivy Vanderbilt, so he decided he would tell Young Bill this morning, if he survived his hangover, after first swearing him to secrecy then naming Wyatt as the gunman who was out to challenge him. It would then be up to Young Bill to pick a place and time to his advantage. If Young Bill downed Wyatt, Sam planned to have the body buried quickly before many questions were asked about who he was if he could get Doc Wedgewood to help and he thought Doc would. If Wyatt got Young Bill, some kind of hell would break loose for Claire when she found out. Sam was beginning to hate Wyatt Winslow, and he didn't like the feeling.

He left his chair unsteadily, for he had not made it to bed. The bottle and his misery conspired to have him spend what was left of the night sitting in a chair beside his kitchen table with his head in his hands propped up on his elbows until he was fully sorry. He had lowered his head and slept that way.

Now, afraid to look in the mirror, he made it to the sink looking for it through squinted eyes. There, he lifted and lowered the pump handle until he felt the water turn cold then he splashed his squinted eyes, face, and hair. He shook his wet head, water flying like a soaked mongrel dog shaking dry, and cried out. His head pain was so intense his eyes flew open. It was then he noted he was only half dressed. With his long johns drooped around his waist, he pumped more water into the sink and splashed his body soaking his long johns and himself completely. Autumn nights are cool, some cold, and Sam, cold as a frog now, shed his underwear and dashed out of the kitchen, naked as a plucked goose, into his bedroom grabbing a towel on the way. Quickly, he found a blanket and wrapped himself then huddled into the chair beside his bed. When he was warm, he fell on his knees beside his bed and said, "God Almighty, forgive me and help me. Amen."

Then he dressed with all the dignity he could muster, left the house without even so much as a cup of coffee, and made the long, torturous walk to Doc Wedgewood's office which was also Doc's home. When he got there, deciding as he stood there waiting to knock it was too early to disturb a man who got disturbed a lot, he shuffled over to Irish Rose's, walked around back to a little cottage where Kerry O'Shea lived, and knocked there instead.

It was almost daylight, too early even for the Bluebonnet Café to be open, and it took several minutes for the bartender to get to the door. When he finally opened it, he said, "I expected you, but not this early. I'll get dressed. Stand there. The cold will help."

Sam shivered.

When Kerry returned, they walked to the back door of Irish Rose's Saloon and the bartender unlocked it. He walked across the stage, Sam following down some steps and on to the bar where the bartender left him standing at the rail as he walked behind the bar and drew a glass of water then poured baking soda into it and watched it foam.

"Drink this," he said to Sam.

Sam eyed it with suspicion but finally drank it.

"Watch this," and O'Shea dropped a bulky green bottle into an oak bucket filled with water then added potassium nitrate, better known as saltpeter, making a chemical reaction where the saltpeter immediately grabbed heat from the water cooling it like ice would.

"Feel this." And O'Shea handed over the bottle for Sam to touch.

"It's cold," Sam said, a surprised look coming from his watery red eyes. "How'd you manage that?"

"It's a bartender secret that came all the way from Paree, France. The elite, those famous and rich ones, ogle over it in summertime. They get their favorite drinks cooled when no ice is available. No extra charge to you, Sam. Dollar covers everything."

Next, O'Shea popped the cork from the bottle of cheap California champagne that was cold now, handing it to Sam while bubbles were still overflowing above the top of the green bottle.

"I don't know if I can drink much of this stuff," Sam managed. "My stomach ain't happy."

"Drink as much as you can. Bubbles will float up your nose, but drink what you can then drink some more. Your stomach will get happier as you get more down."

Sam took several swallows, each one slower than the last until he had finished half a bottle then he pushed it aside. It took several minutes.

Only after waiting patiently those several minutes, Kerry O'Shea asked, "Feel better?"

"Some."

O'Shea pushed the bottle back at Sam. "A few more swallows. I'll make coffee while you drink."

Moments later, O'Shea returned with two freshly made cups of black coffee then asked, "Feel better now?"

"Sure. But I'm drunk again, and I got work to do."

"But you feel a helluva lot better, and it's a fine kind of drunk you have. If you were Irish, you'd be singing. Finish two cups of my Mild Irish Coffee with me, and your footsteps will be so light you'll think you're walking on cotton."

"That good, Kerry?"

"That good, Marshal."

Sam reached in his pocket, got a silver cartwheel and placed it on the bar.

O'Shea took it.

Sam, feeling downright good, like the weight of the world had been lifted from his shoulders when it really had not, would have blessed the wine if he had been a priest. Nectar from the green California bottle made Sam's tongue as glib as a real Irishman's, so glib he asked what the whole town had been too polite to ask for twenty years. "Kerry," he said, "When are you going to marry Rose? I want to be your Best Man."

"Can't. We are married to other people. We're both Catholic. Catholic's don't believe in divorce."

"Too bad. You two make a nice couple."

By Sam's eyes, Rose, when she was young, would have been as cute as Irish lasses get, and Kerry was the jovial kind, easy to like. Both were plump now, but anyone could tell they came by their plumpness happily.

"Thanks, Marshal. A home together is out of the question. This way, we are not living in sin; we are only sinning when we have marital relations. On the Sabbath, if we have sinned that week, and most weeks we have, we ask forgiveness at confession. So far, it works."

"If things change, I'd be proud to be your Best Man. Better hurry, though. Days pass, then years. I can't be here forever."

"I'll tell Rose. She'll be glad to know you approve. As for today, in a couple of hours you'll need what's left in this bottle. It won't look too good for you to walk out with it beneath your coat. I'll leave the back door open, and you can slip in when you feel the need."

They left the way they entered, out the back door, with Kerry going to his cottage, and Sam going to the Bluebonnet Café.

Chapter Thirteen

Daylight had happened while Sam was nursing the green bottle inside Rose's Saloon so the Bluebonnet Café was filling up when he got there. Right away, he saw who he wanted to see, Young Bill and Ivy Vanderbilt. He also saw Wyatt Winslow was not there, and he whispered, "Thank you, Father Almighty."

Wyatt, he judged, was still camping out at the Winslow homestead fighting his battle of morality for what he was about. In the loneliness out there, maybe he would lose some of the bitterness in his soul and relent attempting a killing for a poor kind of revenge that would only bring more pain.

Approaching their table Sam removed his hat and addressed them, "Morning, Miss Vanderbilt. Morning, Bill."

Ivy Vanderbilt turned to see where the greeting came from, and she saw Sam and gave him a smile with such warmth it caused the glow Sam was carrying from the California wine to make him giddy.

"Good morning, Marshal Ordway," she said pleasantly. "Please join us. I love your company," then she turned the smile on Young Bill, adding, "We can take our time can't we?"

No was a word that had disappeared from Young Bill's vocabulary when Ivy Vanderbilt came to town. "Sit down, Sam. Join us," he said quickly.

Sam's stomach was queasy when the day began, now it had regained its love for bacon and eggs with encouragement from the champagne, but as much as he wanted breakfast at that moment, he said "Young Bill, I need to talk to you, and I think the time should be before this day gets any older. Finish breakfast then leave Miss Vanderbilt at the hotel. I'll only need a few minutes. Come across to the jail."

With a very graceful wine embellished bow that had him bending low with his Stetson in his hand, Sam addressed Miss Vanderbilt, "I am sorry to do this, but it's very important or I would share the table with you. I, too, would enjoy your company."

Sam knew his words came straight from the California wine bottle, for never before had he been so eloquent.

Sheepishly, he put his hat on his head and walked to the jail. On the jail step, he turned around to survey Main Street as he usually did, and he saw the wagon he had seen last night at Claire Winslow's house stopping in front of the Bluebonnet Café, and the driver, a young lady, jumped off and went into the Café, and he saw Claire holding the team reins, waiting for her.

The morning sun was rising from behind the jail, and sunlight was pushing a shadow of the building onto Main Street. The sun's light, ahead of the shadow, framed the young woman's profile, so Sam saw plainly auburn hair beneath the little hat perched atop her head. Had not Young Bill been on his way over at any moment, his curiosity about the woman would have sent him across the street. He was glad to see Claire, however. Her being in town was a bright spot; it would save time in what he expected to be a busy day.

As soon as he could manage it, he would show her the letter from Chastity, and it would shine a new light into her world, and the money in it would get her out of town before Wyatt did whatever he was going to do.

Sam examined his grandson as Young Bill was walking from the hotel toward him. As impartially as he could, he attempted to define his strengths and weaknesses, especially his weaknesses if a confrontation with Wyatt Winslow were to take place. For someone who had lived in a lawless and violent land, William McKenzie Foley, known almost from the moment he was born as Young Bill Foley, had never felt a moment of fear or uncertainty. Security was as sure as sunrise and sunset. Nurtured by a mother who was favored with an exotic kind of beauty that was the envy of other women, and protected by a rich and powerful Catholic father as ruthless as the Spanish Inquisitors who had held his own Inquisitions building his empire, Young Bill Foley had found himself insulated yet seeing the lives of other men as perilous affairs. Their experiences remained foreign to him, for he felt none of their fears. That made him vulnerable to overconfidence. Understanding the circumstances of Young Bill's special birth, Sam, having seen it as an insider, knew unhappiness played no part in his nature. And why not? Born into privilege far away from Eastern snugness, living on a frontier where other lives were always at risk; why not enjoy life? Ivy Vanderbilt was now part of Young Bill's excitement, and Sam was not so old he did not remember the glorious feel of it. But, somewhere along the way, he would learn about his mother's infatuation with Bill Waterman. How would that turn out?

Sam turned to go inside the jail then decided the conversation outside would have as much privacy as he would need.

Young Bill was smiling when he hopped from the boardwalk over the jail's only step to meet Sam on the porch, his hand extended.

"What's up, Granddad? You sound serious."

"I am, and it is," Sam replied, shaking his grandson's hand.

"Let's hear it."

"A gunman is in town, or will be back in town, and you're his target."

"Me? Why?"

"Before I tell you, promise not to discuss who with anyone. Anyone, you understand? That includes the Ivy woman. Okay?"

"Certainly. Why?"

"The gunman is Wyatt Winslow."

"I thought he was dead."

"Everyone did."

"He survived the war?"

"He did, but not all in one piece. You might not recognize him. He's twisted up like he's been through a meat packing plant."

"And he wants me?"

"So he says."

"Chastity?"

"Yeah. It's for her, and to save his daddy's honor."

"I see. Is he good?"

"My guess is he is. I never bet against grit, and he has grit."

"I'll be too fast for him. I'm good with a handgun, Granddad."

"I know. I've seen you practice, but you've never shot it out before. Facing another man when he could mean your death can get on a man's nerves."

"I can handle the pressure. I hate to kill him, Granddad. How serious is he? I'll be leaving with Miss Ivy in a few minutes. We'll be gone all day. Tomorrow, I'm due back at the ranch. Roundup is ready, and I always lead the drive. Think he'd get discouraged and leave if I make myself scarce for a couple of weeks?"

"Be my opinion, if he decides he needs to kill you, he won't stop until he tries."

"It'll be tough on Claire either way. Does she know?"

"No. But there's a bright spot. Chastity sent money for her to visit the baby in Saint Louis. I'm gonna see she's on the stage this afternoon with money for a train ticket when she gets to San Antonio."

"That's one good thing about a nasty situation. Claire's a good woman. At least she'll be gone. Sooner or later, she'll find out, and she'll hurt all over again."

"I'm trying to prevent that."

"Chicken's come home to roost, don't they, Granddad?"

"Does that mean you are gonna tell me about you and Chastity?"

"Yep, and I'm not sure why. It's not to justify my part in it. Maybe it'll help you find some way to prevent this thing. I don't want to kill Wyatt. I've hurt Chastity and Claire enough."

"I'd like to hear it. Seems to me, Chastity was pretty enough and woman enough to make a good wife."

"She is. I wanted to marry her and told Dad everything. Next morning, with not a word about it said at breakfast, mother and Dad had me go to town with them in the surrey, and we went to the bank. They went in and came out then we drove to the livery barn where Dad had one of our horses saddled for me. He had me ride behind them, and we went in the direction of the Winslow place. About a mile out of town, we stopped. You'd know the place; it's the first secluded piece of high ground with a stand of trees above the river. Mind you, not a word has passed between us. Dad motions for me to get down. Old Bill Foley does not look up to anybody; we were eye to eye though, and he told me I would be handed an empire, and they were not going to hand it to me if they had to have the daughter of a Hellfire and Brimstone Methodist preacher for a queen. I was to take the money and ride over to meet her, and buy her off. If it took more, come back and get it, but end the affair.

Sam, I ask you, with your father and mother damning you as an ungrateful son, what would you do? For a moment I tried to rebel. My words fell on deaf ears. Then mother took up the verbal whip. I was too young. They had already enrolled me at Notre Dame. I'd be leaving with no need to face a shotgun wedding. The girl was a tramp for having sex out of wedlock. She was a girl of easy virtue, and there were plenty of others like her around, so I could have my pick. I was a fool for wanting to marry a slut, and I gave in. Everything would have been different if Chastity had taken the money and quietly left for Saint Louis. She broke down and told then left. That was her fault. My fault was giving in to my parents."

"Too late to place blame."

"You have something in mind, Granddad. What?"

"I don't have a real plan yet. I want you to have a fair chance against Wyatt, because you've never faced a life and death showdown and he has. Wyatt might be back this afternoon. I hope not. It could make it nip and tuck with Claire taking the afternoon stage. He's camping at Dave's grave at their old home place trying to decide the wrong and right of things."

"I'll handle my end of it. He'll end up dead if he tries me. If you think I'll lose my nerve, I won't."

"Just the same, I'll give you a thought or two. Wyatt sees himself seeking revenge for his sister's disgrace and his father's humiliation, so he'll want a noon or an afternoon showdown, a spectacle townspeople can witness. You are not the saloon type, so he can't go inside Irish Rose's and call you out. You are usually in the bank every afternoon. He'll ask around and learn that, so that's where he'll call you out. Pay attention. Attention to small things can keep bad things from happening, like getting killed. He'll be in the center of Main Street. He'll stand there, waiting like a martyr. When you walk out into Main Street, you will turn to face him. That's when you make your move. As soon as you turn, the second you face him, not a fraction later, make your move. That's your advantage. You had better not hesitate. Wyatt will wait that extra second because he needs the crowd's attention to put salve over a wound he only imagines but he thinks is real. I knew his dad, and Dave would not want it, and Chastity may hate you for deserting her, but she doesn't hate you enough to have you killed or risk her brother getting killed. How can I be sure? Chastity is Claire's daughter, that's why."

"You're a shrewd old codger, Granddad. I owe you. Thanks."

Young Bill turned and walked directly across to the hotel, where Ivy Vanderbilt, seeing him come toward her, left the shade of the veranda and descended the hotel steps to meet him on the boardwalk.

"Bill," Ivy did not say Young Bill because she did not yet know there was an Old Bill, "this young lady," and she waved in the direction of the wagon still parked in front of the Bluebonnet Café, "has asked me for a job. I told her to come back at three. Can we take a shorter trip, have lunch, and return early enough so I can keep my promise?"

So much for trying to avoid Wyatt Winslow, Young Bill thought. Thinking why not today; let's get it over with so I can go back to living my life, he grinned, and said, "Sure."

Then he saw the girl with the auburn hair climb down from the wagon and walk to them, and Ivy Vanderbilt said, "Molly, this is Bill Foley. Bill, this is Molly Gibbs. When I saw her hair, I thought she was your sister. I asked her if she was, and she said no, she didn't know you."

Young Bill was overwhelmed when he saw the young woman. Molly Gibb's hair and his hair were identical in color. What took his voice away was remembering the color of his father's hair before gray dulled it. The three of them were a perfect match. As far as he knew, his father's hair was the only pure auburn hair in the territory when the young woman must have been conceived. For the girl and him to be unrelated was a near impossibility meaning there was a good possibility Old Bill Foley was her father.

Young Bill finally found his voice and said, "Hello. Pleased to meet you, Miss Gibbs. I promise to have Miss Ivy back in time for your interview."

Young Bill, politely tipped his Stetson, then said, "Good morning" to Claire still seated on the nearby wagon, then took Ivy's arm and hurried them past the two women, and they mounted their waiting horses. He made a quick get-away needing time to think.

Chapter Fourteen

Sam Ordway headed across the street when he saw Young Bill and Ivy Vanderbilt leaving. As soon as he was in speaking distance of the two women, with a tone bordering rudeness he said, "What's your name, girl?"

Shocked by Sam's tone, Molly became flustered. She did not identify him by his face, but the star did it. He had accompanied Claire to her wedding. Elder Gibbs was well known and lots of people were there, but she was pretty sure of it. Did he not remember? Those thoughts slowed her reply but she finally answered meekly, "Molly Gibbs."

Then Sam said in the same demanding tone, "What's your daddy's name?"

"Enoch Crabtree."

"From near Bellville? Right?"

"Yessir."

"Pretty far piece from here. You married one of Elder Gibb's boys as I remember."

"Yessir. Cass Gibbs."

"I see. Mind telling me why you're here?"

"To find a job," Molly answered.

Claire could not understand Sam's attitude, and felt it was time to say something. "You know Molly, Sam. Why are you being so gruff with her? Has she done anything wrong?"

"I'm sorry, Claire. No. The child has done nothing wrong."

"I've never seen you so jumpy, Sam. Something's wrong. You know Molly. We went to her wedding. It's the color of her hair isn't it?"

Suddenly Sam wanted a cigarette. He and Old Bill and Dave Winslow began smoking Bull Durham when it became popular shortly after the War of Secession. They had been forced to give it up for lack of money when they went into the Llano Estacado to barter with the Comanche's. After they had land and cattle, and they began to hire cowpunchers, every cowboy they hired, to a man, carried Bull Durham sacks in their shirt pocket, the round tags hanging on strings showing plainly the brand. The men may have been broke but they would manage to smoke; it had become a cowman's badge. By that time, Sam, Old Bill, and Dave, with money in their pockets now, had lost the habit. That was almost twenty years ago, and Sam had not wanted one until this moment.

Sweeping his hat off, he had not removed it because the auburn hair had completely distracted him, he said, "Claire, you're a fine woman, and a handsome one at that. I owe you more consideration than I've shown here. I'm sorry I talked that way to a friend of yours."

"Why, Sam, that's a nice apology, and I'm flattered you think I'm handsome. I'm glad you finally noticed."

"I've always noticed," he replied smoothly.

As soon as the words left his mouth, Sam knew some of them had come from the green bottle. The California wine had allowed him to free thoughts that at his age should remain unsaid. Suddenly, he knew he had to get away and renew his acquaintance with the bubbly liquid. The nectar in the green bottle would replace the Bull Durham he wanted.

"Claire," he said, "I'm going into Irish Rose's for a minute. There's something I need to do. Please go to the jail and wait for me. I have something to show you."

"Is something wrong, Sam?"

"Yes. A few things. But what I have to show you is good. Trust me. Now the two of you get on over to the jail," and he made a shooing motion for them to be on their way, and he headed to the back of Irish Rose's, slipped quietly inside, and finished the contents of the green bottle.

Carrying his giddiness once again, Sam entered the jail. He was almost ready to sing, a chore he had always left to Dave Winslow.

The two ladies were each seated in a barrel chair, one at each end of his desk. Sam passed in back of them and sat down behind the old oak desk facing them, shoved his Stetson back on his head, and reached inside the desk drawer, removed Wyatt's letter, and shoved it toward Claire.

Claire accepted the letter without looking at it. Instead, her eyes fastened on Sam's and said, "You've been drinking, haven't you, Sam?"

"I have."

"What's going on, Sam?"

"Read the letter, and I'll tell you who's going and what on."

Sam was proud of the remark once he made it. It was spontaneous, and he knew the green bottle magic was back in great form inside him.

Claire looked down then. The envelope contained no handwriting, and it was thick with content, and Claire, aware of the subdued undercurrent around her, was inwardly apprehensive, so her fingers were slow and deliberate opening it.

Sam watched carefully. Molly Gibbs was also watching intently.

Claire first removed five twenty dollar certificates, and the thickness of the envelope was reduced to a single sheet of stationary. Claire then withdrew the thin white sheet, and the emotion she experienced when she saw the handwriting caused such a thickness in her voice she could scarcely talk. Unable to form a sentence, she finally managed, "Sam. Chastity?"

Sam, giddy from his recent contact with California, broke into a wide grin. "Read it, Claire."

Claire began, "Dear Mom. I love you," but that's as far as the moment would let her go, and she broke into tears that became sobs, and Sam left his chair and quickly made his way around the desk to hold her. Tender hearted Molly added her arms.

In a few moments Claire regained control, and Sam explained that Claire and Molly were to go home as quickly as possible, because the stage would leave at two. They were to pack whatever clothes Claire wanted to take with her. She was going by stage to San Antonio. Once there, she would buy a ticket on the Santa Fe Railroad for Saint Louis.

"I can't leave Jimbo."

"I'll keep him," Sam said. "I'll see he gets to school every day."

Molly said, "I'll help. If I get work, Marshal Sam can look after him until I get home."

"What about Cass?"

"Cass will just have to get along without me. He didn't worry none about me when he took off for the . . ." the whore in whorehouse was out of Molly's mouth before she clamped her lips shut, but it was too late. Sam had already put two and two together about Molly's visit.

"I don't know," Claire hesitated; her thinking unsettled.

"This is a big thing, Claire. Do it. Don't look back. The time is short. Trust me to look after things."

Claire, wanting badly to go but unsure about her Jimbo, looked down and finished reading the one page letter, then, showing she had not lost her mother hen image she turned to Sam and said, "I've told my children never to send money in the mail. Chastity must have lost her mind," and Claire continued sniffling.

"Don't fault her, Claire. The letter didn't come by mail. A rider brought it."

Walking back behind his desk, Sam sat down, reached inside and brought out a sheet of stationary on which he wrote

> *Theodosia Ordway.*
> *Millefiori Paperweight Factory*

Giving the note to Claire, he explained, "This is the name of my sister and the company she works for. She's a spinster. Couldn't cook and never found a feller who could. She loves company. Tell her I'll come back to visit her one of these days. She'll be glad to help you in any way she can."

Chapter Fifteen

All three left the jail together, had crossed the street, and Sam was helping the two ladies into Molly's wagon when a solitary rider on a black stallion with a white blaze on his forehead turned onto Main Street a block from them. Sam knew the horse. It was Old Bill Foley's. It would be impossible for the wagon to get turned around and leave town without Old Bill seeing that beautiful head of auburn hair on Molly Gibbs head. Only a miracle could prevent it. No such miracle happened, for Old Bill saw Molly's hair and immediately spurred his animal, and he was on top of them, holding up the team and the wagon in the middle of the street.

"What are *you* doing here?" Old Bill demanded in a booming voice that stopped two drovers in their tracks who were just leaving the Bluebonnet Café.

Poor Molly, Sam thought.

Claire thought the same thing, and she defended the young woman, "She's my houseguest, Mister Foley. I'm going to Saint Louis, and she will be staying at my house to keep my son."

Not one to be cowed, Old Bill Foley shot back, "She's got no business in my town."

"My house is mine, Mister Foley. The taxes are paid. It does not belong to your town." Claire's tone was not unkind. Her words were put forth simply, and her voice was just loud enough to be heard by the four of them and not the drovers still standing on the boardwalk in front of the Bluebonnet.

Sam, understanding Claire was standing her ground but did not want to step any harder on Old Bill's sensitive toes, took over and said, "Bill, I'll be back at the jail in a few minutes. Wait for me there, if you please. We need to talk. It's urgent."

Old Bill Foley's face took on a quizzical look. Thinking about Sam's use of urgent, trying to grasp its meaning and his surroundings at the same time like old men sometime do, he left. Unsteady in his mind, he said nothing more and turned the big black and walked him to the jail, tied him to the tie-rail, and walked inside while Sam and the ladies watched.

After he was sure Old Bill was going to stay inside the jail and not bounce back out to pounce on Molly Gibbs once more, did Sam say, "Okay, ladies, not much time to get your work done. Get on with your packing."

Sam watched the wagon for a few moments as it was leaving. When it disappeared around the corner, he walked to the bank and went inside where he withdrew one hundred and fifty dollars from his savings account. Chastity was not as well off as Wyatt Winslow let on. One hundred dollars would not cover rail fare to Saint Louis. His addition would insure a pleasant trip. Leaving the bank, he looked at the envelope with the money. It would put a dent in any retirement he might plan for his old age, but Claire was worth it.

Walking to the jail, a good thought came. Instead of Old Bill Foley, the rider just as easily could have been Wyatt Winslow. Thinking of Wyatt Winslow lessened the glow from the green bottle.

Chapter Sixteen

Old Bill Foley was behind the desk seated in Sam's chair. Sam wasn't one foot inside the door when Old Bill nailed him with his rich Irish voice, "Sam, I want that woman sent back where she came from." His tone was thick with authority.

Sam didn't back down. "Can't. She's broken no law."

Sam was sure Old Bill would bellow like a grizzly bear fresh out of hibernation when he was told nothing could be done. Instead, the old man said, "Sam, how long have I been out?"

Two years was the reply on Sam's tongue, but that would shock his old friend, and he caught himself in time to say, "Quite a spell, Bill. Does Abbey know where you've gone?"

It was a quick diversion, and Sam was proud he had changed the direction of Old Bill's thoughts. The old man was easily distracted now, because the expression on his face showed confusion when he replied, "No, I don't think she does. What you said about a gunman gunning for Young Bill kept me awake wondering if it was real or another dream. I dream a lot nowadays. I was awake most of the night, and I was so confused I decided to come to town and find out. I left before sunrise. She'll come to town looking for me, won't she?"

The pitiful tone of Old Bill's question was like a small child asking his mother to come care for him. Old Bill was two people now. One a grown man with enough power to have decisions carried out no matter the right or wrong of them; the other a helpless child.

"I'm sure Abbey will be along after awhile," Sam replied. "When she finds you gone, she'll come looking for you. Even if they push her team, it will be noon or later when she gets here. Why don't you go on over to the hotel and wait in your rooms. She will go there first. The Town House will be the last place she looks; you never liked the place, and she knows it."

Sam expected Old Bill to leave. Instead, he rose from the chair, but he remained standing stiff like a statue. Sam thought he was dazed. Not sure what to do, or what to say, if anything, Sam, who was still standing, considered walking around the desk to steady the man when Old Bill said in a whisper Sam could hardly hear and had trouble believing after he replayed the old man's words in his mind. Old Bill Foley's words were: "She's mine, Sam. She's mine. What do I do?"

Sam juggled the words around in his brain, but they never organized into the facts as he knew them. Then the picture of Molly's face framed by her auburn hair formed in his mind, he finally answered, "Claim her, Bill."

Sam watched Old Bill Foley considering what claiming the girl would mean, and after several long moments of indecision, he asked, "How?"

"Don't know for sure," Sam replied. Sam knew Old Bill meant how was he to explain it to his wife and son.

Sam knew Old Bill's problem was also his, because Abbey belonged to both of them. Neither man spoke; neither knew what to say or what to ask. Finally, it was Sam who pushed on, "Mind answering some personal questions? They're gonna be real personal for me same as you."

"Nope. This seems to be the time of it. Ask."

"Abbey's mother never refused me. She always made time for my needs, and wishes for that matter, regardless of hers. Is Abbey like her mother?"

"She is. She allowed me to bed her past my eightieth. None of it was her fault or failing."

"Makes it hard to understand. The other woman beautiful?"

"Passable. Not hardly in Abbey's class."

"Strange. Facts say she wasn't rich. Her child is poor as a church mouse."

"True. They're both poor."

"The child is probably sixteen. That's a lot of years for you to think about it. Have you figured out why yet?"

"Why? Because I could, that's why. They owed me. It was in my power. I took the woman because it was my right."

"Your right? Power? What the hell? Just the once?"

"I didn't count the number of times. It was more than a year."

Sam sat down on the corner of his desk to consider what he was having trouble understanding. Old Bill Foley slowly retreated back into Sam's chair, and looking down on the old man, Sam was aware their positions had changed; he was in charge of Old Bill Foley and not the other way around, and he said, "This confession may be good for the soul, but it didn't get us anywhere. We're looking for a decent excuse to give Abbey and Young Bill, including your daughter when she finds out. Was that woman anything special under the sheets?"

"Same as any other woman. You probably had lots like her before you married. Nothing special. She gave in easy. Both of them did."

"Both? Two women?"

"No. Him and her."

"I didn't figure you to be that way."

"Damn it. You got the thing out of shape."

"Then fill it in. Draw a straight line. Abbey will come looking for you, and she's sure to see that girl at some point. We need some kind of explanation."

"The best I can do is place it for you."

"Be on with it then."

Old Bill Foley's eyes moved and found the window beyond Sam, and he began, "That fall, we completed the biggest cattle drive we ever attempted and the reason was the Comanche's kept their part of our bargain and allowed us to cross their territory. Afterwards, the bankers in Galveston said I was the third richest rancher in Texas. The other two being that old outlaw, Shanghai Pierce, and Richard King from the King Ranch down in the valley. That was pretty high cotton for a lad who had been run out of Ireland, so, with plenty of money to spend, Abbey and me began planning the hacienda, and we began building it the following year. Just before the big house was finished, we, Abbey, Young Bill, and me, moved into it. I was not only one of the richest men in Texas, but the happiest. I was living like an English Lord or a Mexican Don. Life was damn good.

"Now, to build a house like that took a big crew of masons and carpenters, so there were lots of Mexican workers living down below where the ranch crew lived. Some we squeezed into the bunkhouse, others were living in tents. I hired an extra cook, and we fed everyone chuck wagon style. You always remember a day like that day was. It was early but daylight was beginning, and I stepped outside with a cup of coffee like I always did. Then I heard a horse galloping toward me, and our *El Jefe* rode into the yard waving an arrow. This is a Mexican who got to be *El Jefe* because he spoke English *and* Spanish, but he jumped off the animal so rattled everything he babbled was Spanish. His words were coming so fast I barely managed to understand an arrow had landed at his feet, between his legs. I figured right off what was happening, and I grabbed the arrow from him. I recognized it as a Comanche arrow. Any man who knows Indians knows a Comanche makes the finest arrows on earth. A brave will spend days and sometimes weeks on just one arrow shaft, so they don't waste them. They hit what they shoot at, and I told *El Jefe* to put his men to work; they were all safe. The arrow was just a message from them to me, and I showed him the small square of buffalo hide on the shaft. It was Indian Western Union sending me a message. Do you remember how we exchanged messages with the Comanche's when we first came to this country and traded mirrors for land rights?"

Chapter Seventeen

Sam's imagination went directly to the day, place, and time, and it was every bit as vivid as when it happened even though his mind had leaped backward twenty years. Sam saw a Comanche chief and Bill Foley exchanging documents made of cowhide. The chief kept one of the hides, and Old Bill Foley the other which he called a deed.

Just as quickly, Sam's mind returned him to the room in the jailhouse where he and Old Bill Foley sat, and he asked, "Bill, do you still have that piece of cowhide stationary?"

"You can bet I do," the old man replied. "It proves my right to the land."

"Good to know, but no help with finding out why you and that woman had a daughter. Move your story along. What happened next?"

"The message that was branded on that piece of buffalo stationary delivered by arrow telegraph that landed between *El Jefe's* legs was a picture that showed three people, a woman, a man, and a small boy. Above them was a circle indicating the sun, I took it to mean a family was homesteading one day away on Indian land. I was to do something about it."

"Seems like you would have got me or Dave to go with you to investigate."

"I thought about it. You and a three man fencing crew were working almost a day's ride south and east. It would have taken an extra day to get you. Dave had gone to bring Claire back, and I didn't trust any of the crew to do what had to be done. It was just a small family. Only one man, so I told Abbey I'd be gone overnight and went myself. With Abbey, I never had to explain my whereabouts running a spread as big as ours."

Sam, sitting on the desk, was letting Bill Foley tell what had to be told at an informal pace.

Bill Foley continued, "I judged them to have settled near the big Bosque where the Indians made their winter home every year. A farmer would choose flat land, not wooded, but he would want water, and there, where the river left the trees, was a long strip of level ground away from the woods of the Bosque, and that was where they chose.

"When I got there, they had finished the noon meal, because the man was heading back to the field when I rode up. He waved. I didn't. I rode over and told him he'd best come back to the house with me. He didn't like it, but he followed, and the woman and boy came out of the cabin when we got there. He wanted to know why I was ordering him around; this was his land. I told him it was Indian land and if he and his weren't out of here by nightfall, in a couple of days there would be more Indians than he could count, and he and his wife and child would be mutilated for sport. He said he didn't believe me. What proof did I have? I told him the proof was in the Colt on my hip which I was going to use to kill him after which time I would take his wife and son with me to safety. That way I'd save two out of three fools. He started mumbling about having sweated for almost a year, and I stopped him; told him to get on his horse and ride with me and I'd show him a thing to set him straight.

He went to gather his animal and I told the lady to begin packing the wagon, and she began to cry, but she started into the house, and the boy followed; he looked to be about four. We rode over a mile deep into the Bosque following the stream bed. I knew there was bound to be evidence of old encampments somewhere down the line, and sure enough, we came on old bones, old campfires, and waste; Indians don't clean up. We rode back. He was quiet as a mouse. At the cabin, he asked what was to be done, and I told him we had to burn the cabin, and the woman began crying again. I told her to hush and move faster if she was going to get her stuff out, because I was going to burn it down after sundown so the flames could be seen by the Comanche.

"They got serious about packing then, and I gathered brush and stacked it beside the cabin's walls wanting to make as big a fire as possible. When that was done, I helped the big fellow tether his animals to the wagon. He had a fine Jersey, and two other cows for milking, and he had a young longhorn bull penned separately. I think the fool thought he could use the bull for breeding. Hell, he'd have been lucky if that longhorn bull didn't kill that poor cow. Another thing was cows will walk behind a wagon, and I suspected he was stupid enough to try to do the same with that young bull. I asked him his name then, and he said he was Enoch Crabtree, and I asked Mister Crabtree if he was going to take the bull. He said he hoped to. He didn't know it would take two good cowboys on two good cutting horses to do that, and I said so. I told him to leave the animal penned and get help then come back and get him when he was settled elsewhere. A bull can be hazed to a different pasturage, but it takes two good men; a longhorn bull cannot be pushed or pulled to one. His pole corral was a good one with poles shaped well and skinned so bark wouldn't rub an animal or a human, showing the man knew what he was about. So were his fields. He had two. It don't take much land to feed a family well. He had water near enough to irrigate if the weather got too dry. Using his plowing mule, he hauled water for his stock tanks and the cabin. It didn't take much extra work for the fields. He had cleared land not far from the creek, not in the woods where the Indians would have camped, but he was too close for them to tolerate. All Indians were being hounded by the Army then, so the Comanche's were taking no chances. They had their own way during the War of Secession with both armies chasing each other, but after the war ended, there were lots of Army officers who had been pushed back in rank and soldiers who didn't have jobs to go back to, so, with the officers looking for rank and glory to get that rank, they were out to get any Indians they could corner. I didn't blame the Indians, and I sure hated for Mister Crabtree to lose what he had worked for, but come sundown, I burned the cabin to the ground. They left before I set the fire, all three of them crying, Mister Crabtree included. Before they left, him and her asked where they should go. I told them to get close to Bellville. I told them a fellow named Howard Bell and a few farmers had a settlement south and west. They didn't go there or the story would be different."

Sam's butt was tired of sitting on the edge of the desk, and it seemed a good time to interrupt Old Bill, so he moved to one of the barrel chairs in front of the desk and propped his boots atop it.

"It's a poor time to move," Old Bill told him.

"I ain't gonna move back," Sam retorted. The California spirit was gone and he was getting a little irritable. "I'm comfortable here. Get on with it."

"The reason I used for going back was I was going to check on that bull. I knew Mister Crabtree couldn't haze that bull, and he would still be in the pen and his water scarce. The truth is I didn't want them on my land. I didn't want anybody on my land except people I chose. I had an itchy feeling they hadn't gone to Bellville. They would have to pay for land there, and I judged them too poor for that, and I figured they'd squat on me again. It was bothersome to me."

"Did you find any reason to scratch the itchy feeling?" Sam asked.

"Damn right, I did. They moved far enough from the big Bosque so the Indians would not to bother them, but they settled on some damn good grazing land of mine. You were never one to roam the land. You went where the work was and worked. Roundup was collecting critters and driving them to whatever railroad was nearest. I'm different from you, Sam. I love every inch of ground I own. I've looked it over time and again just for the pleasure of looking."

"I should have seen that in you, Bill, but I didn't. It was something in plain sight that I never opened my eyes wide enough to see. Go on."

"Well, when I got to the burned out cabin, the bull was gone. Crabtree had come back, but the animal had run off from him. I could make out tracks where Crabtree's horse had tried to head off the critter. The corral poles were gone. He had dragged the poles to his new place rather that fell and strip new ones for his other animals. That made sense. I followed the trail, it was plain enough where he had dragged the poles, and I found the beginnings of a new cabin. They were workers, those three. I'll grant that. A new cabin in one week while plowing a field to get in a crop before winter. I admired them but I was mad. Crabtree came from the field when he saw me. The woman was cleaning out a chicken cage, and she came too. I was not kind when I told them they were on my land and to get the hell off. Both of them said they had rights; they were on Spanish Land Grant land. I told them the Spanish had no rights. Neither Spain or Mexico owned the land; they never found enough people willing to settle it and hold on to it. Me and my people had done it. My grant came from the Comanche Indians who had held the land for hundreds of years. It was my land, given to me by the Comanche, and I had a deed to prove it. Get off now, I said. I knew they had no rights to the land. Spanish Grants and Mexican *Porciónes* required some form of payment, and they didn't have a dime in hard currency. Crabtree had animals and grit, but that's all he had. Government land was a dollar an acre, by law, and they knew I had them. The woman tugged on her man's arm, and they went back and talked underneath a tree and had some serious words. I could tell they were serious words, but they never got heated, just back and forth questions and answers with the woman doing most the talking. When they came back to where I was, the woman did the talking. She didn't know my name, so she said, "Mister, we admit we owe you. We don't have a dime. There's but one way to pay you, and I'm it if you'll have me. She paused and let that soak in. When I didn't say anything because I was struck dumb, she began to explain the she was a dancehall girl before Enoch came along. I'm not a beauty, but I'm attractive, she said, and I know how to treat a man. I'm yours any time you want me. Enoch will take Seth and leave for an hour or so, long enough for us to finish your business. There'll be no hard feelings from Enoch. Seth is not his. Knowing that, he took me and my son as we were, and gave us a better life. He's willin', and I'm willin', if you're willin'."

Old Bill met Sam Ordway's eyes. When Sam said nothing, Old Bill explained, "I left Sam. I told the woman I'd think on it, and left."

Sam found his voice. "Goddamned Bill, if you left, how in hell did the woman have a daughter by you?"

"I went back, Sam. I rode a long way thinking about them and me. I had run off other squatters. Shot and killed some. Those were the dirty, thieving kind. Just trash to begin with. But that was long ago. They were a clean hard working family. They owed me, and I wanted payment. In Ireland, I owed the landlord and couldn't pay, and he shipped me and my family off to certain death to get my land so he could raise beef for the English and get a fancy price. It was harsh, but it was the rules we lived by. We owed him, and we paid. They owed me, and they offered payment, and I took it. That's the way it was. I would have kept taking what was owed me, except one day she said she was pregnant and couldn't be sure who fathered it until it came. I told her I wouldn't be back. She said if it was mine, they would see the child never bothered me or my family. That's it, Sam. None of us thought about the child growing up and getting married."

"Nothing," Sam snapped.

He dropped his chair to the floor. It made a loud clap. The clap showed his displeasure.

Then he voiced it. "Goddammit, Bill, there's nothing in that sorry episode to give consolation to the people you wronged. You traded land for carnal favors."

"Nothing like that. I never gave them title."

"They lived on it long enough so now it's theirs."

"It's only a small farm. Not enough land to miss."

"Well, that's no justification. Young Bill will overlook it because he's a man, but what about Abbey and that sweet young Molly Gibbs. What do we say to them?"

"Damned if I know. That's why I asked you how I was to claim her without doing further damage."

"We'll just leave it like that for now. Get your ass on over to the Bluebonnet. A late breakfast and some coffee will do you good."

"I need to see Father Alfred first. He don't hear confessions as old as mine very often. Until the girl showed up, I had forgotten about it myself. Seems like God didn't forget, did he Sam?"

"I guess," Sam answered absently thinking about Young Bill's earlier remark about him and Chastity and chickens coming home to roost then applying the observation to Old Bill's predicament, and he added, "You can trust someone like The Almighty to keep score whether or not you do. Human's call it payback. I always figured The Almighty used payback a little. You pretty well proved it. Now git."

Old Bill Foley rose from the chair and walked to the door, and Sam remembered why the man had come to town in the first place.

"Wait a minute, Bill," Sam said, and the old man stopped at the door and turned to face him, his hand on the door handle.

"The gunman wanting a face-off with Young Bill is Wyatt Winslow."

"I thought he was dead."

"No such luck. The war maimed him. Maimed him in body and spirit. He wants to kill your son for what he did to Chastity."

"I'll try and buy him off. Where is he?"

"Money won't do it. It's not just Chastity; he's after justice for his father. He says Dave died because of Young Bill's dalliance with Chastity. He wants honor for his father. Wyatt's got nothing to live for, so he's going to spend the little that's left of his life getting revenge. Poor thoughts and reasons, but that's him."

"It was Abbey and me who made that decision. Where will I find him?"

"He's at Dave's old home place. My guess is he won't come back to town before tomorrow. He expects his mother to leave on today's stage. Claire's going to Saint Louis to visit Chastity."

"Do you have any thoughts, Sam?"

"One. I'm not sure about it yet. There's another gunslinger in town. Wes Hardin's brother, Matthew Hardin. I'd say he's for hire. We might have Wyatt go through him. If he gets Wyatt, Young Bill's free. If Wyatt gets Hardin, we find out how fast Wyatt really is and go from there."

"All poor choices."

"Best I can do for now."

"I'd best get on over to Father Alfred."

"No you don't. Don't you tell anyone what you just told me"

"But, Sam, I could pass on anytime. My salvation is at stake. If I don't go to confession, my soul will burn in Hell."

"You waited damn near twenty years before you thought about that. You can take your chances until we can smooth things out some. Leave Father Alfred for the other sinful parishioners."

Chapter Eighteen

Young Bill was quiet. His riding companion guessed his silence was caused by the unexpected appearance of the young woman whose name was Molly Gibbs but who looked as if her name should have been Molly Foley. Molly Gibbs looked like a family secret everyone knew but her. When that young lady walked into the hotel looking for a job, it was a stroke of good luck. The young woman was perfect. She was beautiful, and she was poor. Desperate for any kind of work, she said she would do anything, and Ivy Vanderbilt was willing to test that.

Exactly as Ivy Vanderbilt guessed, Molly Gibbs was at the center of Young Bill's thinking. His mind directed him back to a single wishful thought: Old Bill did not sire her. Her age was clear enough. She was younger than Young Bill. That meant at the time she was conceived, Old Bill had a young and remarkably beautiful woman for his bed; why would he stray and chance an out of wedlock bastard child? If Molly Gibbs was a threat, she would be on the doorstep of the ranch with her claim, yet she had come to town asking for a job. It was simple. The color of her hair was a chance of nature. At ease with his mental detective work, Young Bill returned his attention to his chief concern, the conquest of Ivy Vanderbilt.

"Ivy," he said turning and looking back at her as their horses loafed, "You are the most beautiful woman I've ever seen."

The remark brought a quick smile to her face. "If that's the case, why did Molly Gibbs attract so much of your attention?"

That was not where he wanted this conversation to go, but he responded with humor, "She did attract my attention, didn't she?"

"I'd say that."

"Well, she is pretty. Cute kind of pretty. You're classic. Beautiful like the countryside we'll visit. While we're there, I want to talk about me, and ask questions about you. Are you fair game?"

"A woman loves compliments. Thank you for saying I'm beautiful. And, yes, I'm fair game. I am as ready as a woman gets to be loved then ravished. How does that sound?"

"Brazen and honest. I admire you for it."

"Well, it's too soon in this relationship for me to be ravished. I trust you understand that with your choice of places we visit."

"I do. As much as I would like to hurry things, I can't afford to rush this. I have important things to do with my life. I'm taking you to Tom Silverhorn's ranch. It's less than a mile from here, so we won't be pressed for time, so why don't we run the horses? They need exercise."

"Cut 'em loose!" she replied digging spurs into her animal's ribs.

Both animals were in a rousing gallop, Young Bill leading by a horse's head, until, suddenly, Ivy reined up unexpectedly. Turning back to meet her, Young Bill asked, "Why did you stop?"

"Over there," she said pointing directly north "is what I came out West to find. I love to paint landscapes. Most of the landscapes painted in our country are in New England. That land," she said, pointing, "will make a spectacular landscape when autumn begins to change those Maple tree leaves. Can we ride to where the stream bends back on itself? That little meadow seems like a cool place to picnic. My goodness, I almost missed it. My eyes are already feeding on the colors, and autumn hasn't done its artistry yet."

"Sure, we can. That's part of Tom Silverhorn land. He's not overly friendly, but he's not hostile. Come on. We'll have lunch there."

Approaching, Young Bill could see the limestone cliff that caused the stream to bend was not a high one, probably less than ten feet above them. The cliff was a source of wonder. Studies at Notre Dame had filled in the cause of wonderment. The science of geology was still in its infancy, but men had made observations from as early as Aristotle who guessed the Earth was much older than anyone imagined, and changes had occurred on such a slow scale that it was not possible for an individual to see such a change happening in one lifetime. A moving stream will not change a limestone cliff in a day, month, or year, but in a thousand years or so, it will dissolve and carve the cliff as well as any stonecutter's tool.

Watching the fast moving water with Ivy Vanderbilt next to him, Young Bill looked up at the narrow gorge the stream had carved in the limestone wall, taking centuries to do it, and he asked, "How many years would you guess it took that stream to dissolve that stone and carve the wall across there?"

"Did the stream do that?"

"The moving water in the stream did it, but it took a long time."

"As many as a thousand?" Ivy Vanderbilt smiled at her guess. She knew it was a wild one.

"More than that," Bill added. "A lot more."

"A million? That can't be. It's impossible."

"It's true."

"I'm really surprised. Are you sure?"

"I learned about it at Notre Dame."

"Notre Dame? Now that's something. A rancher's son in college. I thought a rancher's son would learn about animal husbandry or law, subjects that will aid in running a ranch, but I hear you talking about water dissolving stone walls. How is that?"

"I learned about ranch things like selective breeding and land management, but I had other courses. One of my elective subjects was a new science called geology. It opened my eyes to things like the cliff you and I are looking at just now."

"You'll certainly be a different kind of cowboy."

"I intend to be. I'll lay out our lunch over there where we each have a tree to lean against, and, after we eat, we can talk. I'll tell you about me and my plans then you can tell me about your life and your dreams. Fair?"

Ivy Vanderbilt failed to return an answer, so Young Bill turned and walked back to the horses and untied the picnic lunch basket, then returned. Ivy had not answered his challenge, and he decided not to let it drop. He would make it again sometime after lunch.

After lunch, he said, "My mother is Marshal Sam Ordway's daughter. Her mother, Sam's wife, was Chinese. That heritage made my mother an unusually beautiful woman. I want you to meet her."

"I'd love to."

"That will come later. I won't be able to take you sightseeing for a few days. I need to get back to the ranch tomorrow. I lead all the cattle drives, and we have a herd made up ready to move. Nowadays, we drive them to San Antonio and meet the railroad there. I'll only be gone about a week. I'll have you meet mother when I get back. Will you still be here?"

"I expect to. It depends."

"Depends on what?"

"I'm closer to staying than moving on. What I've seen about your town, and the land I'm looking at today, has me thinking this is where I want to settle."

"But this land is not for sale. Anything else I can do to help?"

"It doesn't need to be this land. Land near here could make a beautiful setting for a home."

"You haven't seen my ranch, yet. I'd like for you to wait. I want you to see it. Make up your mind then."

"A woman could think there was a proposal in there somewhere. I find you fascinating, but it's still too early for us."

"Asking you to wait sounded like a proposal, didn't it? I guess it was, although it wasn't meant to be just yet. I'll polish up a better phrase if the time comes."

"We'd better wait on your better phrase. At any rate, it was pleasing to hear. Truthfully, I like you, and I like it here. I paint landscapes, and everything I see pleases my eyes. I do a portrait now and then. Captivating faces attract me, and the moment I saw you, I wanted to do your portrait. If the proposal doesn't happen, will you sit for me?"

"Sure. If you promise not to tell any of the men on our place. They'd ride me something awful. I'd get it in English and Spanish."

"Wish granted."

"Let me finish about me then I'd like to know things about you."

"I'm not sure I want to talk about me, yet. Not today anyway. If there is a later for us, I promise I'll tell you any and everything about me. Will that be okay?"

"I'll settle for that. I want you to know my father is still alive, so the ranch is not yet legally mine. My father married my mother when she was twenty, and he was over sixty. He's been in a coma, or in a comatose state, for two years now. He can't last much longer."

"Are you telling me you will be a rich young man? Is that it? I have some wealth of my own. Are we to match dollars and assets?"

"No. Not at all. I was going to a different place with that information. I'm aware your name is Vanderbilt. With a last name like that, your wealth could easily out distance mine."

"Commodore Vanderbilt fathered twelve children, and eleven lived. He left ninety-five percent of his fortune to only one son. The other heirs split five percent. *If* I'm one of those Vanderbilt's, and I was told my grandfather was Cornelius Jeremiah who spent big and often. He sued for an equal share and lost, so not all Vanderbilt's are filthy rich. I have money of my own. Please accept my apology. I'm sorry I was touchy."

"Accepted. Let me move on. My father and I share the same name, so to separate us we became Old Bill and Young Bill practically from the moment I was born. I want you to know this because the names reflect the vast difference between his old and my new thinking. This land where we stand was a no man's land when Dad and Sam Ordway came this way. The more you look around, the more you'll see what a bountiful land this is, and can be, and it was uninhabited. Why? Plains Indians ruled it, and they are wanderers moving across it like nomads. Their kind of life wasted enormous amounts of fruitful land. Above us, for hundreds of miles upward through Kansas and Nebraska into the Dakotas, this land is one immense prairie of grass. Not too many years ago, every mapmaker pictured that huge oblong circle of land as The Great American Desert, because it was unexplored. Why? Indians hunting buffalo herds roamed here, and those tribes were so fierce white settlers who tried to settle were massacred. I'm sure you know all this. I'm refreshing it because I want you to see what confronted my father, Old Bill, and my grandfather, Sam Ordway, and Dave Winslow when they first came to this country years ago."

"I understand. I really do. I love adventure, and I've been fascinated by everything happening out here, so I read Harper's Weekly faithfully to keep up."

"We get Harper's. What the magazines says about us is pretty thick. My folks and me, especially Mom, keep up with the outside world with it. Mom doesn't care much about reading. She looks at the pictures of the latest fashions, but that's all."

"Do you notice the cartoons Thomas Nash draws?"

"I do. He's humorous."

"I never miss his caricatures. He's really a fine artist. He's famous for political cartoons, but it takes talent to do what he does."

"Dad's favorite is Joel Chandler Harris."

"The Brer Rabbit and Uncle Remus writer?"

"That's the one. Dad can't read well, and Mom reads to him, or did. He follows every word Joe Harris writes because Dad says he's another red headed Irish bastard like he is."

"Really? Joel Harris is really a bastard?"

"True. And his hair is as bright an auburn as mine and Dad's before gray got to it. Dad says we might be kin."

"It's a small world, isn't it?"

"Human path's cross in strange ways. Well, I've let us drift away from my aims. I need to move us back a bit. Its old history, but it's necessary to get us where I want to go. Spanish Conquistadors began our West. They were the first outsiders to attempt to colonize the Plains. They discovered the area was so vast that they drove stakes in the ground to mark their way back, so the area was first known as the Llano Estacado, the Staked Plains in English. Eventually, because the Spanish, and later the Mexicans, had guns and horses, they established settlements as far as Taos and Santa Fe, New Mexico, but the land was too big for them to tame, and the Indians captured guns and horses and drove the Spanish back to Mexico. The two most dominate tribes were the Navajo in the north and the Comanche in the south where we stand. This is where I'm heading with the history: Dad made a bargain with the Comanche, who had ruled this land for six hundred years. He maintains he got title to his land from the rightful owners, the Comanche. After Dad made the land safe, settlers have come claiming rights under Spanish Land Grants. More have been coming lately."

"I'm not sure what you're driving at just yet. Are you saying title to your land is in question?"

"It has been challenged. Old Bill Foley is a stubborn man when it comes to what's his. He refuses to recognize any claim. He maintains he got his title from the legitimate land owners, so everyone who comes here looking for land is trespassing."

"Do the courts agree with him?"

"It never came to that. While I was away at college, Tom Silverhorn's daddy challenged our land rights and won. Fortunately, old Frederick Silverhorn was far from rich, so the amount of land he got was not enough for Dad to worry about, but it worried me about others who thought they might follow his example. It was useless to talk to Dad, so I told Mom. Business is not something Mom wants to understand, but she, reluctantly because I had to pry it from her, loaned me enough to get the process started. She gets her personal money from every trail drive, and she has a tidy sum of her own, but she insisted I was getting a loan not a gift, and I took it.

"San Antonio was too close, word would leak back here, so I went to Austin and hired a young lawyer, Timothy O'Fallon, Irish if Dad found out. Foley is now incorporated and every acre of our land along the Frio and Hondo rivers has been filed on. Control the water and you control the outlying land adjoining it. I'm in pretty good shape land wise, but I have debt to contend with.

"I'm sorry it has taken so much time to tell, but this is what I want you to see. The Land Ordinance allows land for towns, after it is surveyed, for a price not less than one dollar per acre. Each township is a six mile rectangle divided equally into thirty-six sections of six-hundred and forty acres each. The government sets aside 4 of the 36 sections for a post office and public schools. The total amount for the balance of the thirty-two sections is $20,640 dollars. In time I should get my money and more. That's a bunch of township lots."

"I'll say. Do I see you selling town lots?"

"When Dad passes on, that's some of what I intend. I'll keep the ranch, but it's big enough for four ranches. I can run the same number of animals on half the land. By cross-breeding, I can cut the acreage in half again. The land south is excellent farm land; it gets more rain. I can use windmills to water cows on ranch land. That land to the south will attract farmers. As of now, more people are not welcome here. More will come when they know they will be welcome.

Settler's who move here will find a wonderful place for a family. It's the safest place in Texas, thanks to Sam's little civilian army. We have a nice school. I'll see it gets bigger and better, but I'll always keep Foley a small town. My father is Catholic, and he backs the church with his money. We had a Methodist church at one time. I will welcome others.

"Another of my selling points is we have only one saloon, and it's a nice one. It serves as a stage for traveling shows that entertain our citizens. We don't have Big Town entertainment, but most farmers aren't looking for Big City things, anyway. Married women, and nice single girls with their beaux's, come to the shows. Claire Winslow plays the piano when school functions are staged there. My mother has been inside Irish Rose's; so have most of the other women around. It's our Town Hall meeting place, not a din of inequity. Foley, Texas, is a nice family place. I'll get ten dollars an acre. How does that sound?"

"Grand. You didn't mention that other evil place, the one featuring sinful girls of the night."

"None here that I know of; we leave that for San Antonio. I may need to consider one if I can profit from it. I still owe the State twenty thousand. Mom gave me a thousand, but the lawyer demanded his fee up front, so that's gone. He's furnishing valid names for the tracts I filed on, and that's extra. The final price will depend on how many names are gathered. Those are legal voters who are supposed to have filed on each section, and O'Fallon is going to back-date their claim, a slightly illegal proceeding, showing each had abandoned the land before finishing the five year period required for the homestead. He'll get away with it since the old State House burned destroying all public records including old land records; they're building a big new one made of granite that won't burn. He says one of the ranching families set the fire to destroy the records, so we may as well take advantage of what they did and do what they're doing. That leaves me owing extra dollars, in addition to the twenty thousand, plus accruing interest, in debt. Time is short. I have only one more year to pay up. The cattle drive I'm making tomorrow will cover it with money to spare, but Old Bill Foley don't let me touch it. It's wired straight into his bank account and Mom's."

"It's a shame you can't reason with him."

"You forget. He's been in a dreamlike state for two years. We follow orders already in place."

"It's shameful to say, but it would be better for everyone if he passed on."

"For Mom and me, yes. That thought has gone through my mind, but I don't wish it. He's my dad even if he's old. It's a pity Dad isn't younger. She can't handle the ranch."

"The perils of marrying an older man," she said.

Reflecting on the remark, she recovered hastily, "I'm sorry I said that. I'd take it back if I could."

"That's okay. I'm sad Dad's older than Mom, because he's leaving her with a lot of life yet to live. I'm sorry he's leaving us. He made a man out of me. I'll miss him."

"I understand," she replied then added, "Why don't we leave now? We can make it a leisurely ride back."

She arose and he took her arm to help. When she was standing, he embraced her tenderly and kissed her gently.

"Am I that fragile?" she asked.

"Not at all. You're a strong woman, the way I see you. I can't afford for us to enjoy more passion this soon, at least not before I tell you another, much different, circumstance of mine."

His arms were around her waist. He did not release them nor did she pull away, making their faces close and their eyes fixed so that any emotion either had the other would know.

"Today or one day soon, I will kill a man or he will kill me."

Her eyes had been shining, and he watched them changing from happiness to expressionless when he told her. Then she melted against him, her face folding into his chest. After a moment, she looked up at him with eyes that were filmed with moisture. She tried to make words work, and they wouldn't. "Bill . . . Oh, God," was all she could manage.

"It's still a lawless land," he said. "It's needless to discuss the right and wrong of it, because it's simply needless. If I live, I'll explain it all to you. If I don't, it won't matter."

He released her from their embrace and gathered the picnic basket, and they walked to the horses in silence, and rode to town in silence, and he left her at the hotel then went to find Sam Ordway to ask if Wyatt Winslow had come to town.

Chapter Nineteen

Wyatt Winslow entered the jail while everyone was distracted by the arrival of the stagecoach across the street. Leaving his horse in back, he slipped around front using the shady side of the jail to do it.

He eased the door open, walked inside and took a chair across from Sam's, and he watched nonchalantly as two passengers got off and the guard stepped down with the mail sack.

Sam was surprised when Wyatt slipped in but refused to show it. He was damned unhappy to see Wyatt come into town with his mother expected to leave for Saint Louis in just a few minutes, so he didn't bother to greet him, and the two sat in silence.

Sam judged the time was nearing one o'clock. Not much went on in Foley, especially at the marshal's office, so Sam was familiar with day to day activities of the businesses and their people. He watched the guard with the mail sack walk into the Emporium where the mailroom and stagecoach ticket window and its office was while the driver drove off with the stage headed for the livery barn and a fresh team of horses. He knew the guard and driver would have lunch while the team was exchanged and the coach cleaned, and they would be ready to board passengers before the two o'clock departure time.

Meals were available at three places in Foley. The hotel was the finest. Old Bill, when in town, the president of the bank and paying hotel guests, usually ate there. The Bluebonnet Café was busiest; cowhands in town for supplies and most common people ate there. Irish Rose's Saloon had a regular gathering, too, but it was smaller. It had a free lunch of cheese and crackers, hard boiled eggs, biscuits half the size of regular biscuits that Rose made fresh daily to go with small strips of beef and deer jerky that Kerry O'Shea smoked weekly in the smoke house behind the saloon. Pickled pig's feet, for a nickel each, and dill pickles for a penny, were in jars on each side of a large wooden bowl of roasted peanuts which were free. Kerry had a wooden half-barrel at the end of the bar where the hulls of the shucked peanuts were expected to be dropped; he frowned on the man who missed the barrel.

Sam was surprised at the number of men who chose to eat at Irish Rose's, for the free lunch was free only if a drink was first purchased. That seemed to indicate the customers were interested more in hard whiskey, and the word free eased their minds about mid-day drinking. Sam was going to have lunch at Irish Rose's, but he was going to forego whiskey in favor of beginning another bottle of California's mood improver. Wyatt Winslow's appearance put that plan on hold.

"You here to see your mother makes the stage?" Sam asked finally.

"Yep."

"After that?"

"A drink or two. Whiskey keeps me steady. I keep a jug. It's running low. I thought I'd get some saloon food and a drink or two to fortify myself against my ailments."

"It's still almost an hour before your mother leaves. I'm sure she's still packing. She'll make the stage but it will be close. I'm prepared to hold it up if she's late."

"I came to town to make sure she gets on it."

"Risky. Not smart in my opinion. After that?"

"I'll be looking for Young Bill. I'll wait until tomorrow to front him. I'll let him sweat that long. I'll choose the place. Main Street. Everyone can watch everyone."

"Young Bill's always at the bank in the afternoon if you're intent on getting yourself killed," Sam shot back at him. "Call him out when you get damn good and ready; in the meantime, if your aim was to go over for a snort of two at Irish Rose's Saloon, why don't you get on over there then get the hell out of town before your mother chances to see your ugly face?"

Wyatt Winslow smiled. It was the kind of smile that indicated he had irritated Sam just as he had intended. Wyatt evidently didn't want any friends.

"Why not? We don't want Momma to see me, do we?"

The remark edged Sam's temper up another notch. He almost came out of his chair, but Wyatt was baiting him, and he was not going to let it show. Sam had had some feeling for Wyatt because he was Dave and Claire's boy, but Wyatt's conduct had sucked out all of Sam's goodness.

Wyatt stood, turned slowly, and walked out.

Sam walked to the door after him and watched Wyatt crossing the street heading for Irish Rose's. When Wyatt stepped up from the street to the boardwalk in front of the saloon, Matthew Hardin, who was leaving, pushed open the double doors, and brushed him. Words were passed. Sam could not read lips to understand them, but he guessed Hardin was in a bad mood. Ivy Vanderbilt must have told him his services would not be needed when she left with

Young Bill, so Matthew Hardin's anger was for Young Bill who was squiring Ivy Vanderbilt who Hardin thought of as his property, and it appeared to Sam that Hardin may have been trying to take it out on Wyatt.

Sam's mind sharpened his eyes to an unusual quickness, and he began following the scene with intensity. Wyatt Winslow, who was in a frame of mind that resembled a bomb with its fuse lit, was in no mood to be intimidated by anyone, and he turned and walked into the middle of the street while words were still coming from Matthew Hardin's mouth.

When Matthew Hardin discovered Wyatt Winslow was going to challenge him, the look on his face began with surprise and quickly changed to a sneering kind of laugher. Confident that here was a chance to impress the town and Ivy Vanderbilt with his gun prowess, he stepped from the boardwalk into the street, turned and made his move. Only one shot was fired. Hardin's Colt came out of its holster, but it dropped at his feet as his knees were crumbling, and he fell downward. The space in time was less than a second. Sam's visual time clock said lightning quick.

It took a moment for Sam to recover his sense of reality then he rushed from his office and ran across the street.

At a time of high excitement, eyes see things in an extraordinary way, and Sam saw Old Bill Foley come out onto the balcony of his room on the second floor of the hotel with a Winchester in his hands. The image rested in Sam's mind; why he didn't know, because Winchester's were plentiful in all the Foley business places. He was wondering about the curiosity of it as he came to Hardin's downed body.

"He asked for it," Wyatt Winslow said.

"I saw," Sam replied then looked up at the left-handed gunman. "You're fast, Wyatt. I don't know how a man can pull two pounds of iron out of a holster as fast as some men do then control where the bullet is going. I've seen some fast ones. Gomez is one. So is Young Bill. I wonder. If you get Young Bill tomorrow, what's next for you?"

"Don't know. Didn't plan ahead."

"Go to my office. I want the townspeople to see I'm holding you, and your mother could show up anytime, and I sure don't want her to see you."

"Yeah, you're right. She'd recognize this cripple. I'll hide out in your jail. Get me some food, will you? And some whiskey. Please."

"I'll be right back," Sam said thinking about the wine and his increased need for something to smooth a day that began bumpy with more bumps ahead.

At the door he said, "Hear me, Wyatt Winslow. Stay put. Show your face when your mother's here, and I'll pistol-whip you, so help me God."

Instead of walking to Doc Wedgewood's place to have him look after the dead man, Sam elbowed his way through the crowd that was still pouring out of Irish Rose's Saloon. The confrontation in front of the place happened with such suddenness most of the noontime patrons had missed it. The gun shot got their attention, and someone had looked out the plate glass windows and saw a man down, and they all came streaming out.

Sam grabbed one by the arm and told him to go get Doc Wedgewood, and he slipped inside stopping at the end of the bar.

Kerry O'Shea asked, "What happened, Sam?"

"Matt Hardin met a stranger faster than him."

"Stranger that spent one night in the hotel the night Ivy Vanderbilt got here?"

"Same one. How'd you know about him?"

"Homer Flynn."

"At the hotel?"

"No other Homer Flynn I know of."

"Dumb question. Sorry I wasted my breath. I need a carry-out lunch and a cheap jug of whiskey to go, and I want to begin another bottle of California's bottled goodness. Hurry. I got lot's more work to do today, and I don't want that hangover to come back."

"I was prepared for more wine," the bartender said as he reached beneath the bar and his hand returned with a large green bottle, "but I am unprepared for a carry-out lunch. Sam, this is the saloon, not the café. I do not have any way for you to carry a lunch over to the jail."

Sam was already wiping bubbles from his wet nose. "Use your apron. Throw a double handful in it of anything you got left then get me a jug. I'll bring your apron back. Now hurry."

O'Shea hurried to the back. He returned with a gallon jug and plunked it on the bar in front of Sam. "Marshal," he said, "I feel guilty charging whiskey to the jail. We don't usually treat prisoners that well."

"He's not a prisoner. I saw it. It was fair. Hardin got beat and that's the end of it. The lunch is free if I buy a drink, and I'm buying two; this green bottle and that brown jug. Charge 'em to me, not the jail."

Outside, the commotion was beginning to die down with Doc Wedgewood on the scene, and a few patrons were drifting back inside the saloon.

Sam, having pulled on the green bottle as much as time would permit, shoved it back at the bartender, and said, "Kerry, my Irish bartender friend, whiskey will steady a man's nerves but this bubble stuff is better at settling his tail feathers down. I'll be back when my tail feathers get needy again. Thanks."

Doc Wedgewood, when told of a gunfight with a dead man waiting, having dealt with this sort of thing before, came in his wagon, and he was loaded up, leaving, as Sam was passing.

"Do I bill the jail for my services, Sam?" he asked. Doc wasn't one to miss a fee.

"Nope. Bill Miss Ivy Vanderbilt at the hotel," Sam answered, and he walked on over to the jail.

Once inside the jail, Sam didn't waste time on pleasantries. "Here's your damned food and whiskey, Wyatt. The food's free. The whiskey is gonna cost you three dollars. Pay up."

"I usually pay two dollars."

"Delivery charge. Pay up and get out."

"I'm here to see Momma gets on the stage."

"That's a bad lie, Wyatt. You came here to get me riled. You did. You don't want any friends, and you have succeeded. Now get the hell out of here before Claire sees you."

Wyatt smiled. He reached in his Levi pocket and brought out three silver cartwheels, dropped them on Sam's desk, and asked, "Does that include the dirty apron?"

"It does not. Now get the hell out."

"I'll be back tomorrow."

"And probably get yourself killed."

"Either way, I win. You know that, don't you, Sam?"

"I do. Now leave. You've cut it close enough. Claire don't deserve that pain."

"You're right, Sam. I'll slip out on the shade side of the jail like I came in. Even if she was across the street, she'd never see me. Adios."

After Wyatt left, a thought elbowed its way in ahead of the jumble of other thoughts going on in Sam's mind. Why was it he thought so much about Claire Winslow when so many distractions were happening? At that moment, he realized he cared more for Claire Winslow than a man seventy years old should. It was another cause for wonderment.

Chapter Twenty

Claire Winslow worried, after Molly and she had filled it, that her Jenny Lind trunk would break open when the stagecoach men lifted it onto the stage, because the two leather handles were dry from age. The trunk was her treasure. It came as a gift from her parents on her wedding day. They bought it for her when Jenny Lind had just finished touring the States, so it was popular and must have cost them dearly. It was to carry her trousseau in when she and Dave Winslow came out West. It had done its job. It also carried memories.

When she opened the trunk and removed her wedding dress, Claire Prescott Winslow remembered her wedding day. She brought David Winslow a virgin that night as every correct young lady did, but like most young ladies from southern Mississippi, Claire Prescott had lost that nurtured virtue in her dreams on the many warm southern Mississippi nights before a real, live, Dave Winslow delivered her from her wickedness.

Now, opening the trunk, it was Molly's hands, like a child reaching for a Christmas toy, that picked up the dress with all its faded lace and held it against her, and she exclaimed, "Miz Winslow, I ain't never seen nothin' this pretty. I wish I had seen you in it. You must have been special beautiful that day."

The dress was a four tier four hoop crinoline lace, and the hoops had been squeezed to fit into the trunk so now they were oblong instead of round, but Molly was not aware of their deformity, and she made a pirouette with the garment. In another moment, she was reaching in to examine Claire's lingerie. Claire's chemise was a garment Molly was familiar with it, but Claire's was silk, off color now, but it had the soft original exquisite satin feel the young woman had never felt before, and Molly kept touching it's smoothness over and over like a child stroking a kitten.

For Claire, memories came out along with the wedding dress, and she quickly pushed them aside, because they had faded like the color of the dress. As suddenly as the old memories popped out to confront her, new excitement with new expectations replaced them. Chastity and a child she had never seen filled her imagination, and happiness gripped her, and she said, "Hurry, Molly, hurry. You're young. Scramble up the ladder and find my valise. I'll need it to carry my small items."

The attic spanned half the length of the cabin. It was an open space beneath the roof and above the two small bedrooms where Claire and Jimbo slept. The open space above was for an extra room designed that way in the event of more children, and Jimbo came, but he was never moved upstairs because of her husband's death and her daughter's departure. It was used for storage now.

The ladder leading upstairs was on the inside back wall. From the upper rung of the ladder, coming down, Molly turned her head to tell Claire she had the valise, and her eyes ventured across the dining area through the window, and she saw a horseman riding toward the cabin. She knew immediately it was Cass. At the same instant, she knew he saw the wagon outside the front door where they had parked it so they could load it easiest.

Dropping the valise at the bottom of the stairs, she ran to the door telling Claire as she passed, "It's him. It's Cass. I ain't going back till he learns better about me. I promised to keep Jimbo. Tell him that. Help me keep my promise," she demanded, half begging then Molly opened the door.

"I come to get you, Molly," Cass said.

"No need, Cass," and she stood in the doorway, not blocking it but in such a way he knew he was not welcome.

"You're my wife, and I come to take you home."

"No, Cass. I'm not goin'. You took the same vows I took. When you honor them, I will come with you, not before."

"It weren't my fault, Molly. Sid and Everett tricked me."

"Sure. They put the bottle in your mouth and made you swallow."

"Almost. We wuz just havin' a little fun."

"You were through havin' that kind of fun when you proposed marriage. You went back on your vow once, and I forgave you. This is twice, and I don't forgive you."

"That's enough, Molly. You're my wife. You're coming home."

Cass reached out to take her arm, and Molly twisted away.

Claire felt it was time to intervene, and she stepped forward. "Cass, I have a stage to catch. Molly is going to keep Jimbo while I'm gone."

"Keep Jimbo?"

"And I might have a regular job," Molly added quickly further adding to his discomfort. "A lady is gonna see me about one as soon as the stage leaves."

The two women had outmaneuvered Cass Gibbs. His mouth was open to talk, but he was speechless.

Claire pushed the situation quickly adding, "We're running late. The stage leaves at two."

Then directing Cass further, she said, "Take one handle, Cass, and Molly and I will each hold a corner, and that way we can get the trunk onto the wagon bed. Now, be careful, Cass. That handle is old. It's dry with age, and it may break."

Molly stepped aside, and Cass had no choice but to walk past his wife and take hold of the trunk handle while the two ladies took hold of its corners, and they shuffled out to the wagon, and the trunk was placed in the wagon without accident.

When that was done, Claire rushed inside, grabbing her purse and the valise as she did, and rushed back while Cass and Molly were standing beside the wagon looking at each other with Cass trying to think of what to say. The complexity of the situation left him confused, and Claire took control again by simply saying, "Cass, follow us on your horse. Molly, you drive."

Claire hurried back and locked the cabin door. When she returned, they were off. Minutes had been ticking away. She hoped Sam had her ticket waiting.

Chapter Twenty-One

Sam, holding Claire's ticket, was anxiously looking for their wagon to turn from Cedar Street onto Main Street. Seeing a team of horses coming around the turn, he was sure it was Claire, but it was not a wagon behind the team, it was Abbey's surrey. This would be about the time to expect Abbey's arrival. Sam figured she must have had a start when she walked downstairs this morning and found Old Bill missing from his chair. Before anyone would believe he would make the long trek to town, they would have searched the nearby pastures, and that would have taken an hour or so. Finally discovering Old Bill's black stallion missing, town would be the next bet. Abbey was not a horsewoman, and old Felipe, her driver, was not one to hurry a team.

Sam walked to the middle of the street. When he was sure they recognized him, he pointed to the jail and walked to it. Sam waited, and Abbey stepped down, and he opened the door and motioned that she sit in one of the barrel chairs, and he walked around to his. Felipe waited outside in the buggy.

Sam began, "He's here, Abbey. I sent him to the hotel."

"Thank, God. I've been so worried."

"He's upset."

"Oh, God. Does he know about . . ." she hesitated, apprehension softening her voice to a whisper. When she finally found words that would not be so blunt, she finished with, "about yesterday?"

"I don't think so. If he saw or heard, he didn't mention it. It's Young Bill he's upset about."

Abbey breathed a sigh of relief. Her secret was safe. As soon as she felt relief, she realized Sam had said her son had a problem serious enough to disturb her husband from a comatose state, and apprehension gripped her again. "What about Young Bill?" she asked quickly.

"There's a gunman in town. He's gonna call Young Bill out."

"Why? Why would he do that?"

Sam thought it out while Abbey was plotting a course to avoid admitting her infidelity out loud. Yesterday, he needed to know what happened between Young Bill and Chastity. Young Bill had met that need, so he said, "Why don't matter just now, because it's set for tomorrow."

"Oh, God . . . . What can we do, Dad?"

Sam's first plan had just been carried to Doc Wedgewood's to be fitted for a coffin, so he offered the only hope he had left. "I thought we might hire Bill Waterman's *jefe*. Gomez might be fast enough to brace him and win."

"That's a good plan. We'll pay him. Dad, if Old Bill has returned to being himself, I'm still his wife. I will not associate with Bill Waterman under the circumstances. Will you ask him about Gomez for me?"

Sam, thinking he could not understand women, especially his daughter, thought a caustic thought. Entertain was a more accurate word than associate to describe Abbey's relationship between her and Bill Waterman. Sam was considering the unkind remark but fatherly forgiveness had him hastily reconsider, and he said, "I planned to ride out and see Waterman this afternoon as soon as the stage leaves. Claire is going to Saint Louis to visit Chastity, and the grandchild she's never seen. She will be here any minute. I'll see her off. When she's on the stage, I'll go."

"Thanks, Dad," she said walking over and giving him a hug. "I'll go see to my husband now. Do you have any advice about his condition? I mean, does he seem to need special handling? I hate to say it this way, but is he okay mentally? Should I get Doc Wedgewood first?"

"No. I think he's okay. He's lucid. He hasn't had any sleep. He's been awake all night thinking about Young Bill having to face a showdown. He should be asleep over in your rooms."

It occurred to Sam that Claire and Molly would be driving up to the stage station which was next to the hotel, so, not wanting Abbey to see Molly's auburn hair, he said to his daughter, "Hurry on over and see for yourself." Abbey sure didn't need to lay eyes on Molly Gibbs's hair today.

Chapter Twenty-Two

It was not Molly Gibbs who Abbey saw next. Bill Waterman was riding up to the jail just as she and Sam stepped outside.

They waited while he threw reins over the tie-rail then swept off his Stetson as soon as he dismounted in favor of Abbey's presence.

"A surprise and unexpected pleasure to see you here, Missus Foley," he said adding, "since it is the Marshal I came to see."

"I'm here because my husband came to town earlier, Mister Waterman. He has awakened. The relationship that exists between you and me will be forced to wait. I have come to be a faithful wife to my husband."

Waterman was stunned for a moment, but he replied, "Truthfully, I am glad he has regained consciousness. At the same time, I regret our relationship will be discontinued. I will be patient and wait if there is hope for that relationship in the future. Will there be?"

"Dad knows all there is to know about you and me, so I can speak plainly, and my answer is I'm not sure. All I can offer is, I hope there will be, but I am a wife and mother first, and the mother part is heartsick. Dad will explain. Just now, I'll go to my husband. Try to understand."

The two men watched her walk slowly across the street. After she entered the hotel, they turned and walked into the Marshal's Office.

When they were seated, Sam said, "Here's the other thing on Abbey's mind. Young Bill will be called out tomorrow to face a very good gunman. When Old Bill learned about it, he snapped out of his comatose state and came to town hoping to hire another gunman to face Young Bill's challenger and find out just how good the gunman is."

Without adding that one showdown had already taken place, Sam said, "We would like to hire Gomez."

Bill Waterman leaned forward in his chair approaching Sam closer to show his sincerity.

"Sam," he said, "Abbey said you know about us. That means you know what took place the day you and I met at their hacienda. I want you to know it is not a dallying affair on my part. I love her. She's a beautiful woman any man would be proud of, and I'll do anything for her. I am not a man that waits patiently, but I'll wait for her until Old Bill passes on; that's how much I care for your daughter. It pains me to tell you this. I wanted a friendlier relationship between you and me, and Gomez was a thorn to you, so I gave him his wages and a spare mustang and terminated his services. I got rid of him as a goodwill gesture to you. That's what I came to tell you. He's gone back to Mexico. What else can we do? I'll help if I can. If Abbey loses her son, she will be desolate. That means I stay in the background of her life, and that's not where I want to be, so I will help in whatever way possible. Do you know of another way?"

Sam, thinking fate had declared the two men would face each other tomorrow and nothing human could stop it, replied, "None whatsoever. Young Bill's fast, so it will be an even contest. I cannot guess the winner."

Just then, Molly's wagon with Claire in it and Cass following, raced past going in one direction and the stage rumbled past going in the other direction, and Sam jumped up. "Gotta go, Bill. Talk to you later," he said as he bolted around Waterman and out the door.

Bill Waterman, taken by surprise, walked out the door, and it occurred to him that Sam had addressed him as Bill for the first time, and that thought pleased him. All other times, Sam had been formal addressing him as Mister Waterman. It was a good sign.

Chapter Twenty-Three

The stage had stopped in front of the station, and Sam hurried to it waving Claire's ticket. Sam knew when Molly's wagon raced past, Claire was going to the schoolhouse to tell Jimbo goodbye. She was not the kind of mother to leave that undone, and he respected her for it.

"Harley," he told the driver, reaching up to hand Claire's ticket to him, "the lady going on this ticket will be here any minute. I'd take it kindly if you'd wait. How about it?"

"My pleasure, Sam. If it was that young red head that just drove past, I don't get to carry many pretty women. Sure I'll wait. It'll be a pleasure"

"The red head stays. It's the other one. She's pretty, too. You'll see."

"Sure, thing. Like I said, Sam. My pleasure."

Sam walked around the stage and stepped up onto the boardwalk and waited. In a few minutes, the wagon pulled up behind the stage and Cass helped the two men take Claire's trunk as Sam took her hands and helped her step down from the wagon, and they walked the few steps to the stage's door.

As he prepared to help her board the stage by placing his hands around her waist, she turned and kissed him. It was more than a parting peck on the cheek, but it was not a lingering kiss. It had fullness to it. Then she stepped back and said, "Sam Ordway, you've been drinking again."

"I have," he admitted displaying a sly smile.

"It didn't taste like whiskey."

"It wasn't. Champagne. It was champagne."

"Are you celebrating my leaving?"

"Oh, no ma'am. It was Kerry O'Shea's idea, and a pretty good one, if you ask me."

"It has certainly given you a glib tongue. Behave yourself while I'm gone. And tend my chickens. I'd love to be here to watch you gather eggs from my hens. Some of them are pretty touchy. Molly knows where I keep the egg money. She'll show you when you collect from the Emporium on egg day."

Harley had waited long enough, and he yelled down from the box, "I got a time schedule, Sam. Let the lady leave."

"Fair enough, Harley. Thanks. Your next drink's paid for at Irish Rose's."

Watching the stage leaving, Sam waved as Molly Gibbs tugged on his sleeve. "Marshal," she said, "I don't want my wagon to block traffic that might want to come into the hotel or stage depot. I'm gonna see Miss Vanderbilt in a little while. Can I leave my wagon by the side of your jail?"

Cass stepped in. "Marshal, that's my wagon, and she's my wife, and I intend to take her home. No need to park it."

"Young man, you have a horse. She has a wagon. Each of you has transportation. She looks grown-up enough to decide where she goes. She can park it at the jail. It will be safe there."

Cass was at a loss again, but he tried. "Molly," he pleaded, "Honest to God, I was just gonna dance with them girls. After Sid and Everett paid for me to go up-stairs, it didn't seem polite to refuse."

Sam, not one to get into a domestic quarrel but now in possession of a glib tongue by way of California, could not resist, and he said to Cass Gibbs, "Cass, I got ears around the countryside. What my ears tell me is Sid and Everett cut out one of your beeves whenever they get thirsty. They run your cow into the woods and butcher it then bury the hide. I'm told they sell the quartered carcasses to Amos Birdsong at the Bellville Butcher Shoppe. They tell him the beeves come from their papa. It's a lie. No need to be beholden to them. They paid for you with your money. Go home and count your beeves."

Poor Molly. Seeing Cass humbled misted her eyes, and she reached over and placed her hand on his. "Go home," she told him. "Come back in a week. We'll talk then. Care for my chickens and hogs. Weed the corn. Count your cows, but don't do anything rash. Remember your temper gets away easy. Wait a week, Cass, and we'll meet and see if we want to stay married."

"I already know the answer, Molly. I want you for my wife. I love you."

"We'll see, Cass," she said then took hold of a bridle to begin walking the team across the street. She turned back as Cass mounted his horse and added, "In a week, we'll see."

Sam, not really pleased with what he'd done but aware he had done the right thing, turned around and headed for Irish Rose's and the remaining contents from the California vineyards. On the way over, he whispered a walking prayer of thanks to The Almighty. Sam wanted to let The Almighty know he appreciated the delicate way Molly Gibbs' identity had escaped unnoticed by Abbey. Reckoning would come. Sam did not oppose that. A better time would be better.

Chapter Twenty-Four

Molly Gibbs dressed in her best dress for the meeting with Ivy Vanderbilt. The dress was plain gingham. Claire had offered her one of the dresses she was not taking to Saint Louis, but Claire was no longer the slender woman David Winslow had married; she was fuller all round than Molly, so Molly would see the fashionable Miss Vanderbilt in her old worn dress that was clean.

Before dither over Claire's trip began, Molly made sure she was dainty, now she was a little sweaty after all the hurry, not visibly she hoped, but enough to make her uncomfortable about the meeting. Thinking there was a pump in back of the jailhouse where she could get a drink of cool water, she climbed down from the wagon.

The jail was centered as the only building on a block modified for it only. A small cluster of mesquite trees offered shade, and Molly found a pump beneath one, and she pumped until the water ran cool, then she cupped her hands and drank. The water was delicious. Seeing that she had complete privacy under the canopy of two trees, she wet her handkerchief and dabbed it under her arms. She had to do it through the narrow scoop in the front of her dress.

Looking all around, she sensed the slow afternoon pulse of the town and sensed no one was watching, so she dampened the handkerchief again. It felt really good as she reached inside her chemise and used the dampened handkerchief to moisten her breasts, and the tension of her meeting vanished with the water's refreshing coolness.

She walked to the front of the jail, and she was just in time to see Ivy Vanderbilt and Young Bill Foley dismount in front of the hotel. She watched as Ivy gave Young Bill her hand, and Molly guessed she was saying words of thanks because she was smiling graciously. Molly Gibbs wished for a moment she could be that ladylike. In the next moment, she knew she never would, and she crossed the street.

As Young Bill rode off for the livery stable leading her horse, Ivy Vanderbilt saw Molly walking toward her, and she waited on the veranda of the hotel.

"Hi, Molly," she said. "You're here at just the right time. Come upstairs, and we'll talk."

Molly was eager to ask the nature of the job, and she was about to ask as they ascended the stairs, but the desk clerk stopped them.

"Miss Vanderbilt, one moment please," he said. "I've been instructed to tell you some bad news. Will you step this way for a moment?"

Molly was left standing as Homer Flynn led Ivy Vanderbilt to a small vestibule under the stairway where he said, "I'm sorry to be the one to tell you, but a short time ago your bodyguard was in a shootout in front of the saloon. He was killed. His body's at Doc Wedgewood's."

"I'll make the arrangements," Ivy Vanderbilt replied.

As desk clerk, Homer Flynn had seen enough incidents to prepare for most human reactions, but he felt it strange that Miss Vanderbilt was so controlled she was able to take the whole matter so simply. It was obvious. She had her sights on bigger game. And why not? Young Bill Foley was rich Young Bill Foley, so he continued politely, "If there is anything we can do to help, please ask."

"Thank you. I'll take care of things," she replied.

Returning to where Molly had been left standing, Ivy Vanderbilt said. "Molly, my bodyguard has been killed. I need to attend to whatever arrangements are necessary. Can you come back in the morning?"

"Yes, ma'am. I take Jimbo to school at eight. Anytime after that okay?"

"That will do just fine. I'll look for you sometime after eight and before nine. Just come directly up to room three and knock."

Molly, about to walk back across the street to the wagon, saw Sam Ordway leaving Irish Rose's Saloon just as Young Bill Foley was coming down the boardwalk from the livery stable, and she walked to meet them.

Thanks to Kerry O'Shea, who had been hiding Sam's hangover remedy beneath the bar and pouring from the California wine bottle into a clear glass beer mug so the other patrons would not know the marshal was drinking champagne but simply having a beer, Sam's boots were stepping much higher and lighter from his latest fortification, and he said to Young Bill, "You're just the man I need to see. Step over to the jail. Let's talk."

Young Bill politely tipped his Stetson and said to Molly, "It's a pleasure to see you again, Missus Gibbs."

Molly replied, "And you Mister Foley."

Sam said, "Molly, run along. We have serious things to discuss."

"About Miss Vanderbilt's bodyguard?" she asked.

"Yes. And other things."

"How did it happen?" Molly asked, curious as always.

"Not much to it. He tried to shoot it out with another man and lost. Now run along. It won't be much longer before Jimbo gets out of school. Why don't you just go and wait in the schoolyard?"

Molly left them, and Sam asked Young Bill as they were walking to the jail, "You heard what I just told Molly?"

"Yep. Wyatt Winslow?"

"You guessed correct. They bumped outside Irish Rose's, Hardin coming out and Wyatt going in, and Matt Hardin took offense, and his quick temper got him killed. Wyatt is fast."

"You said Wyatt wouldn't be back before tomorrow. Why did he show up today?"

"Said he was out of whiskey, which may or may not have been true. Truth is he wanted to irritate me and intimidate you."

"How so?"

"He got my half done. He irritated me by coming here when his mother was about to get on the stage. He cut it close on purpose. He had no intention of showing himself while she was in town, but he wanted me to sweat him being here under her nose so to speak. I did, and I'll pay him back in kind. I suspect he's hostile to me because I'm your kin."

"How does that intimidate me?"

Sam did not even bite his lip when he told the lie; his California glibness spoke. "Wyatt said he heard about you taking a cattle drive to market. He is going to let you sweat the confrontation the whole time you are on your cattle drive. He said he was going to give you something to worry about every night instead of dreaming about young virgin girls."

"He's not looking for friends, is he?"

"I'd say not."

"By him extending the time, maybe he's losing his nerve. What do you think?"

"I don't think so. He's serious. Deadly serious."

"What do you suggest?"

"Make the cattle drive. See what happens when you get back."

"Guess you're right. I'll head back to the ranch and get ready to move the herd early in the morning."

"Better go by your dad's rooms at the hotel. He's there. He got to town early this morning, bright eyed and sane. Your mother followed a little while ago. They're there now. They'll be glad to know your shootout has been postponed."

Young Bill left and walked to the hotel and knocked lightly on the door of room three before going to his parent's rooms. Ivy Vanderbilt was just leaving, and he said, "I'll be back in a week if the weather holds. When I get back, I'll meet the man who wants the showdown with me."

"I'll be waiting for you. Life always has a twist. One reason I came to Foley is because of its peaceful reputation. Now there's just been a shootout, and you're coming back to one. I don't know what to think. Have you heard?"

"Sam just told me. I'll face the same man."

"Oh, dear God . . ."

"Don't worry. I'm good."

"So was Matt Hardin."

"Cheer up. I was trained by the best. I'll be okay."

Ivy, managing a smile, said, "Well, because of that man, I need a new bodyguard. Do you have a suggestion?"

"Tom Silverhorn. He might do it. He needs whatever cash he can rustle up. He's steady and pretty good with a gun. He's helped Sam. He can't match Wyatt, but he's not going to let himself get trapped into something like that.

He'll protect you and whatever valuables you want protected. You can depend on that."

"I'll look him up after I see to things at Doc Wedgewood's."

"Want me to go with you?"

"No. It's best you see your parents, now. I'll ask Sam to take me. Do you think he'll mind?"

"As pretty as you are, Sam will be delighted to go anywhere with you."

Smiling, she said, "In that case, I'll ask him. Take care" and she kissed him. It was a short kiss, but it was serious. Understanding he wanted a cheerful departure, she left him with the mood he wanted knowing enough about men to help them fulfill their wishes.

She brushed past him, and he continued down the hall to his parent's rooms.

Chapter Twenty-Five

Ivy Vanderbilt tapped lightly on the jailhouse door then walked inside. Sam Ordway looked up, somewhat surprised to see her.

"Sam, will you take me to Doctor Wedgewood's so I can make funeral arrangements for my bodyguard?" she asked.

"My pleasure," he answered quickly.

They walked a block east and one north. Ivy Vanderbilt's hand was on Sam's arm the whole time. Sam was enjoying himself and felt no need to talk.

Inside Doc's Infirmary, Sam waited in the parlor after Doc invited Ivy into his office so the two could discuss what Sam knew would be financial details of Matt Hardin's funeral. Sam knew Doc gave his services without payment to really poor folks, but, for those who could pay, he did not hesitate to ask for his full fee. Doc, acting as funeral director, would also contact next of kin, but there would be an added price for that. Sam smiled thinking Doc wouldn't waste any time naming his fee and additions to Ivy Vanderbilt's bill.

Having learned about Bill Foley's black passion directed against Englishmen, Sam had been surprised when Doc arrived in Foley. Doctor Wedgewood's accent was pure

English, and Bill Foley hated Englishmen. Every Irishman did, but few had hate as severe as Bill Foley had.

Sam figured the why of the hate was something even Bill Foley would never understand. The class distinctions of the English befuddled him, but he tolerated it. The King was in a class above all others, akin to God or the Pope. Next were the noblemen. Every man bowed to every rank above him, and any Irishman was below every Englishman. Thinking it was a divine law from heaven, Bill Foley bowed. Every time he bowed, he bowed with anger, but he bowed.

Doc's arrival came only a few weeks before Foley became a town. Sam, and anyone who was around Doc for longer than two minutes, learned Doc had come to America because his rank would not allow him into Oxford, and his one desire was to become a physician. Since he was not allowed that chance in England, he came to the United States. His continued lack of money made him the only graduate of the Philadelphia Medical College who would agree to venture into an untamed West; the stipend Bill Foley offered was too generous for him to pass up.

Over the years, and Sam watched it happening, an unlikely friendship developed between the Englishman and Old Bill. Old Bill admired anyone who did their job well, and Morris Wedgewood did his job well. He enjoyed the respect of his calling; he loved delivering babies, and, above that, he was quick to learn how to handle gunshot wounds and how to doctor animals.

Idly walking about the room, to pass the time Sam began replaying the incident that endeared Doc to Bill Foley.

It happened about a year after Doc came to town. A Comanche chief brought one of his young wives on a travois to the ranch insisting Bill cast out the demon inflicting her. She was listless and in a coma condition lying on her Indian gurney. Bill Foley had made big magic with his mirrors the day of his treaty with the Comanche, so the chief wanted that same magic for this wife. The Indians didn't call what Bill had done magic they called it *puha* which was their word for power.

Bill Foley knew the Comanche's valued horses more than women, so Bill knew immediately the chief must set great store by the woman since he thought enough to bring her to seek his help. Old Bill was also smart enough to know, if he refused, the Indians would set about raiding his horse herd, treaty or no treaty, so he put her in a wagon and brought her to town to see Doc thereby shifting the burden directly on to the Englishman. He told Chief Sudden Dark Cloud that he, Bill Foley, did not possess that kind of *puha*; Doc, the Englishman, did. Bill Foley deflected the blame. The woman was Doc's baby to cure. If failure was imminent, Bill Foley was going to saddle it on the Englishman.

Understanding exactly what was happening, but unfazed like most Englishmen are, Doc picked up his stethoscope and was about to begin his examination, and Bill Foley yelled at him, "Don't touch her," and that stopped Doc. Comanche custom does not allow a white man to touch an Indian woman, not a private part for sure, and Doc was about to put that instrument on the young woman's breasts.

The young chief had already stepped in front of Doc, and his feathers were up; he was as hostile as a hawk on a nest of young. That left Doc on a high wire with no net below, and Sam had come to the rescue. Sam, knowing the stethoscope was causing the chief's nervousness, took it from Doc and laid it aside. That eased tension for the chief. Doc was beginning to understand that touching was a dangerous thing, and he asked Sam if the chief would let him take the woman's pulse. Using hand language, Sam felt Sudden Dark

Cloud's wrist then pointed to this young wife nodding okay? When the chief nodded his approval, Sam motioned for Doc to proceed, and Doc found the woman's pulse weak and fast. Then, taking a chance, Doc put his face down close enough to the young woman's face so he could smell her breath, and he got a hint of sweetness, and he backed away quickly so as not to excite the chief again.

"I think she's newly pregnant," Doc said. "I can't tell by simply looking because she's lying down and doesn't show. I did smell her breathe, and it smells sweet. I'm reasonably sure she has diabetes. See if you can find out from the chief if she has sweet urine. I'm told Indians don't have outhouses, so when she voided a husband may have noticed the sugary smell was unusual."

How to do that puzzled Sam momentarily, then he pulled the chief aside and, with their backs turned away from the others, Sam put his hand down to his crotch and motioned back and forth with his finger as if he was pissing then turned and pointed to the chief's wife and asked, "Sweet? Sweet?"

All Sam got was a questioning look from chief Sudden Dark Cloud, and Bill Foley took over.

"You jackasses. You got him more confused. Doc, did you say you think the woman is pregnant?"

"It's a good bet. It would surely help to know. If she was standing, I could probably tell. Lying down, not being able to touch her, I can't."

"What's that got to do with her condition, Doc? She doesn't appear to be in labor. Do you think she's trying to abort?"

"Not at this time. However, if its gestational diabetes; and I think it is, she will surely miscarry before she comes to term."

"Then, do something. It's serious business if she loses the child. We can't let that happen here. Comanche's are pure heathen. Other tribes make permanent villages. Some have a birthing house where other women of the tribe help pregnant women give birth. Not the Comanche. They live on the run, and happy to do it. They are chasing buffalo or raiding other tribes or whites for horses, mules, and slaves. Because they live that way, a horse is more important than a woman. Pregnant females squat and drop their child then keep up while the tribe is moving. That's why Comanche tribes never have enough children, but they won't change their custom to make it easier on pregnant women. A boy child is something special. New warriors bring great glory to the parents. Girls become women who become workers for their warriors, so they want every child any woman conceives. What can we do?"

Doc rubbed his chin like Englishmen do when they're thinking then grumbled that he wished he could be sure, but since he couldn't even touch the subject, he'd give it a go nevertheless, so he turned to the chief and, pointing to the woman, made a sweeping motion from his waist with his hand making the shape of a pumpkin. The chief beamed proudly, and Doc knew for sure she was pregnant. Since the diabetes part of his diagnosis was where the risk was, he went about verifying his educated guess. "Sam," he said, "this morning I had honey on my Johnnycakes. There is some in a quart jar on the table. There is also a sugar bowl on the table. Would you get them, please?"

Everyone waited outside until Sam returned with Doc's requested items. With the honey jar in his hand, Doc stuck his finger in it then put it in his mouth. When he pulled it out, he formed the word sweet so the chief could see. Then Doc pointed to the woman and said sweet again, and again, always pointing to the honey in the jar while nodding in a way that was asking the chief if the young woman had been eating honey. Chief Sudden Dark Cloud nodded that he understood. Doc did the same thing with sugar from the sugar bowl. The chief nodded his head yes. The head bob was emphatic. Doc then stretched his hands apart asking if the woman did it a lot. The Chief nodded again. And this time, Doc got another vigorous yes. The Chief had the look of relief on his face. It took a lot of young boys hunting honey in trees to keep her supplied, and the boy's squaw mothers probably complained to him frequently about it. The Chief must also have been sending braves to steal sugar from the fort or nearby settlers, and that was risky, but he had to do it to satisfy his pretty young woman's need.

Doc, looking at the chief eye to eye, held up the sugar bowl then the jar with the honey, and he pointed his finger, and wagged it from side to side indicating no, no, at the woman. To make sure his message was understood, Doc shook his head from side to side indicating another emphatic no. Then he did it again until the chief shook his head up and down indicating he understood she was not to have sugar or honey again. Doc gave the chief the impression that they were the demons, and he got the message over strongly. Satisfied, Doc then pointed up to the sun and back to the woman showing her getting up with his uplifted arms, and using two fingers, indicated in two days she would be well. Then, Doc dismissed everyone with a wave of his arms. Sam was surprised Doc hadn't put his hand out for a fee from the chief. He had built an infirmary with Old Bill's money and added a veterinary unit with his own. Next to Old Bill and the O'Hara Law Firm, Doc was the bank's biggest depositor.

It was Bill Foley's responsibility to take the woman back to the ranch where the travois was, so he missed Doc's lecture on gestational diabetes. Sam did not. The woman, Doc said, probably got a fixation on sweets, and she started eating sugar and honey like other pregnant women do sour foods like pickles. She may not have true diabetes, he said. He hoped she did not. A true case of diabetes was a death sentence, slow but sure. The young Comanche woman, he thought, had a case of diabetes that mysteriously occurs only during pregnancy then goes away when she delivers. It was a mystery why it happened in certain women, but it was not unusual. If that was her case, she would have a normal life after the child delivered.

Doc didn't realize it, but his quick mind in that woman's dilemma, along with Bill Foley's treaty with the Comanche, kept Foley clear of Indian attacks. They honored Bill Foley's *puha* like the Mexican's honored the Pope. Sam's military training did the rest. He created the town's militia. Sam insisted the bank building be double planked around its windows and above the native stone. Narrow slits were made as gun port openings. Across from the bank building was the jail with thick adobe walls also with gun port slits. Both buildings were fortresses. The saloon with its bigger glass windows was vulnerable, but the building front was stone framed with heavy timbers. Across, from it was The Sentinel, and it was built in similar fashion as the saloon without the large glass windows. The town had been planned so Main Street was wide enough for twelve team freight wagons to turn around without going to the edge of town to do it, so it was an extra wide thoroughfare. All the other streets were so narrow a buggy or wagon could pass one way making it difficult for a quick getaway except on Main Street, and Main Street had concentrated firepower every inch of the way, because Sam Ordway taught every citizen, including every adult woman, to use a Winchester, and Bill Foley furnished the arsenal. Sam knew familiarity was the secret to marksmanship. He had the ladies handling weapons, shooting round after round, until they were, many of them, as good as the men.

Word got around. Kinfolk who came to visit relatives, hotel guests, drummers and visitors who stopped at Irish Rose's Saloon were told about Sam's Militia. That way, his dual gender militia kept Foley clear of outlaws and rowdies. Foley was one of the safest cities in Texas.

Doc's office door opened finally, and Sam's memory was cut off when Ivy, with Doc following behind saying thank you twice. Sam knew he meant it because he was holding a handful of twenty dollar certificates.

The three of them parted with Ivy giving Doc her hand then turning to Sam she placed her hand on his arm, and he escorted her back to the hotel then walked across the street to the jail.

Another visit with Kerry O'Shea was in Sam's mind, but he resisted the impulse. He figured it would only be a temporary resist.

Chapter Twenty-Six

Sam had supper at the Bluebonnet Café. When he finished, he walked back to the jail, waited around until darkness had settled in then locked the door to the jailhouse, made his round ending back at the livery stable where he mounted his horse the hostler always saddled about dusk, and he slowly rode the animal home where he unsaddled and fed him then walked as far as his back porch where he stood leaning against a timber support and looked up at the endless sea of stars shining through a cloudlessly clear Texas evening.

His California uplift had left, and his spirit was down. "To be expected," he admitted speaking to himself and the endless sea above.

After a few more moments of reflection, he stepped down from the little porch and walked half-way back between the house and the barn to the center of the yard.

Moonlight was crisp. Only night sounds penetrated silence, and he listened as if trying to hear something more. Removing his Stetson, he knelt.

"Father Almighty, it was just one small lie. I had to stall Young Bill. It took a lie to do it. I need time to figure things out. Sorry I had to do it that way. I'll try and do better next time. Amen."

Chapter Twenty-Seven

Sam knew Wyatt Winslow would be mad when he showed up and found Young Bill was no longer in Foley; in fact he looked forward to Wyatt's irritation after yesterday's carelessness around his mother.

Today, it was Sam's intention to add to Wyatt's displeasure. Sam Ordway was not sure the Bible had a name for the kind of pleasure seeing Wyatt Winslow's displeasure would bring him, but inwardly he knew such a thing must be a sin. If he enjoyed it as much as he thought he was going to, Sam was ready to ask forgiveness from The Almighty again tonight. His imagination had already shown him the look on Wyatt Winslow's face when he found out he had made the trip to town anticipating a glorious shootout in front of the townspeople and found out it had been postponed.

The morning was not going to pass fast enough.

It was only a tad after eight, too early for Kerry O'Shea to be at Irish Rose's. The bartender made the best coffee in town to Sam's notion, strong with a taste of chicory and fresh, so, waiting another hour or heading back to the Bluebonnet created indecision.

Pulling his boots off the desk top and dropping the front chair legs to the floor, he stretched his long legs by walking out front and leaning against a place his shoulder had worn down on his favorite timber that supported the roof overhang, and he idled away some time.

After a while, Molly Gibbs drove by taking Jimbo to the schoolhouse, and she returned a short time later and asked without getting down, "Can I park here again today, Marshal? I'm going to meet with Miss Ivy at the hotel. I might be there awhile. Okay?"

"Molly, this is public property. You can park here anytime. Most folks don't do it, because they don't want other folks to think them or some of their kin are inside. Pick your spot."

Molly parked, and Sam watched her walk across to the hotel, and he noticed she was wearing a different dress from yesterday. Today's dress was probably one of Claire's that she had done some sewing on, but it was still loose fitting for someone like Molly who possessed such a youthful figure.

The little hat she wore yesterday was missing; Sam guessed Molly was fed-up with trying to be lady-like. It was like her to present herself as best she could, for she was not the lazy type, but she was not one to take on airs, so that little hat perched on top of her head must have seemed a touch too much for her to bear again today. Molly was Molly, and her beautiful head of Foley hair was out there for everyone to see even if she didn't know where it came from.

Sam walked over to the Bluebonnet having decided on a quick cup, and Molly Gibbs walked into the hotel and up the stairs then tapped nervously on the door of room three.

Her knock was answered by the stately Negro, Margarite Doss, who said, "Come in Miss Gibbs. We have been expecting you."

Molly's nervousness, high to begin with, increased when she was greeted by the first person of color she had ever seen, and her feet hesitated and didn't know in which direction to go.

Ivy Vanderbilt knew a thing or two about youthful nervousness, and she came across the room quickly and took Molly's hand.

On the bed lay a dazzling white satin gown that immediately captured Molly's eyes, and her mind saw pictures of fancy ladies dancing with gentlemen. It looked like Claire's wedding dress, except Claire's dress was trimmed with lace and this dress was not, but it had all the fullness of Claire's formal gown.

Ivy Vanderbilt did not miss seeing how the gown captured Molly's eyes. "We want you to try the dress on," she told her, "but first I want you to know my associate. Her name is Margarite Doss. We are to be friends, so we'll be Margarite, Ivy, and Molly. How does that sound?"

"Fine by me, but there's no need me trying on that dress. I don't know how to dance."

Ivy Vanderbilt almost laughed but suppressed it. Margarite Doss smiled broadly.

"We're not going to open a dancehall, Molly."

"Not that I don't want to learn," Molly said continuing her line of thought. "Momma was a dancehall girl, and she said she did not want me to grow up like that, so she wouldn't teach me. I think dancing is pretty. I'd do it if I could."

"You will need to dance if you work for us, Molly, but we'll teach you. As a matter of fact, we'll teach you everything you need to know. We want to see how you look in the dress, and we want you to tell us if you enjoy wearing it. Then we'll discuss other things. Go ahead. Slip into it."

Living a farm life all of her life, with only men and breeding animals surrounding her, and her mother as the only female model, Molly had little modesty and would have easily disrobed in front of Ivy Vanderbilt, but the dark skin of Margarite Doss confused her, and timidly she asked, "Where do I change?"

"Here. In this room. We are all ladies. Margarite will help."

Molly turned, slowly and meekly, and Margarite Doss deftly unbuttoned the back of her dress, and Molly stepped out of it to be left standing in her chemise, and she was embarrassed, for her chemise was made of old cotton squares and odd oblong scraps sewed together to fit. She had seen Claire's satin chemise, and she knew her patchwork garment was a glaring admission of its home-made origin.

"There is no need to blush, Molly. If you work for us, you won't need a chemise. For that matter, if you insist on wearing one, I'll give you a nice one I never use. I'm going to guess you don't know why you wear the garment. Do you?"

"No, ma'am, I don't. Momma made me do it. Since I got tits, that is."

Smiling at Molly's tit's reference, Ivy Vanderbilt said brightly, "Not long ago, most people bathed only once a week, and a chemise was worn by a woman to protect her dress from sweat and skin oils. It saved dresses. Later on, ladies who called themselves proper said they wore chemises to hold down their nipples; those proper ladies didn't want men to see the impression of their nipples through the garment then have the men get overly excited and ravage them. In our line of work, we want men to get excited, so we don't wear chemises."

"You're the most proper lady I ever met, so if you don't wear one, I won't wear one either."

"I'm only a proper lady on occasion." Ivy Vanderbilt replied adding another smile, then she added, "Molly, when I work I'm not very proper."

"What kind of work . . . ?"

"A step at a time, Molly. Take off your chemise now, and try on the gown."

"If you say so. Just the same, I think I'll take the chemise like you promised. For when I'm home around other folks."

"You shall have it, Molly. Now slip into the gown. We think you're a beautiful young woman. We want to see you in the dress. It will increase your beauty. Try it on."

When Molly slipped out of her chemise and was bare from the midriff upward, Margarite Doss exclaimed, "Miss Ivy, she's perfect."

"She is, at that, isn't she? Molly, sit down. I'm going to offer you a job."

"Before you see me in the gown?"

"Your figure was the important thing we wanted to see. You'll wear the gown perfectly. Go ahead. We'll wait. Try it on. See if you like the feel of what it's like to be a woman who can afford lots of pretty gowns."

Molly stepped into the gown, and Margarite Doss stepped behind her and fastened buttons.

"Molly," Ivy said, "Many women are hypocrites. Those same proper ladies who wore chemises' to keep from exciting men now wear corsets to push up their breasts. And for what reason? To excite men, of course. Hypocritical, don't you think?"

"Yes ma'am."

"We'll soon make the prim little ladies take notice. A Paris designer has just fashioned what the French call a brassiere. It has cups and straps. No more chemises or corsets. We'll bring some brassieres along with us when we open our establishment."

"Are you gonna have a Shoppe in Foley for ladies?"

"It's possible, Molly. That may become one of our plans. Once we teach you to wear stylish clothes and polish your poise, you can be much more than a salesclerk for old chatterbox women. You're too beautiful for that."

Margarite added, "Don't waste yourself on ladies, child."

Turning to her mistress, she said, "Miss Ivy, Miss Molly has the most beautiful white skin I have ever seen. With her figure and that beautiful hair and our coaching, I think she would be second only to you. Do you agree?"

"Absolutely. Her face is cherub perfect in spite of all this Texas sun. Molly, how do you keep your face as white as it is?"

Molly, obviously enjoying the feel of rich satin, turned her head and said, "I wear a sun bonnet. My face burns and I freckle easy if I don't."

"A sunbonnet pulled tight across your face, I'll bet. Young men wouldn't have been able to see your pretty face or your stunning hair with a bonnet pulled tight. Little wonder a parade of men haven't come to your door. You're probably still a virgin."

"No Ma'am. I'm married."

"Married?"

"Yes, ma'am. To Cass Gibbs."

Margarite Doss and Ivy Vanderbilt exchanged worried glances. "It's our mistake," Ivy said. "We did not see a ring."

"Cass couldn't afford one. He promised to buy one when he sold the first calf crop, so we borrowed his Momma's for the ceremony then I gave it back. Enoch never gave one to Momma, so I figured it to be okay."

Silence filled the room. Molly remembered Cass had not kept his promise, and Margarite Doss and Ivy Vanderbilt had expressionless faces because of a simple oversight.

Ivy Vanderbilt, knowing some boundaries had been crossed but none breeched, recovered, and said, "Molly, you are everything we are looking for, but we want an unmarried young lady."

"That's just it, Miss Ivy. I'm not sure I'm gonna stay married. Cass went to a whorehouse."

Ivy Vanderbilt laughed. It was a good, hardy laugh, and it broke the tension. "Molly," she said, the smile lingering, "a man going to a whorehouse is not such a bad thing. Women make too much out of fidelity. Some women use sex for punishment by withholding it. You don't look like one of those. Were you available for his needs?"

"I'll say. And he did me so much it seemed to be more than just need. I'd have been pregnant a dozen times over without that little sponge Momma gave me when I married Cass."

Margarite Doss and Ivy Vanderbilt, two voices in unison, asked, "Sponge?"

"Yep. Momma said there was nothing like it when she was young. I sure didn't believe a thing like that would work. She said Mae Belle Spell, her friend at the dancehall in Fort Worth, used one and it worked. She didn't want me to get pregnant except when me and Cass was ready. Belle was the only friend Momma had, and Enoch allowed Momma two letters a year after postage went down to two cents, so she wrote off and got it. Momma said the sponge cost twenty dollars. Where she got that much money, I'll never know, and Cass darn near wore it out, me having to wash it so much. I worry it will fall to pieces. I sure need to replace it if I go back to him."

Ivy Vanderbilt's mind was busy. Molly Gibbs had been the perfect answer to her need. Too perfect. Life is never that perfect. So, a husband appeared and blocked everything.

Then Molly's beautiful little tongue directed by her unspoiled mind, gave everything new life by saying the marriage was in trouble. But the husband was still there, so caution meant postponing the next step until she understood the young girl's personal life better.

"Molly," Ivy Vanderbilt began, "how does that gown feel?"

"Wonderful. I never thought I'd feel like a real lady. Every woman needs to feel this way once in her lifetime. It's so soft. It's delicious. My body loves it."

"I'm sorry you have to take it off. Perhaps I can find a way for you to wear it again, and many others. Just now, however, we'll leave things as they are. For your trouble today, we want you to have the chemise I offered you. Margarite, will you get it for Molly?"

With two beds in the room, the extra one moved in to accommodate Margarite Doss, the space was limited. There were two straight-back chairs, a wash basin, and three Jenny Lind trunks, and Jenny Lind trunks as Molly found out yesterday packing for Claire, were sizable trunks.

Margarite Doss had only to take two steps in order to open one of the Jenny Lind's, and, reaching beneath what had to be more than one gown, she found a chemise and gave it to Molly who was then stepping out of the gown. Molly quickly slipped the garment over her head then slipped back into Claire's dress.

"I want to pay you for coming in today, Molly. Margarite, will you open the money trunk, please."

Margarite stepped to the next Jenny Lind, and opened the lid.

With such a compact space, Molly Gibbs had no trouble seeing inside. Inside the large trunk were four soft leather bags that looked to contain jewelry, except they were twice the size of jewelry bags. The bags were a passing curiosity for Molly. It was what was beneath the bags that captured her attention. That large Jenny Lind trunk was filled with twenty dollar certificates leaving only enough room for the leather pouches. Molly had no idea how much money that was. Molly had never seen enough jewelry to know some ladies had enough so it was carried in soft leather pouches, but she knew money when she saw it.

Ivy Vanderbilt, having reviewed all the circumstances in her mind, said, "Margarite, let's give Molly a hundred dollars to hold as a retainer. We may be able to resolve everything and have her join us later."

The tall Negro lady withdrew five bills, and handed them to Molly and said, "It is our pleasure, Miss Molly. I do hope we work together."

Molly accepted the money, and she stood there with the bills in her hand, her opened mouth expressing astonishment.

After Margarite handed Molly the bills, Ivy Vanderbilt stepped to the money trunk and removed a small sponge from one of the leather pouches.

"Molly," she said, "I am also going to replace your worn sponge. Even if you do not go back to your husband, at some point in your life you will need it. Here is a new one. It will not cost you twenty dollars although that is what they sell for. I don't have anything for you to carry it in, however. Did you bring a purse?"

"No ma'am. I never had money, so I never had need of one."

"Dear Molly. I'm also going to give you a purse. Margarite, please get one from the other trunk and give it to Molly. Molly, this will be our understanding. We are giving you one hundred dollars to hold. It becomes yours if you come to work for us. You can earn that much every week.

Call it a bonus. Here," and she reached into the money trunk and got another twenty dollar certificate, "is twenty dollars that is yours to spend any way you choose. You earned this today. The purse, chemise, and sponge are gifts. Wait a week then come back and see us. In the meantime, you must not tell anyone, I'll emphasize this; you are not to tell anyone, what we did or said here today or we take everything back. Sponge *and* money. Do I have your word?"

"Yes ma'am. You have you my word."

Chapter Twenty-Eight

Molly puzzled about Ivy Vanderbilt and Margarite Doss all the way back to Claire Winslow's house where she immediately forgot everything except chores.

When the afternoon reached its hottest, wanting to cool off before she left to pick up Jimbo Winslow at school, she was standing at the kitchen sink pumping water, and she looked into the parlor where Claire's River City Eight-Day Clock hung. Encased in beautifully carved wood, it no longer chimed, but Molly could see the hands were approaching three. She and Cass didn't own a clock of any kind. Then her mind saw her working for Miss Ivy wearing one of those beautiful satin gowns, and the image of the hundred dollars she was holding mixed with the daydream. When the money was hers, one of the first things she was going to buy was a clock. Not one as expensive as Claire's, but a nice one. Shucks, a hundred dollars would buy everything in the world she had ever wanted.

In town, as she was parking the wagon in the same parking place at the side of the jail where she had parked yesterday, through the trees she caught a glimpse of a man leaving on a horse. He would have gone unnoticed except his horse was moving away on the run, and its hasty movement drew her attention. The thing that struck her was she thought the man riding the animal was deformed, and she ducked inside the jail to tell the marshal what she thought she saw.

Sam was seated behind his desk when she entered, his boots elevated on top; it was his usual leisure position. Molly thought she saw a look of contentment on his face.

"I hate to disturb you, Marshal. I just came by to tell you I'll have supper ready about six. Claire told me you usually came by around suppertime. She said she found it easier to cook for three than two. So do I."

"That's kind of you, Molly. I'll take supper at the Bluebonnet. No need to do extra on my account."

"It's no trouble. Matter of fact, I'd love to have you. Claire has the best stocked pantry I ever cooked out of. Having you come by gives me a chance to do one of the things a woman does best."

Sam could not hold back a snappy, "And just what other thing does a woman do best, Molly?"

Molly blushed. It was something she hadn't meant to say, but it had happened and she was caught with a private pleasure thought expressed openly.

She saw Sam's face light up with a wicked little smile, and she came right back at him, "You were married, Marshal. You know. Now don't bedevil me anymore and say you'll come to supper so I can go and get Jimbo."

"It will be my pleasure to be there, Molly."

At the door, Molly turned back, remembering the strange man she said, "I saw a man riding away from the back of the jail when I came in. He was in a big hurry to leave. I thought you should know about it. He looked deformed from what I could see."

"I know about it. He was here. He left mad as a honeybee whose nest has been jostled by a grizzly bear. I'm proud to say this; I caused it, and I'm proud of it. It's called payback. I think The Almighty knows about it."

"Funny. You don't act like the kind of man to prod somebody."

"It was a case of he deserved it, Molly, dear. He came here saying one thing when all the time his mind was made for something else. I don't like the man I found under his words. I disturbed him enough to get him off course, but he'll still be trouble. Now, go get Jimbo, and I'll see you at suppertime."

Molly Gibbs had no idea how much trouble Wyatt Winslow would cause.

Chapter Twenty-Nine

When Wyatt Winslow settled down some, he congratulated Sam Ordway on causing the distraction. The old devil is cagy, he admitted to himself. My plan was to agitate Young Bill before I gunned him down. I wanted to bring Chastity's memory back on him; make him remorseful. I planned for the distraction to slow down his gun hand. Confusion and indecision slows a man's hand. Separate the head from the hand. Well, I succeeded some. I'll sleep on it, and maybe I can come up with another way to intimidate Young Bill some more before I call him out. Well, I have three nights to waste waiting for him to get back here.

It was dusk, and night was coming fast, and Wyatt rode passed his family's old ranch house, not because it had been abandoned to cobwebs, wood rats, coons, snakes and any varmint needing a shelter, but because he could not sleep lying down. Living with Chastity in Saint Louis until her baby had been born was night after night of endured pain sleeping on a flatbed, not that sleeping upright was a comfort, it was not; uprightness simply caused him less torture. When he came back to Saint Louis, certain of his gun speed with his plan laid, he spent only one night under her roof. He felt guilty not staying longer, because he loved Chastity and Cassie, but pain diminished love.

In a small stand of cottonwoods behind the ranch house near the old bunkhouse, beneath one of the old trees, was his campsite. He had packed his camping gear not expecting to return. Now he untied his coffeepot and set it on the ring of rocks that had been his old campfire then went gathering small branches to build a fire, all the time thinking, and thinking got his temper boiling. He had gone into Foley expecting to call out Young Bill and have a showdown then and there. For it not to happen galled him.

Riding back, the thought that Young Bill may have had cold feet and had done the postponing instead of Sam had run across his mind and given him some satisfaction for his disappointment. In the next moment anger was riding on top of his hatred, and he kicked the old cold campfire ashes to relieve some of his disappointment at being put off no matter who did it and why.

After he had a cook-fire going, on his way to get water from the creek, he removed both saddlebags that carried the two pint Mason jars that held his whiskey. As he unscrewed a jar top for a drink, he damned Sam. The old man's ploy had upset him enough so he forgot he was running low on whiskey. A pint and a half meant he would have to ride back into town one more time. He would need another jug before his showdown. Damn Sam. The old devil probably knows how much it hurts to ride. If Sam Ordway wasn't so damned old, I'd call him out on general principles.

Drinking coffee followed by whiskey and whiskey followed by coffee, he said aloud, "It's a wonder I got any kind of stomach left," and built another cigarette.

When it was finished, nursing more whiskey, he decided food was too much trouble and walked to the tree that was his bed, and threw his blanket down then sat against the tree smoking and drinking. In the darkness before the rising moon appeared, he dozed and awakened and dozed again. It was a familiar sleep pattern designed by his twisted body.

"Hello, the house."

Wyatt's gun was in his hand before he was awake. The moon was high and he could make out a man on horseback in the old ranch house's yard.

"Wyatt. It's me. Young Bill. I'm here to talk. Show yourself."

"Up here," Wyatt replied. All trace of whiskey lethargy left him. He wanted to laugh, but he didn't. That will come later, he thought. I'll laugh in his face. He's yellow. He's come to beg.

Wyatt stood rolling a smoke when Young Bill rode up. "Get down," he said.

"No thanks, Wyatt. I have a herd waiting. This won't take long."

"Get on with it. What's on your mind to get you this far off your range?"

"I wanted to see what you looked like after all these years and the War. I see you got it pretty bad. I'm sorry for you."

"I don't need your damned sympathy. Keep it."

"The other reason I took the trouble to ride half the night is to find out if you've lost your mind."

"I'm in my right mind, alright. I want you to sweat for what you did to Chastity and my daddy, especially what you dallying with her did to my Dad, the Right Reverend David Winslow."

"I wish I had your daddy on this trail drive. Rain's coming the next day or so. I can't beat it. Thunder and lightning is a guaranteed stampede. Your daddy had a fine voice, so fine he could sing to a herd and keep them peaceful through any storm. When I was a young boy trail herding along with you and your brother, I remember how he would sing to them at night and they would lay down at peace with coyotes howling all around them. He had a gift."

"And you took it away."

"Chastity and me, not just me; I didn't hold her down. Wyatt, all that's past. That's not why I'm here."

"Just why in hell are you here?"

"To talk some sanity into you. Wyatt, I'm good with a gun. I'm as good as the teacher who taught me, and Lyle Sanford is the best in the world. I matched him. Time after time. Wyatt, I'm fast. Whatever life you have, keep it. I'll help you."

"So that's it. You're going to help me. A bribe, is that it? Call it off and you'll help me?"

"There's no bribe involved. I would have helped you if you had come back without killing on your mind. Forget it. I'm through talking. I rode a long way for nothing."

"I won't forget it. I'll be here when you get back. I'm fast, too. I think I'm faster than you. If I'm not, I'm your equal. Think about that. Suppose we kill each other? It could happen. And listen to this. If I get you, I win. I get the memory of setting you in your place. If we both get it, I still win. I got you, and I got out of this wreck of a body. I don't care a damn about living. I stay alive because I thought since I made it through that bloody War there must be a reason. It's stupid, because there is no reason. So, if you win, I still win. The best of both worlds for me is we both get it. What do you think now?"

"I guess it could happen like you say. I'll be back as soon as I can get the herd to San Antonio, and we'll find out one way or the other, one man or the other, or, as you say, both of us. Look for me Saturday afternoon. I'll damn sure make it back if I have to sweat every ounce of tallow off those beeves. It's your grievance, so call me out when you're ready. Have your gun oiled. Adios, Wyatt."

Young Bill turned his animal, and Wyatt watched him head, not cross-country which would have put him on a direct path back to his herd, but in the direction of Foley. Wyatt speculated about that. Why would Young Bill be going back to Foley this late at night?

Chapter Thirty

It was after mid-night, but Young Bill was not about to look at his watch to satisfy his curiosity when he tapped lightly on the door of room three.

The stately Margarite Doss opened the door slightly, and Young Bill quickly whispered, "I'm here to see Ivy. Would you please wake her?"

"I'm awake," Ivy answered appearing at the door beside the Negro lady.

"I'm here to talk," Young Bill whispered. "Will you take a walk with me?"

"Margarite knows everything about me. We have no secrets. Come in, Bill."

"What if the words I have to say are delicate?"

"Oh, I see. Where will we go?"

"To our Town House in the next block. My parents have our rooms across the hall, or we would go there."

"I'll get a robe."

Margarite Doss disappeared and Ivy Vanderbilt returned moments later in a robe and slipped out the door then closed it quietly. Taking his hand and pulling it so his head came down and his ear was close enough for her to whisper into, she said, "The room next door is mine. I rented it for my bodyguard. As you know, he no longer needs it. It's empty, so we can go there. Will that be okay?"

"It should be."

Once inside, even after the door was closed, Ivy continued to whisper although they now had privacy. "Shall I light the lamp?" she asked.

"The moonlight is bright enough."

"I can't imagine what brings you here this time of night. It must be serious. Is it?"

"It is. It is."

"You said you had delicate words to say. I'm fascinated. What are they?"

"Those words are wrapped around some facts. Facts first. Want a drink?"

"Will I need one?"

"Maybe. I need one. You can decide if you do later."

"It seems strange that you need a drink to talk to me. I'm not hard to talk to. For you especially. You are a very handsome man, and handsome men can always get a lady's attention. You're rich, and that gets attention. For me, you are also intelligent. That gets my attention. What do you need? Ask me."

"Of all the things I'll say, after all the talk, what it will come down to is I will need your body. If that's out of the question, say it now."

"That possibility crossed my mind the moment I laid eyes on you, Bill Foley. You have done nothing to change it. You are an honorable man, and I can be your judge, for I have known dishonorable ones. Yes. It's very possible I'll share my body with you. Now take a drink while I step back to my room and get some protection for us."

"Protection?"

"Yes. To prevent pregnancy."

"I didn't know there was such a thing."

"Men wouldn't."

"No. Don't do that."

"I don't understand. Please tell me what's on your mind."

Taking a flask from his jacket, he drank then offered it to her, and she accepted then drank. Her drink was more than a polite one.

"Thanks," she said with a smiling grimace. "You have me so confused, I think I'll need to match you drink for drink. Now talk."

They were standing so she added, "These chairs are uncomfortable. Let's sit on the bed."

"Let's stand by the window in the moonlight. If we use the bed, we will not be sitting on it."

"If?"

"Come here, and hear what I need to tell you."

Ivy Vanderbilt moved to him. She was wearing slippers, so she was looking up into his turned down face. The expression on it was fixed and serious, and he began to talk. "You know I will inherit the ranch making me wealthy in my own right. You know I have a college degree. Those two things alone tell you I'm not just an ordinary working cowboy. I'll add that my Catholic father saw to it that I worked, and at an early age, so I know ranching. The work is pleasing to me. Ranching is what I do and what I'll always do no matter how much money is in my name at some bank. I became a man earlier than most boys. I enjoy doing a man's work. It gives me a good inward feeling. What that should tell you is I'm tied to the land. I love it."

He continued, but his words slowed as if he was trying to follow an unclear pathway in his mind. "Here's how I see you. I think land has a hold on you like it does me. That's what I saw when we were on Tom Silverhorn's place. Land holds you and me like the sea holds sailors who love it. And you haven't seen the most magnificent part of our holdings yet. I know a mesa that looks down on the Frio River. There's an old Indian path to an overlook where you can see the river as it winds across the land below. Standing up there at night with moonlight streaming on the land, you look down on a flowing silver stream surrounded by a sea of grass that waves gently from the evening breeze that always comes after the heat of the day dies down. The Frio waters are fast flowing and ripples make it sparkle like a diamond necklace. I tell you, it will almost bring a tear to any eye from its beauty. The Indians owned it, and I think, even bloodthirsty as they appear to us, they must have been taken by what they saw. I'm sure they stood where I have stood. Even Old Bill Foley is captured by the magic of this land. After he married mother, he greatest pleasure was riding around looking at it. As soon as the Army captured the last of the Comanche's at Palo Duro Canyon and sent them to the reservation, Dad moved in on the mesa. He saw its beauty. It's easy to understand a man's love for a woman. But can you imagine my Dad, hard Old Bill Foley, loving the beauty of piece of land the way he does? Well, tonight it has become important that you see inside me much sooner than I anticipated. Here's where I'm going. As a rich man's son, I do not intend to be just another wastrel like the sons of most rich men."

"Bill Foley," she said softly, "A man doesn't tell his soul to a woman unless he has deep feelings for her. It is only fair that I speak my soul in return. I want this relationship. Whatever you want from me, I'll give. Go ahead. This is the time our lives have waited for."

"This is what I see. Events give us a chance to shape our lives by making choices. These next moments are for choosing paths. Do you see that?"

"Yes. I do."

"Here's my path. When this land is mine, I will make it into something greater than a place where cattle tromp. There is a place for them, but there is so much land, it's downright stupid to hold it for cows only. In my office at the bank I have plans with details on what I want for this land. My father has forbid this land to outsiders. Catholic Irishmen only. No different, he says, from the German Colony at Fredericksburg. His exceptions were Doc Wedgewood, Dave Winslow, and Sam Ordway. David Winslow would not have had a Methodist Church here except he rode in as partners with Dad and Sam. I intend to invite any honest man and his family, Negro or white, Chinese or Irish, to settle here. As Catholic as Old Bill is, he will not allow a Mexican in his church. Since we are near to Mexico, almost all the cowboys are Mexican vaqueros. They have families, so Dad gave them a church out at the ranch that is too small now. I intend to invite any of them who want to come into Dad's church here in Foley."

Bill Foley paused, took another drink to let his mind fill in. In the stillness, Ivy Vanderbilt matched it and returned the flask with one hand while brushing the other hand across her mouth to minimize what straight whiskey does to an unaccustomed drinker.

"You've said nothing I didn't know or surmise," she said. "You touched on this yesterday. If it is my body you're after, what's holding you back?"

"Another moment or so, and I think you'll understand. It's because of what I'll do with the land in the future. There is risk involved. Title to this land is risky now. You know that because I told you yesterday. I may need to mortgage everything I own, for I will finance men of good faith who come without money wanting to make this their home and raise a family. Trusting people can be risky. It could be a losing proposition. The ranch and all this land could be lost."

"If we make love, I'm not going to make love with you for money. I'll take you if you're broke. Are you saying you won't let me take that risk with you? I'm no child. I'll take the risk, or is this another non marriage proposal? Are you trying to take the long way around saying you want me but will not marry me?"

"No. This will settle it. Before I came here tonight, I rode out to see the man who wants me dead. At first, I took no notice of his challenge, because I know how good I am with a Colt, and I wanted to spare him his life. Then I learned that man was faster than your bodyguard, Matt Hardin, so he's fast. I'm still certain I can better him, but he insists we meet and shoot it out. Here's where it stands. We are good enough to kill each other. It could happen. What I want from you is a child. I want to begin the process tonight and have you meet me in San Antonio the night before I come back here so I can add to the possibility of producing an offspring. I want the child to be a boy to take my place and do those things, and I want you to guide him and do with this land as I would have done."

With his mind unlocked, Young Bill Foley sat down, and Ivy Vanderbilt sat beside him on the bed. Her breathing was shallow. He could hear it. He knew her heart must be beating fast.

"That's a lot to take in," she said after some moments of reflection. "You want me to go all the way, and I will; I care for you that much. I see now why you didn't want protection."

"I want it to be clear between us."

"It is. One thing, I cannot guarantee a boy. Will a girl do? I promise to have her behave in a way that would please you."

"Sure," he said.

"Since a child has implications for a single mother, you obviously have something more in mind. Am I jumping ahead? Like yesterday, I'm not sure if this is a marriage proposal. Is it?"

"It is."

"My answer is I will bear you a child. Gladly. However, I will not accept your marriage proposal. Not at this time."

"Something I didn't consider. You have a past, is that it?"

"All grown-ups have a past. This is not about the past. It's about the future. It's too early in our relationship to add marriage to it. If I conceive, that changes things, and I'll marry you the minute I know. If a child does not come from our two couplings, we will each be free from this obligation. Before you take possession of me, I want to say this: Bill Foley, the way you have gone about this tells me you are a fine human in spite of being a rich and handsome man."

"Before you make me a Saint, I want you to know I have a daughter. The mother and I never married."

"Are we to confess past sins now?"

"What happened between her and me was not a sin. As for your past, a woman as beautiful as you will have been pursued by men from an early age. You are a woman responsive to men, so I don't think you have remained a virgin. Your past doesn't matter to me."

Ivy Vanderbilt took a deep breath then rose from beside him and walked into the pool of moonlight coming through the window. Words were over. Choices made clear.

Standing there, her back to him, she lowered her robe and let it fall. She was naked. She had removed her nightgown when she went back into the room for the robe, and Bill Foley marveled at her brazenness of forethought as she turned to him.

Chapter Thirty-One

Ivy Vanderbilt was sleeping much later than usual, and Margarite Doss who was no longer a servant but had not lost her serving attitude, anticipating her former mistress's awakening, had brought into the room a fresh pot of coffee, and its stimulating aroma awakened her and brought forth a delighted yawn.

"It's delicious, Margarite. It smells like New Orleans. Can it be Bluebonnet Café coffee? No. It's better. And it's not the tepid stuff from the hotel, I can tell. I'm surprised if it's Bluebonnet's. Have things changed at the Café?"

Margarite Doss laughed. White teeth against dark skin made her face a picture Ivy Vanderbilt wanted to capture on canvas when they found a place to settle.

"No," Margarite replied. "Things certainly have not changed at the Café. Honey, that Café never made coffee this good. It came from Irish Rose's Saloon."

"No."

"It did."

"How did you manage that?"

"Marshal Sam saw me at the back door of the hotel when I was getting my breakfast yesterday. You recall they make me wait outside. Along came the Marshal slipping around back of the Saloon, and he saw me waiting. That Marshal. He's nosy in a polite way. He came over and said good morning. Then he said I suspect you ladies have spent some time in New Orleans. Your accents are not hard to recognize. Would you two care for some New Orleans style coffee? I couldn't say yes fast enough and he took me to the back of Irish Rose's Saloon and I waited and he returned with the best coffee I've tasted since we left New Orleans almost two years now."

"And you went back this morning. I'm so glad you did."

"That Kerry O'Shea is a fine man, too. Come any morning about ten, he told me, and I'll have a pot waiting for you and your mistress. Come to the back door. Not that I'm ashamed to serve you, it saves wear and tear on the town's nerves."

"Oh, is it after ten? Goodness. Have I slept that late?"

"Yes, my dear. That you have. And a good sleep as I judge it. You must tell me about last night."

"Oh, I can't tell something *that* private. But I will. Last night I was ravished just like every proper white girl dreams about."

"Ravishing is not just for proper white girls, Ivy Vanderbilt."

Both women laughed.

Ivy Vanderbilt's smile slowly turned to a more serious expression. "Margarite," she said, "we have come a long way from Basin Street. Last night, Bill Foley asked me to marry him."

"I'm happy for you. I expected it, but not this soon. Something has happened to make him come forward at such a time so late at night. Did you tell him everything?"

"Not yet, but I will. I have not accepted."

"I'm surprised. You must have accepted something. I came awake when you slipped back into the room. The time was very late. And you have slept until very late. Ravishing must have happened more than once. Tell me your secret."

"You and I have never kept secrets. We've been open and honest. Let's not change that because of what is happening in my life. Promise."

"Pretty child, yes I promise. Say what's on your mind."

"The plans we made together. It's time to renew our thoughts about them. Mine have changed. If your plans are the same, I intend to honor them in some way."

"I was fearful you were going to ask us to part ways. My dear, I love you. I think you love me too. That love could be called sister love, but it is not that. Sisters fight and squabble. We have not. A truth, no matter how bad, will not hurt the love between us. Dishonesty would harm it, and we both know that. Talk. If we part way, I will hurt. As you know, I have hurt before, and I will survive. Speak freely."

"Where to begin? I suppose first you should know I may be carrying his child."

"That's not like you. Please say that you have not tripped him into that."

"I did not. It is his idea."

"I'm thankful. It disturbed me if you did that. I'm sorry."

"I understand. I must tell you that things began moving so fast I gave no thought to the plans you and I had made. When he called so late at night, I was sure I knew what he wanted, and I was prepared to give it to him because I felt guilty. I never led him on or lied to him, but I did avoid telling him anything about my past or the plans you and I had made, so giving in would help put balm on my sore conscience. Besides, he's a handsome devil. He excites me."

"Child, I was young once. I remember. It's a glorious feeling when you enjoy yourself with an honorable man. I understand. Go on."

"Everything was perfect. Like Molly Gibbs. Everything was perfect with her. Then she said she was married. Not perfect then. Well, in the beginning, both he and I wanted to move into the relationship slowly. Perfect. Just what I needed. No confession. No dark secrets. Those would come later. Tonight, I thought all he wanted was my body, and I wanted him to have it, so I wanted to come into our room to get one of our sponges, but he said don't; he wanted more than just me, he wanted a child."

"Oh, mercy. And you made the decision to go ahead. How brave."

"Not brave. Desperate. Margarite, I love him. I want to please him anyway I can."

"Does he know?"

"That I love him? After last night? I gave myself with such abandonment, he should know, but I never said the word."

"Now, we must make other plans. No. It is I who must make other plans. If love wins out, and it should, he will be yours and your path will be his. It is I who must choose another course."

"I hate that."

"I know, but I saw the excitement you felt the moment you first saw the man, so what has happened to you has not come as a complete surprise to this old soul."

"I hate myself, but I'm so happy, Margarite. I'm already carrying his child. I feel it in my heart, and I'm in the middle of my period, so I should be fertile. He wants me again two nights from now to make certain. I know he'll throw me aside when I tell him my past, but I'll have his child. I'm as happy as I will ever be. He says he doesn't care about my past, but he will when he learns; I know. I'll love him even if he runs me off like a whipped dog."

"My. My. A woman of your experience in love. He must be special."

"He is. I know he is."

"And so your little imperfect world is perfect except for the debt you owe your friend, Margarite. Yes?"

"Yes. What can I do?"

"You poor soul. Let me help. See Margarite through Margarite's eyes. Foley is a wonderful place. Mind you, it is a wonderful place for white people who are Irish. There is not a person of color for thirty miles. Except for you, and a saloon barkeeper, I rarely use the King's English. No one else speaks to me. Honey, I miss New Orleans. I miss those old mansions on Basin Street. I miss the music. I miss the smell of New Orleans food as much as I miss the food. I miss Simon. I miss the people on the back streets."

"How blind of me not to see that. I'm sorry. But, New Orleans is not safe for you. You cannot go back there. What can we do? You have something in mind. What?"

"I no longer wish to build an establishment like we planned, but that may be my only choice. You were to find white maidens for a white clientele, but the business would be mine if we found just the right white girl to take your place and front the business. I could hire people of color for staff and grounds, and my life would blossom again. It was a good plan. But there was a time we thought getting rich was a perfect solution to a perfect life. We had a good plan, and we are now rich. But the plan is not perfect, because we now are faced with what to do with our lives. You are an artist, and if, as you think, your man rejects you later, you will have his child and your art, and you will accept another man as your husband to finish your family. Not perfect, but what is?"

"You're making sense. Go on, Margarite."

"I tempted fate when I went back into New Orleans to sell our sponges to Lu Lu White. Simon taught me there is more to life than money when I offered him more money than he has ever had. No, he said. He had a family. New Orleans was his home. Who leaves his home for another home? One who is unhappy is the answer he gave. He was not unhappy. He loved his wife. His children were not yet ready to leave the nest. Miss Gertie treated him well and paid him decently. I had money, but the question became what do I do now?"

"Yes. What do we do now?"

"What else turned out to be not quite so perfect? Foley, Texas. Foley offered safety, and it was a place virtually unknown. It was perfect for you. You could run away and hide, but we learned only Irish are allowed in Foley, and there is no such thing as an Irish Negro. Not too perfect for Margarite. Then Molly Gibbs walked in. Molly was to take your place leaving you free to pursue your chosen one, but we discovered Molly was married. At this moment, we don't know if she will stay married. If her marriage falters, she may take your place. With jewelry and fine clothes, she can become as elegant a Madame as you; embittered love makes an excellent courtesan. It will be a wonderful opportunity for her. Let us wait and see what happens in that young woman's life. It will give me time to decide what happens in my life. I only know the sugar cane fields of Jamaica and the Houses on Basin Street. What else is there for me?"

"I agree, Margarite, and, as you say, Molly must do it of her own accord. She's lucky. She will not face the ugliness of beginning as a crib girl. She's too pretty for that."

"Like you?"

"Yes. I was fortunate in that respect."

"Since we've put that in its place for a better time, what will we do for two days until your rendezvous in San Antonio?"

"We'll take a quick stroll down to the Emporium. That will get you out for a breath of air and sunlight. Then we'll walk to the livery and tell Claude to get the stage ready day after tomorrow for my trip to San Antonio. Tomorrow morning, I may ride out to Tom Silverhorn's place. We need another bodyguard for our money. Bill told me he was the man to take that scoundrel Matt Hardin's place. One day you may trust banks again. When will you get over a wily older banker cheating you out of your young virginity?"

"When you get over loosing yours to a wily old artist, my dear. We were both fools. No, not fools. Foolish. Enough of this chatter. Your bath has been waiting. The water is probably cold."

"Cold water will be fine. Nothing could make me unhappy today."

Chapter Thirty-Two

Margarite Doss wanted two spools of mending thread when she and Ivy Vanderbilt entered the Emporium. The dry goods section was the front of the store, and an elderly woman clerk with gray hair that was twisted into a tight bun began approaching. A young girl, perhaps sixteen Ivy judged, hurried away as soon as she saw Margarite. It was obvious the young girl had never seen a woman of color, and the appearance of the stately Negro lady unnerved her.

"I'll help you," the lady clerk said, and Margarite asked for two spools of number 40 thread one red the other white.

The grocery section was farther back, and while the elderly lady clerk was behind the counter rummaging through the drawers looking for the right size threads and colors, Ivy wandered deeper into the store where a youngster captured her imagination. An adorable little girl was at the candy counter, and she was looking up at the candy jars. Just as Ivy approached, in an effort to get at the red and white peppermint canes, her rag doll slipped unnoticed from beneath her arm and fell into an open barrel of dried pinto beans as she was stretching for the hard stick candy that was beyond her limited reach.

Instantly, Ivy bent down to recover the doll. With the doll in her hand, rising to return it to the child, she looked up, and her eyes gazed directly into a strange man's eyes that were glued to the crevice of her bosom.

"Do you see something that fascinates you?" she asked. She couldn't help smiling. She was in a humorous mood.

"I do," he replied without the slightest hesitation.

Ivy Vanderbilt removed the jar lid and took a cane from the jar and gave it to the young lady who, hugging her rag doll now, grabbed the candy cane and ran farther back into the store looking for her mother. Ivy then reached into her purse and left a nickel on the counter waving to the approaching young girl clerk who had left the dry goods section earlier, that no change was expected.

Surprised at the ease and evenness of the man's voice since he was caught in a brazen act, her cheerful mood encouraged her playfulness, and she turned back to him and followed up her advantage.

"Was it me you found fascinating, or just that one small part?" she asked quietly.

"You," he replied. "All of you."

The nimbleness of her question had not disturbed his composure, and it surprised her. Most men she met for the first time became easily flustered. She was standing face to face with a man who owned a handsome face filled with freckles. Expecting to put him on the defensive, she asked another question, "Are you a cowboy? To me, you look too neat, like you never touched a cow."

His smile came quickly. "Yes, Ma'am, I *am* a cowboy, a hard working one at that. My name is Tom Silverhorn, and I'm a small rancher, so small I'm my only ranch hand, so I do all the labor. Want'a see my hands?"

Turning them upwards, exposing calluses, he met her eyes again wanting to see that he had proved his case.

Their toughness was apparent, then her eyes glanced downward, and she saw a Colt revolver leaning outward from a well oiled holster, and her mind asked, is this the Tom Silverhorn Bill Foley recommended. Is this the gun fighter she wanted? He knows how to use the Colt, I'm sure of it. Bill Foley has no idea how much money Tom Silverhorn will be protecting. Wanting to be sure this man was trustworthy and not just a cowboy with a glib tongue who might do them harm or rob them which she suspected Matthew Hardin would have tried later on, to bring out more of his personality, she began with questions again. "I have been looking at ranches to buy. Do you know of one?"

Before he could answer, Margarite Doss joined them.

"Mister Silverhorn, this is my business associate, Margarite Doss, and I'm Ivy Vanderbilt," Ivy said.

"It's a pleasure to meet you ladies," he replied and added, "It's a bit unusual for ladies to be businessmen."

"We are not businessmen, Mister Silverhorn. We are business ladies," Ivy pointed out quickly.

The snappy remark was meant to put her in command again, but he only laughed at her catching his mistake. "That you are," he said. "There's no mistake about that."

Ivy Vanderbilt was serious, and she continued to study the man. His reply had been even and smooth. Was he too smooth? Or, was he simply adept at handling sticky situations? Trust was as important as ability if she were to choose him as their bodyguard. Matt Hardin could have been a mistake she did not want to repeat. She and Margarite had confessed to each other that the gunman the sheriff in Fort Worth had recommended might actually rob them instead of protecting them. That was the reason his permanent departure had not been greatly mourned.

The Emporium always had customers, although this was a time of day when traffic was only a trickle. Store activity always had a low hum from employee voices mingling with customer voices. Tall Tom Silverhorn with equally tall Margarite Doss surrounding a beautiful Ivy Vanderbilt had caused voices to cease, and Ivy Vanderbilt heard silence, so she made a quick assessment. Tom Silverhorn's land was a picture she wanted to put on canvas; for him to choose such scenic land said something good about him. Too, as his employer, she should get easy access to it. Tom Silverhorn also appeared to possess a great measure of levelheadedness since he handled their chance meeting so easily, so she made the decision.

"Mister Silverhorn," she said, "we need a bodyguard. Bill Foley has recommended you. Are you interested?"

"I'm surprised. Young or Old Bill?"

"Young Bill."

"I'm interested, alright. Old Bill's bank won't loan me a nickel for improvements or stock, so any money I can make I'll be obliged for. But, two things you should know; first. I'm not a gunfighter. I shoot straight and often under pressure, so I can protect you and your property. Second thing is the Foley's are not friendly to me. Especially Old Bill. He's downright nasty. My dad was a cowboy all of his life, and between us, we saved hard wanting to buy our piece of dirt and grass. Dad worked on one of Shanghai Pierce's ranches down near Galveston, and he was allowed to build a cabin on a small plot of land and run a few head of maverick longhorns when he married Momma. After she died, bunkhouse talk led him here. It was whispered that Old Bill Foley didn't have title to his land anymore, and he doesn't, not all of it anyway. Some of this land is part of a Spanish Land Grant. A judge named Chambers was given an *Empresario* contract by the Mexican government to bring in eight hundred settlers before the war for Texas Independence. He never fulfilled his contract, but the grant was officially recorded. When the Republic of Texas became part of the United States, the treaty noted that Spanish Land Grants were to be honored, because those Land Grants had been faithfully recorded, and all other titles were muddled with uncertain boundaries. Spanish Land Grants assured clear titles which could be transferred honestly. That treaty is the law of the land made so by the United States. We got clear title to our land. Old Bill knows about it because he withdrew the case without a trial on his lawyer's advice. With Dad gone, I'm in debt to the First National Bank in San Antonio. I admire Old Bill Foley's claim so I keep quiet. If I go around bragging, others will try to do what we did. Those were scary days for Old Bill, and he faced the Comanche when no other man would, but the State of Texas says different now. I'll finish by saying, I don't know Young Bill that well, but, if the Foley's are your friends, you should know that about me before you hire me."

"You have just told me you are an honest cowboy. I trust you now. We need to discuss salary and duties. We are in room three at the hotel. If you have time, we can go there now."

"Anything else I had to do can wait. A full-time job paying cash is more important."

"You will earn it. The job has long hours. Come along, Mister Silverhorn."

Walking to the entrance, she said, "Foley seems to have honest men. Are you really one?"

"I am. And most of the people here, women and men, are straight up honest."

They took to the boardwalk and walked to the hotel and up to room three.

Chapter Thirty-Three

"**Mister** Silverhorn, those three Jenny Lind trunks you see are valuable to us. One is more valuable than the others, but you will not know which one. You are to protect all three. You will be expected to guard them and us twenty-four hours a day. We furnish room and board, and the pay is one hundred dollars a month."

"A hundred a month? Are you sure? That's twice what a ranch foreman makes. I'd be a fool to turn that down."

"Well, let's settle things. Can you handle twenty-four hours a day with a ranch to run?"

"I can if I can go out there once in awhile to check stock and fences. It's roundup time, but without another hand, I can't make up a herd, so I'm not selling anything this year. I'll need to go back to the ranch for my gear. I want my shotgun and Winchester. Can I do that tomorrow?"

"Tomorrow will be fine. We'll leave Margarite here, and I'll ride out with you. I'd like to paint a landscape on your place. With your permission, I'll start tomorrow."

"Anytime, Ma'am. I'm proud to say there's some right pretty places on my place. Better have a slicker, though. Rain's coming."

"That could be a problem. The work of an artist is to bring light and color together. Wait. If I use oils painting rain droplets clinging to autumn leaves, they would have unusual color. I may discover something unique. I'll give it some thought when I look the landscape over tomorrow."

"Are you an early bird or a late sleeper?"

"Early bird. Once I slept by day. I have changed that habit completely. The Bluebonnet is open at six. We'll have breakfast then."

"And you pay for our breakfast. Room and board, you said. I like this job already. If I'm your new bodyguard, how do we address each other? I'd prefer Tom, but you may want us to be more formal."

"Tom it will be, and we would prefer to be Ivy and Margarite, but we are ladies, so in public, Miss Ivy or Miss Margarite would be more respectful, don't you think?"

"I do. Next, I'll go over and tell Sam Ordway so he'll know I'm your new bodyguard."

"After you see the Marshal, walk down to the Livery and tell Claude to have our stagecoach clean and be ready to drive me to San Antonio Friday morning."

"You have your own stagecoach?"

"We do. Claude is our driver, and he prefers to sleep in the coach. It's a Concord, so he can sleep in it. He hates hotels. He's crotchety. I think whiskey plays a part in his likes and dislikes. He's a good driver, so we tolerate him. Let me emphasize the job is twenty-four hours a day."

Tom Silverhorn made no comment, and Ivy Vanderbilt added, "Your room is next door to ours. When you need a break or we send you on an errand, Margarite or I will help. Each of us carries a Remington Derringer .41, a more powerful model than John Wilkes Booth used to take Abraham Lincoln's life."

Margarite Doss produced her hide-out gun. It appeared from a hidden pocket cleverly sewn into her dress. It appeared, not as quickly but as easily as a gun drawn from a gunman's holster.

Tom Silverhorn was surprised at her dexterity. The expression on his face said so; the expression also asked what kind of women are these that I have just agreed to work for?

They both saw his uncertainty, and Margarite Doss, to ease the cowboy's mind added, "Mister Silverhorn, a woman who has once been a slave will have come in contact with unsavory men and women. I introduced the weapon to Miss Ivy and instructed her on its use. She, too, is also very good with it."

Not every word was an outright lie, because her mistress was skilled with the little gun, but it was not Margarite, but Ivy Vanderbilt who had learned about the weapon from a wealthy planter's pudgy son when he laid it aside as he was undressing to take on the entertainment he had purchased from her. Escape plans, always close in her mind, had her ask about the gun. The next afternoon, she sent Margarite to purchase two of the weapons. The pair had cost twenty-five dollars, and they were not the old black-powder single-shot weapons, but the new Remington Rimfire double-barrel model. The planter's son's weapon had cost twice the cost of the pair because it was inlaid of German silver.

Ivy quickly added facts to Margarite's little lie, "We were told that a gunsmith by the name of Henry Deringer, spelled with one r, made the first hide-out weapon. When Lincoln was shot with one, a reporter wrongly spelled Deringer's name with two r's, so the copies of his design were called Derringers. These are the modern Remington Rimfire .41 caliber Derringer's, not the Philadelphia Deringer .40 caliber that John Wilkes Booth used to kill the president with. Abraham Lincoln didn't have a chance, and our weapons are even deadlier."

Margarite Doss handed Tom Silverhorn her Derringer to examine.

"Quite a piece," he said. "Got to be up close to do damage. This is the first one I've seen. Neat. Just the thing for a woman."

Ivy smiled, and asked, "Does that mean you have not visited a brothel, Mister Silverhorn? I'm told ladies of the night carry them hidden in their undergarments."

"No, ma'am. I know of such places, but every nickel has been dear to me. Dad was on every trail drive I made, and as soon as we were paid, we rode home while the other drovers ran wild. I've no regrets. Dad lived to see the land we worked for. I have the place now, and pretty soon I'll have it paid off. I still owe five hundred dollars. If I work for you for a few months then sell off a few pairs, a pair meaning a heifer and her calf, I can be out of debt."

Beautiful Ivy Vanderbilt was a woman who enjoyed men, and she recognized Tom Silverhorn was sharing his dream telling more about his life than he would ordinarily tell a stranger.

"And after that?" Ivy asked playfully.

"I'll find a woman like you. Not as pretty, but she'll be enough like you so I'll never need to visit a whorehouse."

"You mean brothel, don't you Mister Silverhorn?"

"I do," he replied, and he added, "Sorry, Ma'am."

"In that case, we will forget you said whorehouse in front of two ladies."

"Please do. I apologize again."

"Please don't."

Ivy and Margarite were enjoying themselves, and Tom Silverhorn, failing to understand their humor, could only smile weakly.

Life does not pair us correctly, Ivy Vanderbilt thought. If it had, Tom Silverhorn would have won Molly Gibbs.

Chapter Thirty-Four

Sam Ordway was seated in his chair behind his desk with his booted feet propped up on the twenty year old relic reflecting on the cooking difference between Molly Gibbs and Claire Winslow. His reflection earned him this conclusion: Molly was not Claire's equal, but she was as good as second gets.

Adept at reflecting since he had spent twenty years as a town marshal who had very little to do except reflect, he watched Tom Silverhorn leave the hotel and begin walking across the street, headed for the jail, and he waited.

"Howdy, Marshal Ordway," Silverhorn said when he opened the door.

"Come in, Tom. Have a seat."

"Thank you, Marshal. Thought I'd drop by and let you know I have a job."

"Bodyguard for those two women?"

"Yep. I'll be toting iron. Okay?"

"Yep. Permission granted. You're mindful before you pull a trigger. Can't say that about their last employee. It would be my guess the ladies are lucky he was quick to take offense and got himself killed. Once he discovered where they hid their valuables, he would have relieved them of them. Most of the Hardin's are church deacons or preachers, but others like John Wesley and Matthew are tough citizens."

"I'm proud to get his job, although everything about those ladies causes me wonderment."

"Me, too, Tom."

"That Ivy woman is one handsome creature. A genuine pleasure to look at, but she'd not be for just a plain cowboy like me. Even if she could cook, no rancher would want her in the kitchen or chasing chickens looking for eggs, not to mention milking a cow or slopping hogs."

Sam's laugh was brief then his face took on a serious expression. "My grandson may be the rancher that fits your bill. He's not a plain cowboy, and I think he's taken with the Ivy woman. I'll ask a favor of you, Tom."

"Let me guess. You want me to tell you if I find out anything unusual about my employer ladies. Is that it?"

"It is."

"Not likely, but I'll help if I can."

"The trouble is, the Ivy woman seems to be the genuine article, all woman, and wholesome as women get. But, why doesn't she talk about herself? She doesn't mention her money or where she got it. Did her daddy leave it to her? Is she the widow of a rich rancher? Why all the mystery? I have a hunch, but I won't say it out loud just now. Maybe it's simply that she's not been here long enough to find friends and talk about her past."

Sam had been intent on their conversation, and his gaze out of the jail's plate-glass window was a vacant one so that a rider dismounted at the jail's tie-rail, and Sam was not aware of it happening until the door opened.

"Howdy, Marshal Ordway."

"Miles Petty. What brings you all the way from Bellville? For you to get here this time of day means you must have worn down a good animal."

Sam did not rise from his chair, and Miles Petty, weary, took the chair next to Tom Silverhorn directly across from Sam.

"I left before daylight," Miles informed him. "I understand it won't be long before this hick town gets a railroad which means a Western Union Telegraph and us civilized people can get in touch with you the modern way instead of wearing out horseflesh."

"I've heard that business about a railroad and a telegraph station before. Surveyors come through every year or so, but nothing happens because Old Bill Foley won't let them cross his land. Only two ways it can happen. The legislature condemns the land, and they won't do that because they'll have to pay for it. The other way is when Old Bill passes then Young Bill will give it to them. Now that's put to rest, speaking of wearing out horseflesh, if you lost a pound or two, it would help any animal's back you crawled on."

It was good natured ribbing, and Miles Petty knew it, so he replied in kind, "Sam, if you were to get married again, you would cast a bigger shadow. I gotta a good wife. If I pass her cooking, it would hurt her feelings. As you know, a Deputy Sheriff don't make a helluva lot of money, and I'd have a hard time attracting a new cook. Good wives are hard to find."

"He's right, Marshall," Tom Silverhorn butted in. "Not that many available females around. If my new job holds up, I'll be on the lookout for one, and I don't need competition."

"Miles," Sam said, "The young feller next to you is Tom Silverhorn. Tom, this is Miles Petty, deputy to Sheriff Ed

Beck over at Bellville. Miles, what brings you here in such a hurry?"

"Bad news. Maybe good bad news for young Silverhorn here if the young lady I'm looking for came to Foley. A new widow woman was made yesterday."

"Cass Gibbs!" Sam exclaimed, and his chair legs dropped to the floor. "Sid and Everett?" he asked. It was more a statement than a question.

"Yep. Looks that-a-way. Army patrol saw a horse with a broken rein trying to crop grass. It looked suspicious, a horse with a broken rein dangling and no rider. They looked around, made a wide circle, figuring the rider might have been thrown, but there was no evidence of anything like that, so they brought the horse to the Sheriff's Office. Ed recognized the brand and the animal, and he came out and got me, and we went straight to Jubal Spence's place, it being a lot closer than Cass Gibbs's new little ranch. Jubal was expecting us. His boys had killed Cass, he admitted, but it was not their fault. They had left the country, he said, but they came by to tell their daddy the truth of what happened so he could tell the sheriff the straight of it."

"You reckon Jubal can tell the truth?"

"He'll dodge it some, but he tells most things straight now. He learned respect for the law at Rusk. Do you know him?"

"Never met the man. Sid and Everett came to town with Cass before Cass met Molly. Sid and Everett got rowdy over at Irish Rose's, cussin' and bullyin' a male clerk from the Emporium partaking of Kerry's free lunch and having a jolt. I promptly ran 'em out of town. Kerry O'Shea told me Cass moved to another table by himself, so he was not party to it, and I told Cass he was welcome, but pick different friends. If Jubal is like his boys, I know him without ever seeing him."

"Nature gives different men different ways, but the apple never falls far from the tree, so those two sons of his are natural night owls like their daddy. Jubal was one to sleep all day and prowl at night. He first came to Ed's attention when a little pot and pan peddler was robbed in the middle of the night while he was asleep at his campsite about ten miles above our town. Several other little jobs sprang up, one being the poor box at the Catholic Church that got Ed plenty mad. Then Ed set a trap and caught him breaking into Pruter's Saddle Shop after word was let out old man Pruter kept his money in a shoe box. Our jury sent him to the prison at Rusk; it was new then, the big prison at Huntsville got overcrowded. Rusk sits on red clay, and the State built a smelter to mine iron ore from the iron in the clay. Short of it is, they worked hell out of the prisoners, daylight to dark in boiling hot heat tending a white hot smelter, and Jubal came back a different man. Not Christian, mind you, but fearful of the law and not eager to take another trip back."

"Sid and Everett didn't give me the understanding they ever learned discipline or manners."

"Good guess. The boys were almost gown when Jubal got released from Rusk. They hassled every girl at school until the teacher rode out and told the parents not to send them back until they learned some manners. Jubal and his wife may have tried, but his wife is a mousy little woman not given to say no or much of anything to anybody, so the boys got kicked out of school. Jubal rode in and told Ed he wasn't responsible for them anymore. He sent them packing. He told Ed he was not going back to that blast furnace, and his two boys were bound to get in trouble and might drag him into it."

"Miles, I know where they went to live after Jubal kicked them out."

"They sure didn't go anyplace and work it."

"No, they didn't. Listen to this for gall and dumb luck. You know the old line shack on Old Bill Foley's range that butts against Jubal's, maybe two or three miles from Bellville, don't you?"

"Sure. It's been abandoned half a dozen years."

"One day a pair of Old Bill's riders who were scraping the range for stray's saw the place was occupied and rode over to evict them, and Sid and Everett told it that Old Bill Foley, himself, came riding out to the line shack checking his range and found them. They told it that Old Bill said they could live there as long as he was alive."

"No way he'd do that. Not Old Bill Foley. That's real brass."

"Young Bill knows his daddy. Old Bill Foley was not one to tolerate anyone on his land that didn't work for him. Old Bill Foley did not give gifts to strangers, but Old Bill was down, sleeping most of the time, but he did ride the countryside once in a while, so Young Bill said he would tolerate them until Old Bill passed on if they behaved."

"Well, they misbehaved. Even Jubal admitted it, although it was said sideways."

"How's that, Miles?"

"Jubal told it that his boys said Cass came to the line shack just before dark with a cow hide that he had dug up. The cow hide had his brand on it, and he accused Sid and Everett of butchering it and selling the meat for whorehouse and whiskey money. Cass added four other cows were missing, but he was not going to try to find old hides, he just wanted forty dollars for this one cow or he was going to bury the two of them where his cowhide had been. Sid and Everett denied everything, Jubal said, but Cass was hot-headed and wouldn't listen. He drew his Colt and fired at Sid's boots as a warning saying he wanted his money or else. That's when Everett shot Cass out of the saddle."

"Do you and Ed think that's the straight of it?"

"Not by a long shot. Jubal didn't either. Cass was not known for stupid. Quick temper, yes. He probably didn't fire any warning shot knowing those two boy's never had a dime ahead. He probably issued a deadline ultimatum. Ed told Jubal he figured Everett fired the shot that killed Cass, and Jubal allowed he might be right. Those two boys would be highly nervous about someone who had evidence they were cow thieves. That's hanging evidence."

"Go on, Miles."

"Jubal had Cass's body at his place. His boys must have brought it with them from the shack. They said they wanted to show their daddy they had told the truth, and sure enough, he pointed out that Cass had not been shot in the back. Ed examined the wound. He wanted to make sure Cass was not shot in the back, either. Well, he wasn't. He was hit in the chest, so Ed was satisfied. No matter how it happened, Ed would not be able to prove the shooting was murder. Incidentally, we didn't find the cowhide. They took it with them or took time to rebury it."

"I can guess why the boys are leaving the country even if they are innocent of murder."

"Can you now? Anybody who knows Elder Gibbs knows that."

"Yep. I understand Old Elder believes in an eye for an eye and a tooth for a tooth. Just black and white. No in-betweens."

"Give Jubal credit. He went with us to tell Elder about Cass. He told Elder it was a sad thing, but he didn't beg for mercy for his sons, and he defended them saying the shooting was pretty much an accident. Elder disagreed politely. Told

Jubal right out his sons were cow thieves, but thanked him for coming to express his sympathy. He then told Jubal he would send his sons after Sid and Everett just as soon as Cass was properly buried. Jubal said he gave his boys food as they were heading for Mexico, but he didn't think Sid would make it far. Cass had somehow got off a shot and hit him high in the chest. The bullet may have hit his collar bone or a rib. Sid was hurt but he was going to ride as far and as fast as he could; he knew Elder. That was the end of it, except Elder asked us to ride to Cass's place and tell his widow. It was late when we got there then we found out she was gone. Ed asked around town when we got back, and she hadn't been seen, so he judged she had come to Foley for one reason or another. I'm here to find her and take her back. If Foley had a telegraph, I could have wired you to find out if she was here and saved the horseflesh that worries you so much."

"She's here, Miles. She's looking after Jimbo Winslow. Claire Winslow went to Saint Louis to see her daughter and grandchild."

"Do you mind showing me the place?"

"Sure. It's just outside of town. I'll go with you."

Tom Silverhorn had been a silent listener overlooked by the two lawmen. With Miles Petty's recounting finished, the three of them stood, ready to leave, and only then did Sam and Miles become aware of his presence again.

Miles, bringing humor, said to Tom Silverhorn, "Young man, you should come along. You won't need to wait on a payday if you can marry this widow. She's inherited a nice small spread with fifty cows less a few that have mysteriously disappeared lately."

"I can always use more cows, but I don't need more land. Land's not important. At my age, what is important is a proper woman that can have kids and cool my need. I'll have to meet the widow another time, though. I agreed to do a job, and I'll do what I agree to. Right now, I need to get over to the livery stable and see that a stagecoach gets ready for the Ivy lady."

Sam's mind was busy as the three of them shuffled to get out the door without bumping each other. Ivy Vanderbilt was not going to be the only wealthy woman in Foley. With Cass gone, Molly Gibbs had just made a small start in the Ivy woman's financial direction. Now, if Old Bill Foley claimed her as he said he would, Molly was going to become seriously wealthy, and she didn't have any idea it was happening.

Chapter Thirty-Five

Tom Silverhorn stood in the hall in front of room three and waited for Ivy Vanderbilt to begin his day. It was not yet six and darkness made the corridor dimly lit, and he hesitated about knocking on the door fearful his new lady employer had overslept. His hesitation grew, but he found himself approaching the door to knock when the pretty lady slipped quietly through it facing him directly.

"Good morning, Tom," she said pleasantly, her voice hushed.

"That depends, Miss Ivy," he replied keeping his voice low. "Rain's started, and it's gonna rain all day, maybe longer. Personally, I kinda like a day like this. Others hate it. Are you still of a mind to go with me?"

"Of course."

Ivy Vanderbilt was carrying a long leather case instead of a purse, and he took the satchel-like container from her, and they walked downstairs, where Tom Silverhorn asked, "If you ride with me you'll get soaking wet before we get back. Your coach is ready. Do you want me to have it brought around after we finish breakfast?"

"Of course not. I've been rained on before. I didn't melt."

Walking past the front desk now, Tom Silverhorn opened the door for her, and they paused on the veranda and watched the slow drizzle for a moment or two.

Wordlessly, Tom Silverhorn unrolled a yellow slicker from under his arm, and they huddled beneath it and walked down the steps, then turned left and walked quickly to the Bluebonnet Café next door.

As the first and only guests, they were served quickly, and ate with only necessary words passing between them. Ivy Vanderbilt's mind was filled with thoughts about her relationship with Bill Foley. Her concentration was not on food. She ate well, but she ate absently. Tom Silverhorn knew serious thoughts were crowding her mind. He could only guess at what they might be, but her kind of woman would always be a mystery to him, and he knew it.

After his employer signed the breakfast check, he said, "I'll walk to the livery and get our mounts if you're still of a mind to ride. Do you have a slicker?"

"Yes. See that I get the same animal I ride when I go with Bill Foley. There's a slicker tied behind the cantle along with two canteens. Please see that the canteen on the right has fresh water. I drink from that one. Don't worry about the other one. I use it to clean my brushes when I use watercolors which I may or may not do today. There will be enough rainwater any place I stop, so it really doesn't matter if that one's empty."

Tom Silverhorn reached down and picked up Ivy Vanderbilt's leather case, and she said, "Oh, I almost forgot my case needs a slicker, too. The leather will soak through eventually, and it carries my portable easel and a canvas that could be ruined. My brushes and paints will probably be okay, but my working smock and shoes are squeezed in there. Naturally, I prefer they stay dry. There are two extra slickers in the stage for use by Margarite and myself. Claude knows where they are. Have him get one for my case."

A few minutes later, they left Foley. Riding through intermittent drizzle that made conversation a poor choice, words were not exchanged until they crossed onto Silverhorn land and Ivy again saw in the distance the place where she and Bill had stopped and they had kissed beginning their serious relationship.

"There," she said, pointing north, and they rode toward the curved limestone cliff that Bill Foley told her had been carved by the Frio River. He failed to say where the water came from that challenged the stone wall, and she began to wonder about that. Logic said it came from high up, a place where snow melting on some mountain top began running downhill gaining enough speed to begin dissolving the cliff that stood in its way.

Tom Silverhorn could see the cliff was not entirely vertical. The slope allowed trees to climb it, but the trees were not scrubs like the mesquites and oaks, they were beautiful maples with leaves that glistened from today's mist and rain. All along, he had known the grove was there, but as a cowman, trees, especially a thick grove of trees, had no interest. Cows ate grass, and grass didn't grow under the thick shade that maples made.

As they rode in, to his surprise, a small glade began to open. It was such a small clearing it was not possible to see it from any distance away. The shape of it made a triangle with rounded corners, and the ground had a grass carpet which was luminous green made so from a bountiful supply of water nearby. It was very pleasing to the eye.

Tom Silverhorn knew water had been responsible for all this; even on a hot day this place would be cool, and Tom Silverhorn said, "I've been here almost five years and never came out here. I was always too busy working cows on open rangeland. Look what I've missed."

Ivy Vanderbilt smiled. "I understand, Tom," she replied adding, "This has become one of my all time favorite places. It appeared just like magic, so I'm hoping to find magic when I paint it. I'll buy it if you'll sell."

"Probably not," he replied.

They dismounted, and Tom Silverhorn withdrew the leather case from its yellow slicker that held his employer's easel and paints.

"It won't be necessary for you to hurry. So I won't worry about you, how long will you be gone?" Ivy asked.

"Two hours or more. It's still almost a mile to the ranch. It would be closer if we had gone directly to it. I worry about leaving you here alone."

"But I wish to be alone. I came to paint this place on this kind of day. The first time I came here, I saw this landscape on a bright day. The colors seemed to dart out at me and dared my imagination to capture them on canvas. That's what an artist does, Tom. Capturing colors by blending paint to match nature's colors is what I do. It occurred to me yesterday when rain was coming that almost all landscapes by other artists' are painted on days bright with sunshine. I want to capture leaf colors when cloud overcast and rain droplets clinging to the tips of them magnify their gold's and rust's.

See," and she pointed. "Over there are vines of wild grapes. And, over there," and she pointed again, "lower to the ground are blackberry vines with fruit almost ripe so the berry colors are mixed. Some berries are green, some bluish black, others are green and purple. There's color everywhere. Some are muted, and some jump out like the flowers on the honeysuckle vines. The contrast of the yellow stamens inside the flower against the brilliant white circle of the petals is simply daring me to paint it. An artist lives to capture color, and color is constantly changed by light. And light moves. Light is never still, so shadows are formed. Shadows allow an artist to show depth, and depth gives life to a painting. So, you see, today's light is different from ordinary sunshine. I'm going to try to capture colors that are seen as normally bright but are now subdued by rainy grayness, and I'm going to attempt putting emotion into it by changing the depth of the field. I'll move the trees nearer, leave the carved limestone where it is, and I'll move the cliff farther back. It will not be an easy task, but I'll thoroughly enjoy attempting it."

Having given what amounted to an art sermon, she smiled at her own seriousness at having done such a thing to a cowboy who had not asked to be in her temple, and she sent him away waving her hand at him, and said, "I don't paint very well with someone watching, so, go, and take your time. I'll be okay."

"I'm not so sure. I'm uneasy about leaving you."

"Don't be. I have my hide-a-way Derringer."

"With only two shots."

"Tom, even your cows have not found this place. The only living things passing here have been deer and squirrels."

"I'll hurry."

"Don't. I'll use every minute of your two hours. I won't mind if you are gone three hours. Light makes shadows walk. Chasing shadows is something I love. I won't even know you're gone. Now, git, cowboy."

"I did overlook the fact you're the boss."

"I am, at that. Before you go, would you cut a sturdy stick about two feet long for me? Make it as straight as possible. I overlooked bringing a mahl stick. It's a stick used to steady an artist's hand. I need one to do what I intend. I'll tie a cloth on the end of the stick that touches the canvas."

While Tom Silverhorn walked to a nearby maple tree looking for a low branch suitable for a mahl stick, Ivy unpacked the box that held her brushes, tube paints, and palette knife. Past field experiences taught her that a French easel is best since it makes everything an artist needs portable and the whole tripod affair collapses easily for travel.

After firmly placing the tripod easel, when that was done to her satisfaction, she took out an old paint splattered smock and a pair of shoes that were also old and paint splattered. Pulling the smock around her riding outfit without bothering to tie the ends, she smiled. Her memory reminded her, the shirt she was wearing today was fastened at her throat; the shirt she was wearing when she came riding here with Bill Foley was purposely opened two buttons down.

She was removing a pre-stretched canvas when Tom Silverhorn returned with a suitable imitation of a mahl stick, and she said, "One last thing. Help me spread this slicker between those tree branches. I need a shelter for my canvas when more of those little showers come."

The cowboy tied four corners of the slicker to low hanging tree branches, then, mounted up to leave, looked back and saw Ivy Vanderbilt sitting on a small portable stool under a bright yellow poncho for shelter with a long brush moving briskly against a canvas, painting happily.

Almost an hour later, Ivy Vanderbilt, after her landscape had taken shape, reached into her leather case and got several small sponges from it. Each one was a mix of many hues of a single color. The blue sponge was bluish and the green greenish. Black was blacker than black because purples were seeping through. She called them her cool color sponges, and she kept them separate from her hot color sponges, the reds and oranges.

Using sponges to paint background images was a technique she had learned from George Inness at The Hudson River School, the first place she had run to when she left home impulsively and angry. Reaching for a sponge to apply color to her canvas, she looked at it and found herself remembering her internship at The Hudson River School where George Inness already had a reputation as the Father of American Landscape Painters. And she asked silently, what would my life have been like if I had stayed at the school? She had left when George Inness frightened her out of her wits by having an epileptic seizure in a flower field when she was painting with him.

Pushing unfinished thoughts away, she painted the background on her canvas just as George Inness had taught her, using sponges. The background at the base of the cliff was blurry underbrush and berries, so she used her cool sponge colors first then the hot color sponges. Onto the background image, she drew lines, some straight, most curved, for trees and their branches.

While she painted, George Inness stayed in her mind. Knowing him had changed her life. A Sunday newspaper article with a likeness of him at his summer home in Tarpon Springs mentioned he had found just the right sponges there for his work. It was a fortunate circumstance for her and Margarite, because his remark became the gateway that led them to riches and out of human bondage.

After her memory of George Inness, a second image of another man always came. He was Duc Josef le Tourneur. After Duc Josef, sponges, word or image, sent an emotional dagger piercing her soul. After five years the memory of Duc Josef was painless now, still her ears still took on a warm twinge of embarrassment when she remembered Duc Josef's handing her a sponge. Even the nightmare of Simon Doss was no longer a nightmare, it no longer caused sleeplessness.

Tom Silverhorn found her as he left her, seriously painting. She looked up and acknowledged his presence with a smile then went back to work. The cowboy had thoughts of his own to occupy his mind waiting for his employer. At his ranch house, selecting weapons for his new job, he faced the fact that he could be called upon to kill a man or men protecting his employers and their valuables. The thought caused him some hesitation, for he had not killed a man. With the image of the two women he was to defend in his mind, he knew with certainty, that he could do it, for any man or men who would harm them, would be evil. With his thinking clarified, he chose a Greener shotgun instead of his Winchester. If it came to killing, it would be close work, and a shotgun was his weapon of choice.

Chapter Thirty-Six

Rainy weather continued. It was intermittent, duplicating yesterday. Wet weather was giving needed moisture to grazing land that was hungry for it, but it was going to slow her ride to San Antonio, and muddy rain-filled ruts were going to make the ride an uncomfortable one, but Ivy Vanderbilt left with a smile of resignation having decided how she would handle her meeting with Young Bill Foley.

She was wearing riding Levis and a western shirt, nothing frilly or feminine. They were clothes proper women would frown upon, but, if her stagecoach got stuck she was dressed to help out. If it became seriously disabled, a saddled livery animal was following on a lead rope; she was determined to get to San Antonio. In her mind, the relationship that had cascaded so quickly must be decided one way or another; her heart said one thing, her common sense another, but her history had to be told, and she realized this was the time to tell it.

A Jenny Lind trunk was riding in the stage's boot, sheltered because it held a seductive ice blue satin evening gown with midnight black accessories necessary for a lady to precipitate a male's seduction. Even knowing the male would be a willing participant, rain and mud could lay in ambush to prevent it, so if an ambush happened, her resort was a black negligee folded in a saddlebag on the livery horse.

Since rain was an off and on again kind of thing, it made the ride slower than either she or Claude had anticipated so it was late in the day when they crossed the little bridge over a curve in the San Antonio River leading downtown.

She had not been to San Antonio, but Claude had, and he navigated the coach past intersections that crossed at strange angles, and they came to the Alamo, but they were also in front of the Menger Hotel which was only a stone's throw away from the historic shrine. The Alamo was forty years old now. The Menger hotel was twenty years newer. William Menger originally had a brewery and boarding house on the property. Business success brought with it money enough to convert the old boarding house into a two story hotel that was the finest in the southwest. Robert E. Lee and U.S. Grant had been guests there. At different times, however.

Ivy Vanderbilt, made aware of the hotel history by her driver, stepped out of her mud splattered coach and was greeted by a doorman. Claude waited for a bellhop and handed down her trunk to the young man when he arrived then left to take the coach around back to the stable.

Walking ahead of the bellhop, she passed through the grand Victorian lobby that was richly furnished with plush chairs, love seats, and sofas done in a fashionable color but one she disliked which was a dark red maroon that fairly glared under the Pintsch gaslights.

She approached the desk nervously, thinking she would soon have an answer to her first little dilemma; did Bill Foley have reservations?

"May I help you?" the desk clerk asked.

"Reservation for Bill Foley," she said in a quiet yet demanding tone. She did not end the sentence with a question mark. She did not say please.

Turning the register book to her, the clerk asked, "Your name?"

"Mrs. Foley," she answered. Her voice was steady, and her eyes were focused on his.

"Room twelve. Downstairs as requested," he replied. "Will you be staying all three nights?"

Three nights was a surprise, and she answered, "I hope so," and she signed the register. She wrote *Ivy Vanderbilt Foley* and turned the register back to the clerk who took one look at the name and quickly came from behind the desk, and the three of them hurried down the richly carpeted corridor to room twelve. The business of names always brought a hidden smile, or a smirk. She knew Vanderbilt got the clerk's undivided attention.

She settled into the room quickly. It was a typical room with a single bed and two wing-back chairs adjacent to a small table in front of a large window. After the two men placed her trunk, she asked, "Which California wines do you serve?"

The bellhop answered quickly, the prospect of extra money apparent from his eagerness, "Inglenook, Beringer, and Paul Masson. We also have French Champagne."

Her New Orleans experience had not been limited to the inner workings of the Bordello industry. French influence in New Orleans was everywhere. French wines, French perfumes, French fashion, and French Maisons de Tolerance, simply known as whorehouses in America, found a second home in New Orleans. She had learned about wines. The Inglenook, Beringer, and Paul Masson vineyards had root stocks that came from France and Germany. Inglenook originated as a Bordeaux wine from the South of France where mostly red wines were made. A red wine would not fit tonight. Beringer and Paul Masson were German Rhine wines from the Rhine section of Germany. Both vintners made a sparkling white wine just as bubbly as champagne. Champagne, in the strictest sense, was wine that came only from the Northeastern section of France. Wine called California champagne was not named properly. It was only a matter of naming, because California made excellent sparkling white wines with taste equal to the proper French champagne.

"Do you have ice?" she asked.

"Certainly," replied the desk clerk, indignity in his voice.

A way to make ice had been discovered years ago, and ice houses were in every big Eastern city, but her travels in Texas had shown her the scarcity of ice in the State, and there was none in Foley she knew of. The Menger was a grand hotel, but it was in the center of what was still a wild state. Ice had been readily available in New Orleans and her home in Baltimore for many years. Entering the hotel, availability of ice became a question for her. Chilled wine was to be her crutch. It was something she counted on to help her tell Bill Foley what she had to tell. Afraid her tongue would back away from the confrontation, she needed wine to loosen it and her tension. The wine was to settle nerves that were making her hands shaky and her inner self panicky. Without ice, she would have to chance warm bubbles floating up her nose causing tears or making her choke when she talked to him. She was determined Bill Foley would hear her confession clearly.

"No French Champagne." She did not want to give Bill Foley the impression she was celebrating. "I'll have a bottle of Rhine wine iced," she said. "I want one with a plain name. Beringer's will be fine."

In truth, Beringer's was the newest of the wineries, less than ten years old.

"Beringer's," the desk clerk said to the bellhop who nodded indicating he knew what to bring.

"And a bottle of Jack Daniels whiskey," she added. "I'm not familiar with bottle sizes. Just bring a small size, please"

After both men left, walking aimlessly about the room waiting for the bellhop to return, her memory, badly needing something to occupy it other than the dread from the consequences of her confession, carried her to a morning when the Baltimore Sun's headline said the Ice King, Frederick Tudor, had cut ice from Walden Pond. Tudor insulated ships with sawdust and shipped ice from the frozen ponds in Maine, Vermont, and Massachusetts to southern cities, making him extremely wealthy, but the part of the article her memory was interested in was Walden Pond. Before Simon Doss entered her life, Walden Pond had been of no interest. After Simon Doss had done his deed, Henry David Thoreau's words meant something, which was a surprise, for she was at the time the article was written a headstrong girl whose head contained only self-centered ideas. The article said Henry David Thoreau went to Walden Pond seeking to live life at its deepest, to drive life into a corner, and if it proved to be mean, to discover the full meanness of it. Meeting Simon Doss was where her life got mean. Simon had driven her life into a corner.

Ivy Vanderbilt, in a lonely room with her thoughts magnified out of portion, found her agitation lessened when the wine crutch was delivered.

The bellhop offered to open the bottle, but she declined. She would wait until Bill Foley got there to use her crutch; she did not want to be tipsy. Her question now was how late would he be? She knew rain would slow the herd so he was sure to be late, so, when and how would they eat? She did not want to sit in the dining room alone dressed formally with people staring at her. Little decisions became big dragons.

A knock finally came about nine. When she answered the door, it was Bill Foley, and she folded into his arms.

Waiting had been a torment, and she lost her resolve. Giving way to her nervousness, she tried to pry the cork from her wine bottle and failed, so she had nipped at the Jack Daniels bottle until only half remained, and she was tipsy.

He was dirty. His clothes were caked with dried mud. His face had been wiped clean, but there were places missed during the wiping. She was completely unaware of its dirtiness; her mouth went to his searching and pleading, thankful he was finally there for her to touch.

"Bill, oh Bill, thank God you're finally here. I was going crazy waiting. My head is dizzy with all the questions that will find answers tonight, and I'm afraid of them. I was almost delirious when the room clerk said this room is yours for three days. Is that true? Please say we will run away from that man tomorrow. I have money. I can make more. Don't go back and face that man."

Without answering, Bill Foley moved past her to sit in the nearest chair. "I'm bushed," he said wearily extending his long legs and booted feet. "We pushed hard, before daylight and after dark. I'm exhausted."

"Too exhausted to do what is expected of you?"

"No. I'll manage fine with a bath and some whiskey. Reminds me. Did I taste whiskey in your kiss? Your mouth is sweet."

"It's whiskey. You're creating a mental wreck of me."

"Never meant to. Meant to go slow."

"It would have been nice to get to this point slowly, but it didn't happen that way. I'm learning life marches to its own cadence, so here we are. Our personal crossroads. Choose your direction, life says. Do we go together? I'm going to tell you who I am, and I'm afraid you will choose to go a different way. We'll see."

"Your worry is about nothing. Look at us. We're a sight. I'm a cowboy in dirty range clothes and you're a beautiful woman in that gown. I almost hate to ask you to take it off."

"Don't worry. I'll gladly take it off when you're ready."

"Some of my dirt rubbed off on it. I'm sorry. Have you eaten? I've been worried about that."

"No, I haven't, but I can't eat anything. I'm too nervous. My stomach is in little knots. Fear does that to me now."

"You're afraid? Of what? Me?"

"You? No. Tomorrow, yes. You haven't answered me. You have my hopes up. Are we going to run away and leave that horrible situation in Foley? Please say yes. We can spend tomorrow and Sunday here enjoying each other. I'll give you all the female body your male body can take, then we'll head for Colorado or California, or any place you want. My stagecoach is here. We can leave anytime you're ready.

"I'm sorry my reservation got your hopes up. This hotel is always booked, especially week-ends. I asked for three nights because I wasn't sure how long it would take to get the herd through, and I wanted to be sure of a room. I'm going back to Foley tomorrow, and I can tell you why. Point one. I've worked hard for the land I will inherit, and I intend to claim it. Point two. Even if I knew Wyatt Winslow was faster than me, I'd face him. I'm not afraid if people think I'm yellow. I'm afraid to live yellow. I won't do it. I'll die first."

Bill Foley was talking sitting in a slouched position, his legs stretched out while Ivy Vanderbilt had been moving about the room slowly touching things here and there as the conversation progressed, and she was at the window looking through it into the Menger Courtyard when her hopes of leaving ended.

She stood in silence for a few moments then pulled the drapes together tightly. "All along I knew it was a false hope," she said simply. Then she turned and asked, "Have you eaten? I should have asked sooner."

"That's okay. I ate with the boys. Most of them are Mexican, and we ate at a little Mexican Café down by the loading pens waiting on the tally. I had *arracheras*, Mexican steak strips. As late as it was getting, I figured you had already had supper. I wish you'd let me get you something."

"I have something," she answered, and she walked to the table where the wine sat.

"I planned for this bottle to stand as my supper. See. I know to call it supper here even if we call it dinner back East. I look forward to sharing your life although it may only be for tonight and tomorrow. Now open my wine and I'll drink supper while you bathe. The water is tepid but plentiful, or it was when I bathed. Afterward, you can undress me, and we will proceed with parenthood. I have a small amount of Jack Daniels left to help you past your tiredness."

The room was lighted by gaslight. The fixture had been turned on but low when she entered much earlier with the bellhop, so now they cast shadows when they approached the table from different directions.

Ivy, finding her precious ice melted, dipped her fingers in the cool water, and playfully flipped droplets from her fingertips into his face and with her handkerchief cleaned the last smudge spot from his face. He frowned as she did it then picked up the green bottle and fumbled the cork from its mouth letting bubbles foam over for a moment then filled a wineglass for her.

Her mouth was dry, and she drank as if it was water. After she sat the glass on the table, she said, "There, for a few moments, I was in a near panic. I'll be fine in a moment. Go bathe. Then undress me. I may not respond like the first time. Emotionally, I think I'm wound too tight, but I want you to do with me as you please."

"I'll be delighted. You are a beautiful woman," he said filling her glass again. "I've dreamed about you. Not just at night."

"Thank you, but stop babbling and bathe. Everything inside me is coiled up ready to jump out. I can't calm down until I tell you the story of my little rotten life."

"For a beautiful woman, you have a low opinion of yourself. It's needless. I have a pretty good idea of who you are."

"It's possible. Women like me are easy for men to figure out. What other men see, I want you to see, but I want you to look inside, so I must tell you who I am. I cannot live an honorable life with you if I don't. Understand this: I want you, and I want children and a home. I would live with you if you were a shepherd and lived in a hut as long as you said you loved me, but I won't live a lie to get you. You don't love me, yet. A man can't love what he doesn't know. I'm not just another woman. There are times I wish I was, then I remember when I was just another woman; I was pretty, spoiled, and completely self-centered. I don't really want to go back there. So, before morning, I'll know if you love me or if you're just another man having a good romp because I was a handy body in your quest for a family."

"I'll listen. It needs to be done. I see that now. I'll bathe while you drink. Drink slow and I'll bathe fast. Mind if I finish your whiskey?"

"I'm sorry I drank so much. It was meant for you. I didn't want to call the bellhop to open the wine bottle when I couldn't, so I drank what I meant for you."

"No harm done. I have more in my war bag. Clean Levi's, too."

"You won't need them."

"I will afterward."

"Hurry, dammit. I don't want to be drunk when we do it."

"I'm almost out of my clothes already. All I need is a moment to soap and splash off."

Anxious waiting time was short. Only a half-glass of wine was consumed when Bill Foley said, "There. I'm out. Let me towel off. I've dipped steers longer than this. Now, what?"

"Don't dress."

"Okay. What next?"

"Turn the gaslight up."

"Up?"

"Up. As bright as it will go."

Chapter Thirty-Seven

Ivy sat up and looked down at Bill. "Now that we've done our part at becoming parents, I'll tell you why I wanted the gaslight so bright."

"You said I was to look you over from head to toe, and I did."

"Did you see any scars?"

"Not a blemish. Only a beautiful body."

"Good."

"There's more, isn't there? What did I miss?"

"Nothing outside. I have a scar inside I want you to see. I'm going to tell you about it. You can turn down the gaslight now."

"It's late. Why not open the window and turn off the gaslight? The window faces a closed courtyard and no one will be passing out there this late. We're both sweaty. A cool breeze will feel nice. Our bodies will thank us."

"Yes, do that. On your way back, bring what's left of my wine. It's warm, but I'm thirsty, and it will help my tongue talk."

Bill Foley, barefooted and bare, stepped to the window, pulled the drapes aside then stood there breathing the late Hill Country breeze that comes up every evening to cool the land. It caressed his body, and he stood there reflecting on where he was, how his life had pointed him to this hotel room with this woman, and how it might all come to an end, and his eyes focused on a thin crescent moon that was slowly making shadows with light passing through scattered rain clouds coming to earth and crossing the courtyard on its way into the room, and he wondered if he had a future. Then he picked up the wine bottle, walked to the bed, and gave it to her.

Ivy Vanderbilt, propped by two pillows, took the big green bottle and patted a place next to her. "Come lay beside me," she said softly.

Drinking wine by holding the heavy bottle with both hands, she said, "There's a lot to tell, and I'll get this over as quickly as possible, because you need rest for tomorrow if I can't stop you."

He took his place lying beside her, and looking up at nothingness, he put words to more of his thoughts. "No. You can't stop me. As spent as I am, I won't sleep much. This may be it for me. I don't think so, but the man I face doesn't care what happens to him. I care about living. I have everything to live for. Not him. Death is better than a life the War forced on him. Life holds only two pleasures for him, whiskey and confrontations that furnish excitement. His body is twisted. He's pitiful to look at. He may have been robbed of his manhood. Once he could have had a woman who would love him. Not now. The War robbed him of that, too. If he can, when he pays a woman to fuck, it's over in minutes. When intimacy is not part of it, what does he do with the rest of his time? What's left? Calling me out is a Hell's Inferno in his mind. He's burning for it to happen. He wins if he wins. He wins if he dies. I lose either way. If I win, people will say I killed a cripple."

"If you kill the cripple, will you come back to me?"

"That's my plan."

"Kill the cripple, Bill. Kill him. Kill him for me and our baby."

"You're sure? Most women won't touch killing. They'd say back away and save the wretch. Not you."

"No. I'm a weak. Like most women, I'm afraid of killing, but the man's a fool. He owns a life not worth saving. If he's determined there's to be a death, I want it to be his, not yours."

"When you arrived in Foley, I knew I was seeing a woman who was not afraid of life, and life's a hard road. It takes courage for a white woman to travel in this country, even with a bodyguard, and you showed loyalty to your Negro friend in the face of White disapproval. Most people never learn to look life straight in the eye. You'll take the good life gives and say to hell with everything else."

"Most men don't think like you. Cowboy's especially. You have a philosopher's soul, Bill Foley. From the stern way you describe your father, I'll guess it didn't come from him. From your mother, perhaps?"

"Nope. Most cowboys are born philosophers, but a woman is really responsible for whatever else I am."

"Ah. The one who had your child?"

"No. That was the result of two children playing at a grown-up's game and getting caught. This was a woman I met at college."

"Tell me about her."

"Sure. It's not the kind of thing to make you jealous."

"I'm not jealous. She would be here now, but she isn't, so I'm not jealous of her. She sounds interesting. What happened?"

"She died."

"Oh. I'm sorry. Were you in love?"

"No. She was. I cared for her, but not enough to make a life with her. We met in English class. I didn't like the subject. With a test coming the next session, walking out into the hall when the class ended, I commented something like how the hell do you study for an English exam? It's not like math or history where you can follow a formula or a timeline. I'll likely fail. Iris, her name was Iris Cavanaugh; I didn't know her name then, overheard me and invited me to study with her. It was forward for a girl to do that. Heads turned. I was impressed by her making the invitation in front of all her friends and smart enough to know it was a chance to avoid a failure, and I accepted before she could change her mind.

"She was a local girl, born in South Bend. Her family lived in the Little Dublin part of South Bend, on Hill Street by Saint Joseph's Church. South Bend, Indiana, is half way between New York and Chicago. Irish labor built most of the roadbeds for American railroads, and, instead of going on to Chicago, a good many Irish laborers settled South Bend so it became a Catholic town founded by Irish railroad workers. Father Sorin's Subdivision and Little Dublin are where the poor families live. Seems like I live well with poor folks. I've spent nights in a Mexican *jacale*, that's a mud-brick house poor Mexican families live in that's cool in summer, warm in winter, and hell when it rains.

"Well, Iris loved to read. She studied everything, even things only men studied like geology and animal husbandry, because she enjoyed being around men and animals. She wanted to be a school teacher. She loved kids and was always talking about books she had read or was going to read. She loved everything Charles Dickens wrote. She read A Tale of Two Cities twice. She loved English, and her enthusiasm rubbed off on me. One day, she missed school. When she was absent the second day, I went to their little house on Hill Street, and the family told me Iris was dead. Her appendix had ruptured. The night before, she screamed out around mid-night with stomach pain. Her parents gave her laudanum and more laudanum, and in the morning went for the doctor. He brought his nurse and instruments with him prepared to do surgery in their house, but she was already burning up with fever. It was too late, the doctor said, the appendix had already burst and contagion had set in. For her to have such a high fever so soon meant the contagion was so virulent she didn't have a chance. It was time to pray the doctor said, and they sent for the priest. She was gone, but I learned something from her life that I'm not sure has a name. Because of her vitality, there is unrest inside of me, but it is not an unpleasant restlessness. Yearning is a word that fits in somewhere; yearning to know."

"She sounds wonderful. I'm grateful fate passed you from her to me, but I'm not sure if I have a chance to keep you. I'll tell what you need to know about me then you decide."

"Take your time. I know this is important to you. Don't be afraid. I want this to work out."

Tilting the green bottle up, she swallowed the last drops in it then sat the bottle gently on the carpet beside the bed and began.

Chapter Thirty-Eight

My first memories are of Cos Cob, Connecticut. Cos Cob is a small artist colony in the town of Greenwich, Connecticut. My mother was an artist's model, and all the men in the colony were fathers to me. I thought that way of life was the way all people lived. When I was about nine, maybe ten, we left there and went to live in an art colony at East Hampton, New York. Mother had found another, wealthier, male companion who fancied himself a sculptor. I was told they had married and my name was Vanderbilt. I did not have a last name before, just Ivy. There was no school at either colony. I learned to read and write and do numbers from mother. Mother's name was Jessica but no one called her that. It was Jessie or Jess. No one used last names. When I thought about it later, I thought it strange, if mother was married to a Vanderbilt, why we continued to live in the artist colony. It didn't bother me. We did live in a mansion one summer. It was in North Carolina. There was only a caretaker and his wife and two Negro stablemen who looked after a stable of thoroughbreds and several teams for the carriages. Both those guys were little so they could work the animals like a jockey would, and it took awhile for me to make them my friends, but they finally taught me to ride, and the stable was where I spent my time, and I roamed the estate by horseback. I had a good time that summer. In fact, it was a wonderful time. The weather was always pleasant. When summer ended, we went back to the colony, and I was immediately sent off to a girl's school in Baltimore. I had visits from my mother but not very often. At school, I was a good student when I wanted to be, but that was not very often. I was at the beginning of my rebellious teens, so mother withdrew me from school, and I began living with her and a new husband who was an art teacher at the Maryland Institute there in Baltimore. That marriage lasted until mother ran off to Santa Fe with a rich student who fancied himself good enough to be recognized in Santa Fe, Santa Fe being a Mecca for artists of all crafts. She left me with Henry William Bryan, who was not a gifted artist, but he was a good teacher; good enough so one of students was Henry Bolton Jones who has an international reputation now. I owe Henry William Bryan a debt I can't pay. He created a better understanding of art for me by explaining what goes on in an artist's mind when he or she paints. To do that, he taught me poetry and a great deal about writers; an artist does on canvas what writers do with words.

"Well, I was just beginning to awaken inside then Henry William died. I think mother's leaving had something to do with it. She was a pretty woman, and he cared for her more than she deserved, because she was flighty and bratty. I was like her until my meeting with Simon Doss."

"You're not flighty and bratty now. You've certainly changed."

"I have."

"Go on. I should not have interrupted."

"It's okay. Well, Henry William owned a small art gallery that did decently financially. I could have stayed, but it wasn't good enough for me. Better things awaited me. No one could tell me differently. No one did, of course. I found out that most people, men especially, will tell a pretty woman anything she wants to hear, and I listened to those petty things. I was determined to leave, but Santa Fe was out; mother was there, so I picked Saint Louis because Samuel Stockwell had gathered several other artists, and they had painted murals of places along the Mississippi River. One famous canvas was The Falls of Saint Anthony at the mouth of the Ohio River, and it got lots of newspaper and magazine publicity, enough so I wanted to join them. I was after fame and fortune. Actually, fame was more important. I loved being admired. Couldn't get enough. Silly girl.

"Mother left a thousand dollars for me, money she got from her newest paramour or probably what she got from Vanderbilt, so I always had money, enough so it was never a worry. Well, fame wasn't in Saint Louis. Paying customers were dwindling so the panorama moved to New Orleans. The mural is a series of paintings that are connected and rolled past a paying audience. The canvas is twelve feet high and over six hundred feet long. Twelve feet high, mind you. Since painting the canvas had been completed, artists were needed for touch-up only and I certainly couldn't get famous doing that, especially at twelve feet up on a step ladder. My work as a muralist lasted one day, then I quit."

"Granddaddy guessed you had spent considerable time in New Orleans."

"He's right. I spent five years there."

"With Simon Doss?"

"No. Not Simon. Not exactly. When I left Stockwell's Panorama, I began looking for a studio where I could show my paintings. I was ready to be *found* by the world. I was a beautiful woman *and a brilliant* artist. I couldn't worship myself enough.

"After Santa Fe, New Orleans is a great a haven for artists, but Paris, France, with the Louvre Art Gallery, is the ultimate place to be recognized. In New Orleans, I found a unique art gallery that belonged to Duc Josef le Tourneur. Duc Josef was brilliant enough to *discover* me; he was one smooth French nobleman. His Duc title is French like the English title of Duke. With a name like that, he could claim, and he did claim, the acquaintance of the Haute Bourgeoisie of France, and to prove it, he had paintings and sculpts he had done of some of the most famous French nobility. He had letters addressed to him from people like Lucien Bonaparte, Francois Rene de Chateaubriand, and Jeanne-Francois Juliette Julie Recamier to prove his bald lies. He was a master seducer using those letters although they were really simply notes responding to his correspondence. He finally admitted, on one of the days he had too much wine too early, he copied the portraits of those people. He had claimed they sat for him. I'll give him credit; he was a good painter to do such wonderful imitations. It was the best work I'd seen in New Orleans.

"The day I entered his shop, he was in the rear, and he was cleaning a canvas. We exchanged names, and I told him about the places I had lived then said I was available to pose. He smiled such a genuine smile to this day I still find it hard to believe how quickly he could invent a lie. "How fortunate you have arrived at this time," he said. "My model just informed me today was her last day." He was a smooth one. Smooth enough to fool me. And he lied with the nicest voice and sweetest accent imaginable. He dismissed his model the next morning, and I, without knowing, was at work the following day.

"He did two portraits of me. The first one took him almost two weeks. Throughout every sitting he complimented me over and over. I was a unique beauty. I had the face of an angel. He and I would be famous. He had been on the verge of greatness, now with me as his model we were going to be rich and famous. We would go to Paris. He would introduce me to Julie Recamier. I knew about Julie Recamier. Anyone in the art world knew of Juliette Recamier. Her portrait reclining on a sofa hangs in the Louvre in Paris. She married at fifteen. Her marriage was to a very wealthy banker who was thirty years her senior. It was first whispered, then later taken as truth, that her husband was her biological father who married her to make sure she would be his only heir. Soon after the marriage, with all that money and her looks and intelligence, she became the center of art and literature in France. Those who were her friends were known as the Haute Bourgeoisie. The sofa in the painting is now called a Recamier, named after her; she is that important in our world.

"I was impressed every time Duc Josef compared me to her. Duc Josef was setting me up. He had help, of course, because all of my life I had been told of my good fortune to be born such a beautiful woman. "Ivy," he said, "I must do a nude of you. Then we will be famous, I as an artist and you as my model. Remember Goya's Nude? Goya painted *la maja desnuda* and it upset every member of the Spanish Crown. He was their court painter, and they insisted he paint clothes on her. He knew he had a masterpiece. He was not about to destroy it, and he refused. What did he do? He painted the same model in the same pose clothed. Then he had two masterpieces."

"Mother had posed nude. Frequently, as a matter of fact. I saw nude models, women and men, all the time, so I agreed. I said yes immediately. I didn't even blink I was so flattered. I was off on a journey to be famous.

"It took almost a month, and Duc Josef was professional in every way, but the morning he finished, he didn't tell me the painting was done. He simply walked from behind his easel and handed me a sponge, and so help me, I swear to the Virgin Mary, I had no idea what his intention was. Up to that point in my life, a sponge was used like George Inness has used it, to dab paint for backgrounds. The sponge Duc Josef handed me was new. If I was to use the sponge for painting, it should have a color or colors in it. I was confused, and Duc Josef saw it, and he smiled a wicked little jeer, and he took great delight when he put it bluntly, "Sweet little Ivy, you needn't look so innocent. An artist fucks his model when he finishes a nude. Every model understands that. It's an honored tradition, and you know it. I don't want more children at my age. Insert the sponge so we can prevent that.""

"I knew the tradition. Truth is it had never crossed my mind. I swear. That had never entered my mind. My mind had been looking at my portrait hanging in the Louvre. At that moment, standing there naked with a sponge in my hand and my mouth half opened with a silly look on my face, I knew I had made an implicit bargain when I agreed to sit for the nude, so I let the old Duc have his way. It was not a pleasant way to begin a sacred part of a woman's life. There I was, beautiful me, allowing my body to be humped for the first time by a spindly legged old man."

"Is that all your uneasiness has been about? We're not children. We left childhood years ago. I didn't expect you to be a virgin."

"It doesn't end there. There's Simon Doss. Remember?"

"Go on."

"While the Duc was having his way with me, I was becoming furious. He was taking forever. I wanted it over, and I threw him off and punished him with hot words. "*You lecherous old bastard, you had this planned all along. The painting was a ruse. It was me you wanted, but you've got all of me you're going to get!*"

I grabbed my smock and stormed out. I was so furious I didn't take time to slip into it. I was wrapping the garment around me as I ran, and scenic portions of me were left for afternoon bystanders outside the gallery to see. I didn't care. I had rented an apartment on Chartres Avenue only two blocks from the art gallery. It was early afternoon, and not many people are about in the French Quarter at that hour. A lot of people are just waking up so my partial nudity didn't cause a stir. I don't think New Orleans police arrest naked people anyway.

"In summer, New Orleans weather is warm and muggy, and I went directly to my bathroom to take a cold bath. The cold water cooled my temper for a moment, but I started another temper tantrum when I couldn't get my bath soap to lather enough, and I threw the bar against the bathroom mirror and broke it. I shrugged and thought so much for trying to wash away a bad experience.

"Then a vile thought reheated my temper. Angrily, I removed the sponge, washed it, went to the cupboard and took out a saucer and placed the sponge on it. Then I ran into my bedroom and ripped my brightly colored bedspread from the bed and placed it over my night-stand and sat the saucer with the sponge on top of it.

"I was still dripping wet, mind you. I didn't even take time to towel off, and I put my painting smock on and grabbed a clean canvas and unfolded my French easel and began painting with oils.

"Every artist does a bowl of fruit at one time or another. The sponge on the saucer was my fruit, except my bowl was a saucer and the fruit on the saucer was a sponge.

"I was angry and painted with anger, so I painted with angry colors. I finished about mid-night. There's no way you can color a sponge to make it angry, but I painted an angry bedspread using Goya's nightmare colors, shades of violet, blue, purple, and black, and I drew dragons with heads breathing fire using my angry colors, yellow, red, and fireplace fire-like orange. The bedspread was alive when I finished. It was my masterpiece. Those vivid colors on the bedspread thrust the white saucer and sandy sponge into the face of the viewer's imagination. I painted with oils so I could use a palette knife like Vincent Van Gogh to give texture to the sponge so it could be felt if a finger was run across it. That sandy sponge stood out, I'll tell you. The sponge became an object that could not be ignored. Like any good artist, I gave it a name. I called it Virginity Lost. And, like any good artist, I signed my name."

"I'd like to see it. Do you still have your masterpiece?"

"No. You would have to travel to New Orleans to see it. It hangs next to the portrait of me as Goya's nude."

"I thought you were never going to see the Duc again. If you left the nude, and he had it, how did you get it?"

"I didn't. You'll see in a moment. In a way, I wish I had never seen him or the painting again. Then I have second thoughts and wonder if I would ever have found the woman I am now without that next meeting which was Sunday morning. My mood had improved, and I was having a leisurely breakfast in my little garden courtyard. In New Orleans, in the French Quarter, homes are built around small courtyards, similar to the Moorish style buildings in Greece, Spain, and Mexico, but much smaller. The courtyard opens directly to the sidewalk and street, and an ornamental iron gate, locked for protection, allows people in the courtyard to see and talk to passersby. I was enjoying a second cup of coffee when a carriage pulled up in front of my gate, and I looked out. None other than Duc Josef le Tourneur was climbing down with a canvas tucked under his arm.

"Wait, Mon Cheri," he said quickly as I was getting up to leave, "I have good news," he said. "Our painting has been sold."

"I was trapped. I walked to the gate and opened it. He didn't enter. Instead, he said, "Come, Cheri. I have a patron waiting. She wants to see you and the painting. My carriage waits."

"His carriage took us to Basin Street. Have you been to New Orleans?"

"No. Sam has. More than once, I think. Go on."

"The houses on that street are old mansions. Some of them are four stories. I spent enough time on that street to know the names of all the owners. Josie Arlington owns a four story house. Kate Townsend the three story one across the street."

"Sam's not the kind of man to tell his grandson about places like Basin Street, but his grandson is a big boy who has been to big cities. You can go on, but you don't need to."

"No. I'm not about to duck this."

"I didn't think you would. Not the woman I know. Go on. It's interesting."

"Well, the old Duc made a fool of me once, and my greed to be famous let him make a fool of me a second time. If I met him today, I'm not really sure if I would kill him or thank him. That's some kind of quandary for a young girl to have who has been seduced from her virginity by a lecherous old man, isn't it? I don't know if what happened is a blessing or a curse. In a few moments, you will give me the answer. I want only the truth from you, Bill Foley. Nothing noble to spare me. Just the pure truth as you see it. Agreed?"

"Agreed."

Ivy Vanderbilt took a deep breath. Bill Foley heard the inhalation and felt the body next to him grow tense. Then she said, "I think you know all the mansions on Basin Street are whorehouses."

The words were whispered hoarsely. He knew she was ashamed to say them, and silence followed.

"I swear by The Virgin Mary, I didn't know the houses were whorehouses. We got down from the carriage and walked to the front door, and Duc Josef pulled the bell cord. We were standing in front of a beautiful old two story mansion, and a Negro butler answered the door. He was the biggest man I have ever seen. Not an ounce of fat. Just big. I wondered how he could find clothes to fit. He let us in and ushered us down the entrance hall. The walls were done in a gaudy color I never liked. The color was deep mauve, a color of purple I hate. It has no class. Several framed paintings of nudes hung on the walls between velvet drapes of the same ugly color, so my mind was asking questions as we walked. Then a short dumpy lady came out from the parlor on our right to meet us.

"Ivy," the Duc said, "This is Gertrude Spivey, our patron. Gertie, this is the model for my nude."

"You're right, Duc," Gertrude Spivey said. "She's worth a thousand dollars."

"I thought the woman meant the painting, but the Duc unwrapped the portrait, and she didn't look at it; she only looked at me. I should have tried to run away then, but mind was distracted by the thousand dollar figure. I was overwhelmed by the high price.

"Step into my office, and I'll get the money," she said, and Gertrude Spivey led the way, with me, the huge Negro butler following me following her, and the Duc following us with the painting under his arm, but it wasn't an office we stepped into. The room didn't have a desk; it had a bed.

"Gertrude Spivey stepped into the room, and I was next. I wanted to bolt. My mind couldn't comprehend anything, but it told me to run. I turned, but big Simon Doss, the butler, was standing in the door, and he filled it. I was blocked. With no place to run, I took a step into the room, and Gertrude Spivey grabbed my forearm and pulled me in all the way. The Duc slithered in after us.

"My heart began beating as fast as a rabbit's, because I saw a White man and an Oriental, not as huge as Simon Doss but muscled heavily, standing on each side of the bed. I didn't know what was coming, but I knew it was bad, and I was probably going to be the victim.

"Gertrude Spivey, with her hands on her hips, addressed me roughly, "Young lady, we are going to make a whore out of you. I've had little brats like you before. I know how to tame a haughty bitch," and I turned to run and ran into Simon Doss's big arms. He held me as easily as a man would hold a doll.

"Simon's arms bound me, and Gertrude Spivey continued her lecture. "A girl like you thinks she's something special. I'm going to teach you you're nothing. You are going to learn, in the next minute mind you, to service any man, black, white, or tan, who can pay. You have a choice. Surrender meekly to a fucking with Simon Doss once, or be held by two men while the third pleasures himself until all three are serviced. You will be forced into sex three times, and more if you resist. After they finish with you, you will understand that you are not special anymore. If you are still haughty, they will fuck you until you learn. You will be at the service of any man who pays. Now, make your choice. Simon or all three?"

"I'll scream.," I said. "I'll scream and kick and bite. Someone will come."

"Just where do you think you are?"

"It's a nice neighborhood. Mansions everywhere. The police will come."

"This is Basin Street, dear. This is the Red Light district. Anything goes. The New Orleans police never come here. Now chose. I'm tired of your foolishness."

"No!" I screamed out.

"I see you have a temper. You will not have one when I finish with you. I have agreed to give Duc Josef one thousand dollars for you, so you are my property. You are my whore. I am your madam. We will not leave this room until you are properly soiled so you will gladly do your job, and your duties will begin tomorrow night."

"No. I'll run to the police the first chance I get."

"Why? You will have been soiled. The police cannot change that. Nothing, no power on earth will change that. Spare yourself. Nothing can save you. You will leave this room a soiled dove."

"Simon. I choose Simon. Not with the Duc watching. Everyone else, okay. Not the Duc."

"As you say. I'll give you that much. You see him as a traitor, and you are right. Here is your payment, little man," and Gertie Spivey took a roll of twenty dollar notes and counted until they totaled one thousand dollars, and she added, "Leave."

Gertie Spivey ushered the Duc all the way to the street entrance then returned to the room, pointed her finger at me, and said, "Now it's time for some old fashioned, German discipline, and you need it, you spoiled child. Simon, do your job!"

"Simon did his job, Bill. I was a whore for almost four years."

After a moment spent in silence, Bill Foley left the bed and walked to the window. Ivy Vanderbilt could see him outlined in the dimness, and she waited.

Looking for a path to follow for what he wanted to say, he finally found words he thought would work, and he turned and said, "You may not like this, but I've learned there are things a man and woman cannot see alike. This is probably one of those times. Here is the way I see it.

"Inside scars are a fact of life. All of us have them. Some scars are bigger than others, but size doesn't count. Life makes no promises about size, only a guarantee that scars are going to be, and everyone gets their share. I'm a rich man's son. Rich has its privilege. Rich has its curse. Just being Old Bill Foley's son has meant I've taken beatings from men, and boys when I was young, who just wanted the pleasure of whipping a rich man's son. It's always more than one against you, and you put up a good fight, but you always lose because they gang up on you. I have visible scars to prove that's the way life is. You were born beautiful. Beautiful has its privilege, but beautiful also has its curse. You proved it. What you've told me may be a complaint about the injustice in life, but injustice is part of life for everyone. Here's what I see. I don't see any visible scars. It's not like you had chicken pox, and you were left with scars all over your face and body. When you fall down and skin your knee, you get up and move on. You did that. You're not looking for pity. At least I don't think so. I think I'm in love with you, but it won't work if you're just another confused woman with a willing body. Just what the hell are you trying to tell me? Make yourself clear."

Slipping from the bed, grabbing the sheet and wrapping it around her as she ran to the window, she pulled his face to hers, close enough so he could see her sincerity even in the dimness, and she said, "Bill Foley, you sweet man. The scars mean nothing to me anymore. I'll tell you why. Simon Doss and Gertrude Spivey made a new woman of me. The new me is kind and understanding. I never was before. My temper isn't vile. It was before. I'm broken. I'm a good saddle horse now. I work under bridle and saddle. A wild mustang is beautiful to look at, but why own one? A man needs a horse to ride, not just to look at. I'm both those things now. I came to Foley, money in hand to buy a small ranch and marry some unknown cowboy to have children with. It was to be my attempt at becoming anonymous, because the Pinkerton Detective Agency is probably looking for me right now. Gertrude Spivey is the kind of woman who will spend her last dime to recover her investment, although I made her plenty before Margarite and I slipped off in the middle of May when she was on vacation. I felt so stupid. Dumb me. My way out had been staring me in the face all that time and none other than Duc Josef had furnished it. I had money; Gertie charged three hundred dollars a night for my services and gave me fifty so I would be pleasing to her clientele. I had no expenses other than art supplies; yes I continued to paint. I had lots of spare time; my body wasn't rented out every night, not at that price. Gertie furnished everything including my clothes. She is not pretty, her figure is kind of boxy but she loved pretty clothes and shoes. Every time she bought something new, and she loved to shop, and the Shoppe's were expensive ones, she always bought something for me. I was her reputation. After she got me, she was up there with the other ritzy madams. When she showed me off, she was showing herself off, too.

"I'm taking too long. I don't mean to. I'll hurry."

With words coming quicker now, she said, "I was deathly afraid of getting pregnant. As much as I hated the old Duc, I went back to the gallery when it came time for a new sponge. He crowed about me coming back to see him, then he had the gall to charge me fifty dollars claiming the only place in the world to get a sponge like I needed was in the islands off the coast of Greece. I made inquiries, and other ladies of the night who could afford them told me he was telling the truth.

"One Sunday morning, like a gift from heaven, while I was reading the Times-Picayune, I saw an article about George Inness that told what a wonderful place his summer home was. I was interested because I had worked with George Inness. A copy of one of his paintings the newspaper printed was of Tarpon Springs where divers were climbing out of crystal clear water with sponges. When Gertie left on vacation, Margarite and I left for Tarpon Springs. We bought a trunk full, and we went back for more. We sold ten thousand dollars worth before we left Florida. In Mobile, we began selling in wholesale lots, so I bought a stagecoach and had it refurbished there. We slipped back into New Orleans and drove up to Mahogany Hall and Lu Lu White, an Octoroon lady friend of Margarite, took one thousand of our special sponges and paid us ten thousand dollars, cash. Lu Lu bought wholesale and sold retail. She bought for ten dollars and sold for twenty, and she had inserters made. Simon Doss is a whittler, and he gave me the idea for our product. The sponges from Greece have a small ribbon sewn on them so they can be removed, and that ribbon tangles. I had Simon fashion a curved inserter made from polished oak with a blunt hook on the end like a knitting needle for easy removal, and it works perfectly. No more tangles. He sells them for one dollar and splits with Margarite. All the Call Girls on the Street were glad to pay twenty dollars apiece, and they knew friends in the smaller towns and word spread just like it had in Mobile.

"Well, with all that money, Margarite and I went looking for a place to call home, and we heard Foley was a safe place. The Pinkerton's would never consider an unknown small town like Foley; they'd look in the big cities. So, here I am, and I wonder about the good and bad of it, but coming to Foley brought me to you. I didn't come here looking for you. I came looking for someone entirely different. A woman has a body she can't ignore when that body demands children, and my body had been shouting at me. When she sees one particular man, she's vulnerable. She will damn near stand on her head to get him into bed with her. The more I saw of you, the more I wanted you. In fact, you made me nervous inside the moment I saw you. Now, here's your dilemma. You're rich, or will be, and you are well known. With your plans, I know you will be meeting bankers in the future, influential people like governors and senators. Men who took me to bed in New Orleans were well known, rich and influential. Sooner or later, I'll be discovered. Do you want me for your wife when that happens? Here's your choice: If you ask me again, I'll marry you. Or, I can have a child then disappear. I'm waiting. Tell me what you want."

"Tell? No, I'll show you."

"Anything. Just get it over with."

"I need to go to the bathroom first," and he was on his way almost before his words were finished. In a moment, he reappeared holding his Levi's. "Here," he said producing a jewelry box from a dirty Levi pocket.

The box was smudged, but she failed to notice, because he was taking her hand, and he fumbled finding the proper finger to fit a ring on.

"Ivy Vanderbilt," he began, "You had the courage to tell me about a past I suspected all along, and I tell you it doesn't matter. I love you because I think you face life like a courageous woman should. People will find out about you, and people will talk. Behind your back or to your face. People will talk about me, probably behind my back. It won't matter. If you're the strong woman I think you are, we can dismiss all of it as chatter. That's my sermon. Now, will you marry me? Yes or no."

"Yes. Hell yes. Thank you for choosing me."

"Well, it's after midnight. It's a new day, and it's the day my life could come to a sudden halt. If that happens, you'll have my child to take care of. I'm not sure mother, or Dad if he's still alive, will look kindly on another child born out of wedlock. You may be on your own. I'll draw my money out of the bank and leave it with Sam before I meet Wyatt. It's not very much."

"I won't need it. I have some, and I can make more."

"As the mother of my child, I'd prefer you don't go back to your profession."

"Don't be silly. I'll sell sponges. I probably have ten thousand dollars worth in my trunk."

"Well, that leaves us set for life. If I live. Now, I need to try for a few hours sleep. After the four or five hour ride back to Foley, I'll need time to do the bank thing, and I want a few minutes with Sam before my confrontation. Your stage is too slow. It'll be over one way or the other when you get back to Foley. Remember I love you. Love the child."

"Bill Foley, you are not going to leave me. I brought an extra horse as insurance to get here. I'll go back on it. We'll ride back together."

Chapter Thirty-Nine

Sam Ordway was as nervous as a momma Dominiker with a brood of biddies when a coyote begins pawing the ground outside the henhouse.

Wyatt Winslow had just left, and Sam was watching him through the jailhouse window heading for Irish Rose's Saloon to partake of Kerry O'Shea's free lunch and whiskey. It was Saturday, his chosen day for glory, and Wyatt had come into town early to agitate Sam and work up more anger toward Young Bill to add to his pleasure prior to the big confrontation.

Once again, Wyatt had succeeded to Sam's displeasure. Sam had come out ahead on one point, however, and that's what was causing his nervousness. He had asked to examine Wyatt's Colt. It was a hunch only, a little more than idle curiosity. Samuel Colt's first weapon was manufactured in Paterson, New Jersey, and he named it the Paterson Colt. It was not very successful. Later, Captain Samuel Hamilton Walker of the Texas Rangers worked with Colt on a new design, and the Walker Colt .45 was born. It was so successful one thousand was ordered for the Mexican-American War. The Walker Colt had an extra long barrel that gave it as much range as some rifles. After the war, the barrel was reduced to seven and one-half inches and became known as the Shopkeeper's Model. A Sheriff's Special came three inches shorter than the Shopkeeper's model. A Banker's Special was featured next; it had a barrel between the two. The Sheriff's Special, with the very short barrel, was lighter and faster. The Sheriff's Special was less accurate, but accuracy was not important at close range, and there would only be a short distance, fifty feet or so, between Young Bill and Wyatt.

Wyatt was toting a Sheriff's Special. Young Bill carried a Banker's Special. The advantage went to Wyatt.

The thing Wyatt had said when he entered the jail that stirred Sam's anger was, "I'll lay odds your grandson doesn't show today."

Almost as soon as he said it, the big McClintock clock on the bank building chimed. Both hands were straight up showing high noon. Its hands had been moving steadily since then. They were up and down now, and Sam stepped out on the porch of the jail, already a bit anxious about Young Bill's whereabouts.

Waiting was trying, and eating was something his stomach wouldn't allow, so he decided it would be a good time to check on his daughter and Old Bill. Old Bill had been wide-eyed for almost a week now. Abbey said he slept with one eye open if he slept. It concerned her enough so that yesterday she had Doc Wedgewood over to look at him.

Wyatt Winslow had slipped into town after more whiskey day before yesterday and let it around that he was going to call Young Bill out on Saturday if the pampered rancher's son was not too yellow and didn't stay in San Antonio after his trail drive was finished; Wyatt wanted a crowd for his show.

Doc Wedgewood was as capable as Kerry O'Shea at collecting gossip, so he heard the taunt, and he asked Abbey if Old Bill knew about the coming gunfight; if he did, that might be the cause of his restlessness. It was the first Abbey had heard it was set for Saturday, but Doc didn't know that. She needed a Bromide to settle her down. When she was calmer, Doc told her that old men coming out of a coma usually experienced extended episodes of sleeplessness, and he whispered to Abbey that sleeplessness would be hard on Old Bill's heart. Old Bill was across the room sitting in front of the window watching Main Street, and Doc walked over and tried to give him a Bromide and he flatly refused.

When Sam knocked, Abbey answered the door, and Sam said, "Young Bill should be here anytime now."

"Oh, dear God. I hope he has the good sense to stay away."

"He'll come. He knows Wyatt will dog him until they meet. Young Bill is not going to back down."

"Daddy, can't you do something?"

"Out of my hands. It's in the lap of The Almighty."

Abbey sat down on the sofa; having just had a Bromide, it was more like she folded onto it.

She was listless from the effects of the sedative, so Sam walked across the room to where Old Bill sat. Old Bill did not acknowledge Sam's presence. His eyes never left Main Street.

Sam placed a hand on the old man's shoulder. "Howdy, Bill," he said.

"Howdy, Sam," Old Bill replied, and he looked up into Sam's eyes for just a moment. The old man's eyes were bloodshot and spacey. Then he looked away giving Main Street his undivided attention again. Sam saw the Winchester was still beside him.

"Have you forgotten about Molly Gibbs?" Sam asked.

"Nope."

"After the shootout?"

"Yep."

Sam turned to leave. "Have you seen the O'Hara Law Firm about it?"

"Not exactly. I got a meeting set for Monday morning but didn't say what for."

Sam stood there for a moment. There was nothing to be gained by staying. Abbey was sedated, a tad less than drunk, and Old Bill had his eyes glued to Main Street.

At the door, as he was closing it, he looked back for, and saw the butt of, Old Bill's Winchester beneath the window drapes. Sam figured it was there to be used later on today. Old Bill always carried the rifle with him. Everyone in Foley had one handy. Just the same, Sam knew he should come back to watch the proceedings from this hotel room.

Sam left the Foley suite, stepped across the hall to room three, and knocked. Tom Silverhorn answered the door. Margarite Doss was standing near the window across the room.

"Tom," Sam said, "I came to ask Margarite a question. I'll come in, if you please."

Silverhorn stepped aside closing the door after Sam was inside. Sam went directly to the Negro lady, and asked politely, "Does Kerry's New Orleans style coffee still meet with your approval?"

"Yes, indeed, Marshal," she answered smiling. "I've been in this room so much I think I'm going to turn white. Seeing Kerry and drinking his coffee reminds me of home. It is one of the few pleasures I have."

"Have you lived in New Orleans long?"

"It's been my home for over twenty years. Simon and I were sold at the slave market there two years before the war."

"You were a slave?" Tom Silverhorn asked.

"Yes. A ship's captain bought us in Jamaica, and brought us here. He knew he would get top dollar for us in New Orleans, because it is the largest slave market in the South.

"My memory is very keen on the day we were sold. Before the auction, Simon and I were separated, and I was afraid we would be sold separately. We women were made to bathe and the men to bathe and shave. Men were given suits and shoes, cheap but new, and women were given new calico dresses, shoes, and handkerchiefs to tie around our heads. In New Orleans, they wanted us to look nice for the sale. We had heard about how bad it was in other places, because other slave markets didn't care."

Sam knew what Margarite had experienced. Tom Silverhorn did not, and Tom found himself interrupting, "Did Miss Ivy buy you?"

"No, Tom. A lady who owned a mansion on Basin Street bought us."

"Have you known Miss Ivy long?" Sam asked quickly.

"Four or five years, I think. She's a good woman now."

"I understand," he replied. Margarite Doss's adding she's a good woman now meant they understood each other, so Sam said, "My main reason for coming here is to ask you if you would be kind enough to keep a young man for me this afternoon. Molly Gibbs was keeping him, but her husband was killed, and she's gone back to Bellville for the funeral. I stayed with him this morning until I had to come to town. You know what's taking place, don't you?"

"Yes, Marshal. I won't watch. Tom will; I'm sure. I've met Molly Gibbs, and I'd be proud to give her a helping hand."

"That's all I ask. Jimbo's got no business watching. He knows Young Bill. The boy don't need any more memories of somebody he knows dying. Word gets around fast in a small town. Kids overhear and tell other kids. This room is on the opposite side of the building where it's going to happen. Even the gunshot will be just a little pop from here. Will you keep him until it's over? I'll be needed out there."

"Go get him, Marshal."

"I'll be back in a few minutes."

After delivering Jimbo into the custody of Margarite Doss and Tom Silverhorn, Sam went back to his jail.

Chapter Forty

Walking across Main Street to the jail, Sam saw a horse tethered out back in the shade. He recognized the animal, so he was not surprised when Bill Waterman greeted him when he came through the door.

"Hello, Sam."

"Hello, Bill," Sam replied and took the cattleman's hand when he offered it.

"Sam, I know what's happening. I came to ask a favor."

"You can ask, but today I don't reach out ahead. I don't grant anything to anyone. Best I will do is say I'll listen. What is it, Bill?"

"I want to be near Abbey. I don't want to interfere with her and her husband, but I can't help wanting to be near her. Can you help me?"

"I don't know, Bill."

"I'll put it this way. Will you help me if the opportunity comes?"

"Yes, Bill. I will. Abbey can use all the comfort she can get if Young Bill goes down."

"I want to be your friend, Sam. We're not friends yet, and I finally understand why you're standoffish. It came to me where I've seen you before. You were an Army guard at my trial in San Francisco. Am I right?"

"You are."

"A man can change, Sam. I have. I was young and had not learned to question the whys in life. I played by the rules I was taught. I was wrong, but Sam, I'm not sorry. I did what I knew to be right then. My knowledge of right and wrong is different today. I love Abbey, and I'll do what's right even if it means stepping aside for now. I know my wait will be worthwhile. She will come to me when Old Bill moves on. I admire her for waiting. Help me if you can, Sam. That's all I ask."

"I'll see. Wait here. I saw Young Bill and the Ivy lady when I came across from the hotel. They just pulled in at Martin O'Malley's livery stable. It's important for me to see him. I'll be back."

Sam walked to the center of Main Street and waved until he was sure Young Bill had seen him then he walked on across to the hotel and up the stairs where he waited on the veranda. The veranda was empty; it would be crowded soon. The hotel lobby, however, housed a gathering of chatting townspeople who wanted to witness the lawful violence.

"Hi, Granddad," Young Bill said pleasantly.

"You're pretty damn cheerful for a man about to be shot at in less than an hour."

"He's impossible," Ivy said the expression on her face anything but cheerful. "I've offered him everything I own to run away with me. He won't."

"I only offered her *half* of everything I own, Sam. I asked her to marry me. She has accepted."

"I'm guessing she's told you."

"About Basin Street?"

"About Basin Street."

"I've changed," Ivy said defensively.

I just heard that a few minutes ago, Sam thought, but his reply was sincere. "I wish happiness for both of you."

"Now all I have to do is kill a man and we can live happily ever after," Young Bill added.

"And not get yourself killed at the same time," Sam cautioned then added, "Wyatt's carrying a Sheriff's Special. You carry a Banker's Special, don't you?"

"I do."

"Do you know what that means?"

"Sure. His gun has a shorter barrel. Less weight might make him a fraction faster."

"That's right. Here's my Sheriff's Special. You'd best use it."

"No, Granddad. I know this one. Yours would be new. I'll go with what I know."

"Maybe you're right. Are you afraid?"

"Some."

"I would be if I was in your boots."

"There's something you can do for me, Granddad."

"What would that be, son?"

"Watch Wyatt. If he pulls a fraction before I turn, and I go down, kill him for me. Okay?"

"Sure. But I may not have to. I think your daddy will do it. He has his Winchester loaded and sitting next to the window next to him, ready to use. I'm going to watch everything from up there to make sure he doesn't plug Wyatt before the play begins."

"Interesting. We're going to see Mom and Dad. I want them to meet Ivy. Come on up with us."

"Wait a minute. Bill Waterman asked to be with me."

Sam waved to Waterman at the jail, and kept waving until the rancher noticed, opened the jail door, and walked toward them.

"Go on up," Sam said. "We'll be right behind you."

Abbey answered the door and quickly embraced her son. She immediately overcame her Bromide induced sedation.

"Please don't do this," she begged with tears in her eyes clutching her son so tightly the door was blocked with Ivy, Sam, and Bill Waterman behind.

Unlocking the embrace, Young Bill said, "Sit down, mother. I have things to say and not a lot of time to say them. First, Dad and Mom, meet Ivy Vanderbilt. Ivy, this is my mother, Abigail Foley. Across the room by the window is my Irish father, William McKenzie Foley."

Abbey extended her hand, and Ivy took it. Old Bill managed to stand. Ivy went to him, and he extended his hand and she took it then returned to Young Bill's side.

"Mom, Dad, I've asked Ivy to marry me and she has said yes. We will have a Catholic ceremony as soon as possible if I'm still available after this gunfight is over. If I don't survive, I want everyone here, as my witnesses, to know she is probably carrying my child who is my heir."

It was too much for Abbey to take in, and she sought the sofa again. Old Bill Foley began walking toward his new daughter-in-law to be, and Ivy met him. He embraced her, and said, "Make him happy and I'll love you."

"That's fair. You can count on me. I'd take him away from this if he'd go."

"Don't. My son will face things square on. That much of me is in him. He'll be free to marry you before the afternoon is over."

"I hope so."

"Time is short," Young Bill said addressing Ivy, but speaking in a voice loud enough so everyone in the room heard. "I'm going downstairs to the bank. I'll add your name to the documents I told you about earlier in the week. I'm also going to add the possibility of a child and my desire to marry you. That will serve as my Will. It should only take another few minutes for both bank clerks to sign and notarize the papers. Ivy, you stay up here with Mom and Dad."

"Not on your life." Ivy, realizing the phrase she used was a poor choice, changed it to, "I'll go where you go."

Young Bill embraced his mother, and Ivy and Abbey embraced, then the couple walked to the window where Old Bill Foley waited, and the three shared a final embrace, then Young Bill, holding Ivy's hand, walked out the door. He did not say goodbye.

Chapter Forty-One

After the documents were signed and notarized, Young Bill Foley waited in silence standing in the Foley National Bank lobby holding Ivy Vanderbilt's hand.

The bank building was on a corner, and its broad plate glass windows gave the couple an unobstructed view of Main Street, and they saw Wyatt Winslow, early and eager, push open the batwing doors of Irish Rose's Saloon and walk out leaving the doors swinging behind him. He walked to the center of Main Street and waited. His facial expression shown with sinister enjoyment; a single thought was in his mind, only good can come to me from this. High excitement was running throughout his body and it blocked out every shred of pain, and he laughed out loud to be free of the demon, and Ivy and Young Bill could see his laugher.

Just then the McClintock chime clock on the corner of the bank building began to chime its first of three chimes, and Ivy clutched Young Bill's hand then quickly released it so he could leave her.

Neither spoke. The moment between each chime was too tense for words. When silence followed the third chime, Young Bill Foley opened the door and walked through it.

Ivy Vanderbilt attempted to follow.

243

Young Bill looked back, saw her, and his eyes narrowed demanding she not take another step, and she stopped, a lone girl standing on the boardwalk under a bank clock.

Wyatt Winslow saw them and yelled, "Yea, Young Bill. I see you have another pretty woman following you. Does she know about Chastity?"

"That's none of your affair, Wyatt," Young Bill answered. "Our affair begins and ends when I reach the center of Main Street."

"Then get on with it, damn you. You Foleys got the best of everything while the Winslow's got nothing. You didn't even leave us self respect. I'm here to collect. Make your move."

From the boardwalk in front of the bank, it took fourteen steps to gain the center of Main Street. Knowing this moment would come, Young Bill had counted them every time he crossed the street after Sam Ordway told him about Wyatt Winslow's challenge. He knew he was as fast as any man alive. If Wyatt allowed him to turn so they faced each other, Wyatt was a dead man. If Wyatt drew when he was turning, everything would be in doubt.

His heart was beating faster and faster, but with the thirteenth step next, his mind turned to ice, and every move he made went back to timing so automatic there was no need to think, and he took the last step.

Wyatt was a showman, for he waited until Bill made his pivot and they were facing each other dead on then they both drew and fired.

Upstairs, Sam Ordway watched. Anticipating Young Bill would begin his walk from the bank to the center of Main Street when the clock chimed, he edged closer to the window where Old Bill Foley sat. When the first chime began, Old Bill reached behind him only to feel Sam's hand clasp his hand.

Sam knew his hunch had been correct. Old Bill planned to put a bullet into Wyatt Winslow.

When the second chime sounded, Old Bill slumped over. Sam, Old Bill's hand in his, tried to keep the old man from falling to the floor but couldn't. He did ease the fall so Old Bill didn't fall face down. His face was looking up, and his eyes were open but sightless.

The third chime took place without Sam hearing it. Awareness returned when he heard what sounded like one shot.

Time was suspended for a moment, and Sam organized his thoughts, and he realized Old Bill had died, and two shots, not one, had been fired, the sounds coming so close together as to seem simultaneous.

Sam stood. He saw Abbey huddled in Bill Waterman's chest shielded by both his arms.

Tom Silverhorn had been watching through the window, and he said, "They're both down. They've killed each other!"

Sam threw open the door, dashed downstairs and began pushing through bystanders on the veranda until he was out into the street.

There was a throng around Young Bill, and Sam could not see into it. Beyond the throng was Wyatt Winslow, but Sam could not see past them to tell whether or not Wyatt was dead.

"Don't touch him!"

Sam recognized Doc Wedgewood's voice. He was an angry doctor. "GawdDammit, don't move him. Not one inch, mind you."

When Sam pushed his way into the center of the circle, he saw it was Ivy Vanderbilt Doc was cussing. She was on one knee trying to clean muddy streaks from Young Bill's face. He had fallen forward, and the ground was not yet dry from yesterday's rain. It was a good guess she was attempting to pull Young Bill's body against hers when Doc stopped her.

"He's not dead, no thanks to you," he lashed at her still. "He will be if he's moved. There's no place in the body with more contagion than the bowel, and he's been gut shot. Move him with his guts opened from a gunshot wound and all that ugly contagion will spill inside him and spread like wildfire. He's in shock now. I intend to sew him up out here. It's his only chance."

Chapter Forty-Two

Waving his hands like a farmer shooing chickens from corn, Doc Wedgwood scattered bystanders.

Ivy, Sam saw, was confused. She could not decide if she was to go or stay. Doc said one thing; her heart said a different thing. She had somehow managed to change from range clothes into a proper dress anticipating the meeting with Young Bill's parents. How and when she found time to do it, Sam could not guess. What was plain was her dress was muddied, probably ruined.

Looking up, she saw Sam. "Give me your knife," she demanded. She had made her decision. It was evident; Doc could bellow all he wanted. She was not going to leave Young Bill.

Sam gave her his knife without thinking. He even opened the blade for her without thinking.

Pretty Ivy Vanderbilt, with bystanders murmuring and milling around her, began to cut her dress. At her waist, she made a circular cut half way around then sent the knife blade downward then made a similar downward cut on the other side of the garment exposing a fluffy white petticoat but having made a large cloth she folded into a small bundle. On her knees, aiming a stern voice up at Doc Wedgewood, she said, "Moving his head won't upset his guts. I made a pillow for him."

"Good show," replied Doc, relenting,

Young Bill Foley's beautiful auburn hair was mud caked, his Stetson thrown aside by the fall, and Ivy Vanderbilt was not going to leave that head and hair in such disgrace.

After placing her pillow under Bill's head, she looked up for Doc again, but Doc was gone. She looked around and found him down the street just then rising from over Wyatt Winslow's body.

"This man's dead," Doc said loudly. "Is there a next of kin here to claim his body?"

And Sam Ordway said, "I'll claim him."

"In that case, do I charge the town for my burial service?" Doc asked.

"No, you damn Englishman with your Scotch ways," Sam replied. "I'll be responsible for everything as a private citizen, and I want him buried proper. Include a gravestone. He's not going to be treated like a pauper without a marker."

Satisfied, Doc then motioned to two men who had been waiting for his direction, and they picked up Wyatt's withered body. "Take him to my office," Doc said, "You know where to leave him. My nurse should be on the way here. If she's still there; tell her to hurry."

Ellen McNulty, puffing from more weight than her frame demanded, was carrying an armful of blankets and sheets when she appeared from the alley between the Café and the hotel, her Irish legs pumping as fast as a pudgy girl can move them. Out of breath when she reached them, she was ready to unload her burden on any person other than her Doctor. Ivy and Sam were nearest, so she chose them.

Doc Wedgewood had been waiting for his nurse. Now he began cutting away at Young Bill's Levis and giving orders while he was doing it. "I want every inch of his body, except around the wound where I'm going to work, covered with sheets. Leave his head and face open. I want blankets placed on the ground and tucked gently under his body."

"Miss," Doc may or may not have remembered Ivy's name; when he was working everyone became Miss and Mister, "you may remain where you are. You will assist my nurse, her name is Ellen McNulty. Ellen is going to use ether. You will aid her. Ether has been proven a godsend for this kind of surgery, because it relaxes abdominal muscles and chloroform does not. Here's the problem. As yet no one has formulated a plan for its use, and if we use too much the anesthesia puts the patient into such a deep sleep, he dies. Use too little and the patient experiences pain and begins to fight blindly, and the surgeon could accidently kill the patient he is fighting so hard to save. Ellen will put a thick gauze strip over his nose and drip ether on it. His lips are not to turn blue. This is very important. If pink begins to leave his lips, warn Ellen, and she will stop the ether. Ether is difficult to add by the drop because it pours so freely and evaporates so quickly. You two must work as a team to control an uncertain drip."

Continuing to address Ivy, Doc, using his impressive professional voice added, "Your other responsibility is his pulse. It is slow and steady now. I want it to stay that way. If it becomes fast or weakens, warn me."

Looking up at the men surrounding him, he said emphatically, "Not one of you is to light a match. Ether fumes will explode."

Doc's hands were busy bathing Young Bill's abdomen around the wound with denatured alcohol, and his eyes were focused on his hands, but his demanding voice gave the townsmen surrounding them more directions. "I want two men to a blanket, and I want a square or a circle formed. Give us plenty of room but keep us protected from the wind and dust by holding those blankets up. For all I know, horse-shit may be sterile, but I'll not chance it. Others of you need to block traffic."

Sam knew his job. He sealed off Main Street with eight of men he had not assigned to be blanket holders, and he had others stop pedestrian traffic on the board-walk. By the time he slipped back to the circle and peaked in on Doc's work, Doc had already made a small working incision.

Doc talked to the ladies as he did his work; Doc enjoyed explaining. "I have cleansed around the entrance wound and swabbed inside as far as I could with Carbolic Acid to kill contagion. Carbolic Acid is the chemical Sir Joseph Lister began his antiseptic technique with. Now, I'm adding a new chemical called Gentian Violet. It's to stop contagion but does not irritate as much as Carbolic Acid, so I can use it liberally," and he poured a thin stream of the liquid into the bullet hole until it bubbled out.

"Gentian Violet is a dye, so the young man's skin will be purple for a few weeks to come, if he lives."

Working carefully, he then sutured the small wound.

The blanket holders, men who had skinned deer, cattle, and pigs, as part of their everyday living, understood Doc's procedure and knew he had accomplished the easiest part. Using that same knowledge, the men knew if the contents of the injured bowel spilled over into the abdominal cavity, Young Bill was in serious trouble. It was Doc's next procedure, where the bullet made the exit wound, that would be Doc's big test. If the bullet failed to go through and was lodged inside Young Bill and Doc ruptured any gut probing for it, his death would be probable, and it would be painful.

"Ladies," Doc said, "help me move the patient. We'll turn him up on his side a bit, just enough for me to work. Be gentle as possible. We'll prop him with folded blankets above and below the wound."

Doc, working on his knees in stocking feet having removed his boots before stepping on the clean sheets, helped turn the patient then cut away more clothes and exclaimed, "We may be in luck. The projectile came all the way through and did not hit an artery. There's bleeding but it's minimal for this type of wound. It appears the pathway was through the proximal part of the small intestine, that's a very good sign. There's very little damage it will do there. Had the gentleman who made this hole been just a trifle faster, I would not bother sewing it up."

Chapter Forty-Three

Young Bill awakened an hour later, but he did not know it. He moaned then returned to the unknown place called unconsciousness.

He was now in Doc's infirmary with Ivy, Abbey, Sam, and Bill Waterman. They were keeping silent watch along with Ellen McNulty who was checking his vital signs while she waited for him to revive enough to be in conscious pain then she would give him an injection of morphine.

"Low grade fever is expected with surgery, Nurse McNulty said. "Higher fever will come, but not until tomorrow evening or night. If his fever climbs sooner, it will not be a welcome sign."

Adding directions, Nurse McNulty said, "I'll need the help of everyone here, because this patient's care is beyond one person's endurance. The first lesson begins now, because in a few minutes he will be coming out of the ether fog, and he will need an injection of morphine."

Nurse McNulty motioned them together and deftly demonstrated the preparation of a morphine injection. What she did was drop a very small salt tablet and an even smaller morphine tablet into a glass syringe filled with water that had been boiled. She easily injected the contents into a vein in Young Bill Foley's arm a short time later when he moaned but did not move.

"We boil these two devices immediately after each use, and we put them under a clean linen towel to be ready for the next injection."

She passed both parts of the unit to each person wanting them to hold the syringe so they would be familiar with the feel of it. Then she had each one draw water into the metal device and push the plunger as if they were injecting the contents into a patient. She did not let them dissolve any of her tablets; morphine, though not that expensive, was too valuable to waste. Satisfied they could give the injection when it came their time to do it during the night she sat down by Young Bill's bedside.

After several minutes of silence, with an unconscious patient and four silent observers, Ellen McNulty felt it was her duty to talk. With a captive audience, her only subject, other than food, was medicine, and she said, "Doctor Wedgewood believes British medicine is the best in the world. That may be true, mind you, but it was an American, a dentist who used ether for anesthesia, and it was a Scotchman, Alexander Wood, and a Frenchman, Charles Pravaz, who showed the medical world how to make an injection of morphine by inventing the screw type syringe I just showed you. Before that, we used a trocar, and I'm here to tell you it was too cumbersome for such a delicate job. Lately, we used a smaller Southey tube, but once an incision was made, we had to leave it open, and an open incision admits contagion. We lost patients to contagion just trying to relieve pain."

Sam had heard rumors he thought were unfounded about Doc taking his pleasure with nurse McNulty. Before today, his observation was Ellen McNulty's only pleasure was food. Now he knew medicine was another of her pleasures, for she could have only have gained her knowledge of medical history by reading Doc's books and journals, and Doc did not let them leave this building. Just maybe she had another pleasure, and Doc, with his long nose and lanky frame like most homely English men, had found that pleasure to each other's satisfaction.

Satisfied she had impressed her two teams with her brightness, Nurse McNulty suddenly remembered to ask, "Do any of you know what Mister Foley's food intake was earlier today?"

Ivy Vanderbilt replied quickly, "He had breakfast. Scrambled eggs, toast, and coffee."

"No lunch?"

"No. He didn't have enough time for it."

"Wonderful. There will be very little bowel content; one less burden on Mister Foley. Doctor Wedgewood will be happy to hear it."

Then, to dismiss them she said, "Get some rest. The next three days will be important to Mister Foley and trying for me and the Doctor. Beginning now, we will awaken the patient every four hours, day and night. It is also very important he take quinine to prevent the expected fever spike. Morphine, as you have seen, is soluble and can be injected, but quinine cannot. It must be given by mouth, and it's too bitter given as a powder alone, so we mix it with a small amount of wine. He will get no other food or liquid. The bowel must stay clear. Doctor Wedgewood will decide when it's time to begin broth feeding. If nothing bad happens, our patient may begin to have soft foods like scrambled eggs in a week to gain strength. Doctor Wedgewood will make all feeding decisions in the weeks to come."

If Doc's still here, Sam Ordway thought. He's been saving his money to go back to England. Lack of money and status kept him out of Oxford, so he came to the United States for training. With what Young Bill's surgery is going to cost and preparing Wyatt Winslow's and Old Bill Foley's bodies, Doc should have his money to go back home in style. He's not the kind to leave without a replacement, though. I wonder; will he take Nurse McNulty?

Chapter Forty-Four

Sam and Ivy left together saying little except goodbye when they parted at the hotel; today had worn them.

Heading for his cabin on Cedar Street, Sam remembered Jimbo and turned around. Back at the hotel, he knocked lightly on the door of room three, and Margarite answered the knock.

"He's sleeping, Marshal Ordway," she whispered before Sam could speak. "Leave him tonight. He can sleep in Miss Ivy's bed. She won't need it. She's changing now to go back. She will not leave that man. Jimbo bathed, and he's wearing one of Miss Ivy's negligees as a nightshirt. I had to cut some of it off so he would wear it. We had a good time today. He ate supper with me in back of the hotel kitchen and enjoyed every minute. Jimbo would make a fine Negro."

"I'll see him tomorrow," Sam said, then turned and headed once more for home.

One of Sam's thoughts before sleep was Foley had been fortunate to have the likes of Doc Wedgewood. Another thought, hidden beneath the day's dramatic activity, had come the moment Old Bill Foley died. What about Molly Gibbs? Old Bill had gone to his grave without acknowledging her. Sam knew the thought would come again, and he could deal with it better later.

There was a bigger question causing him a major consternation. It was a question that had been surfacing from the moment Wyatt Winslow made his appearance to begin this fateful day; how will I explain this to Claire Winslow? Wyatt sure didn't give her much thought planning his dramatic departure. Wyatt's only comment was her hair can't get any grayer. Sam added this thought: When she hears the truth, there will be another scar on her soul and the lines on her face that had turned to laugh lines were going back to being sad lines. There was no way he could help, but he wanted to.

Chapter Forty-Five

Shortly before four in the morning, Sam slipped quietly into the parlor of Doc Wedgewood's Infirmary where Ivy Vanderbilt was awake but visibly tired. Her eyes, even in the dimness of the room, were weary and red. The different dress she had changed to when she went to her room was rumpled.

She had been expecting Sam, and as soon as he got there, they walked into the room where Young Bill was, and they exchanged places with Abbey and Bill Waterman.

Ivy would have fared better by getting a little sleep in her room, Sam thought, but he knew she felt she had to be near if anything went wrong or if Bill awakened and asked for her.

Bill Waterman and Abigail Foley left moments later.

Waterman walked Abbey to her hotel suite then he walked to the Foley Town House to rest. Abbey had given him a key not wanting him to stay in the hotel where she was. She was trying to retain as much propriety as possible.

Sam and Ivy began their watch wordlessly. Young Bill Foley was due more morphine and quinine. They accomplished the procedures, and Young Bill came into and out of consciousness, staying mostly out, and in the darkness of early morning, minutes began moving slowly toward daylight.

Searching for fever, Ivy touched her face against Young Bill's, may even have brushed him a kiss, Sam couldn't tell in the dim light, then the two of them began their silent watch again.

Both she and Sam were still worn from yesterday's high emotion so talking wasn't considered until daylight began lifting the darkness and sunlight drifted through the Infirmary window curtains. Sam considered walking to Kerry O'Shea's and waking him. Ivy could use a cup of coffee, and so could he. Looking at his watch, he found it a few minutes before six, and he decided to let the bartender sleep.

"The Bluebonnet Café will open in a few minutes; I'll get us some fresh coffee," he told Ivy in as quiet a voice as possible.

"That would be wonderful. Thank you," she replied, and Sam left to stand at the Bluebonnet's front doors.

When he returned bringing fresh coffee, they drank. When her cup was empty, Ivy said, "Sam, there's little to do but talk. I'm curious about something Wyatt Winslow said yesterday."

"And what would that be?"

"Out there in the street in front of everybody, he accused the Foley's of cheating his family. That man was bitter with hatred. I don't believe his accusation. Did Bill or his dad do something to cause it?"

"No," Sam answered without the slightest hesitation. "Wyatt was flat out mistaken. I know. I was there every step of the way."

"But he was so bitter. Real bitter."

"It's a long story."

"We have nothing but time, Sam. Will four hours be long enough?"

"Four hours to tell twenty years? Sure. It can be done. First, tell me what Wyatt said. I was upstairs in the hotel."

"He said the Foley's took everything and left the Winslow's with nothing. Then he said the Foley's didn't even leave the Winslow's self respect. What did he mean, Sam?"

"Has Bill told you anything about Chastity?"

"He said he had a daughter but had not married the child's mother. Is Chastity her name?"

"It is. She is a Winslow, Wyatt's younger sister. I think Chastity was only a small part of Wyatt's anger."

"If the child out of wedlock was not the cause, what was?"

"Birthright is my bet. Birthright is something Old Bill Foley dearly believed in."

"I'm not sure what you're getting at. I can't see the connection to Wyatt Winslow. I'm pretty, so that's my birthright. What was Wyatt Winslow's birthright, and how does it fit the circumstances?"

"Pretty is something you were born with. Others are born homely. Those are natural things. We all start out with what nature hands us. That's not it. Birthright is something handed down. The difference is rich and powerful people who want to hand their wealth and power down to children who have not earned it. Unearned money and power are not good gifts. Old Bill Foley did not make that mistake with Young Bill. That young man earned his."

"I think so, too. But what does that have to do with Wyatt Winslow? Where did his hate come from?"

"Think of kingdoms if birthright is sketchy."

"Do you mean Wyatt expected some of the Foley cattle kingdom?"

"He did. That's it exactly. For you to understand, I'll need to go back a bit."

"I'd love it. I'd dearly love it. I'll get the Foley history. Take your time. Tell me all you know."

"I know all of it."

"I'm alive with interest. I'll be a good listener."

"You may need to be. If I go to the beginning, it's a long way back, and once my mouth and memory get started, they're hard to stop."

"Sam Ordway, you're not the kind of man to bore a lady. You're smooth. Don't keep me waiting any longer."

"Well, it began at Irish Rose's Waterfront Saloon in Galveston where I first met Bill Foley. She's the same Irish Rose O'Grady who owns the saloon here."

"How unique. It's not a coincidence, is it? How did it happen?"

"Old Bill Foley willed it."

"I see. He was a strong willed man. Is that it?"

"It is. Hardship will do that for some men. Others are like spring flowers that wilt when they meet a frost. The Bill Foley I met that afternoon had another thing to harden his will. He had hate."

"I thought this was about Wyatt's hate. Now it's Bill Foley's. If that's the issue, Wyatt should have taken it out of the father, not the son."

"You're jumping ahead. Bill Foley hated a system, not a man."

"A system? That never occurred to me."

"Since this is about Old Bill Foley, Dave Winslow, and me, you need to know a little about each of us. You've met my daughter, so you can understand when I say I was married to a very beautiful woman."

"And she was Chinese."

"She was. Young Bill has been talking about me, I see."

"Some. Not enough, though. I'll hush now. Go on."

"I was in the Army, planning to make it my career until I met her. It was during the war with Mexico, and I had been sent to California, and the Gold Rush began."

Deciding the Waterman trial was a side-track Sam brushed it aside and continued.

"As soon as Chan Li and I married I asked for a discharge and bought a small claim that turned out to be a pretty good one. We had Abbey and life was good until it took a week for Chan Li to die. Why she got cholera and I didn't is a mystery I never solved. If it was The Almighty testing me, I failed, because I took to drinking hard whiskey. A retching bowel sending out a foul smelling odor is an ugly way to die, especially for a sensitive woman who loved the fragrance of jasmine. Chan Li had that special dignity Orientals have, and it stripped her of all of that dignity, and stripped her bare. Watching her die humbled me. I was a broken man."

Sam Ordway's words softened as the past unfolded. When his telling stopped entirely, Ivy reached over and placed her hand on his. She knew his memory was still moving even if his words were not.

After a moment, he began again, "Finally, old Chang Wu and madam Wu, her parents, called me to task for neglecting Abbey in favor of strong drink, so I gave up whiskey. Abbey was ten when her mother died. Twelve came overnight, and she began showing womanhood. We realized it was time adulthood was addressed, and education attended to. That meant leaving the Wu's. They were as reluctant to let us go as we were to leave, but the Wu's were intellectuals, and they were Orientals, and they had taught her English and numbers well, but they had no other knowledge of culture except their own, so they saw the need for an American education. They were right. California functioned by Spanish custom. Her choices for a mate were Mexicans or rowdy miners.

Rich Spanish families sent their young back to Mexico City for schooling. My Anglo status would not allow that, and neither would my pocketbook, so I wrote my younger sister, Theodosia Ordway who lived in Saint Louis, and she was delighted to have Abbey. Did Young Bill tell you any of my family history?"

"He did. Some. I know your father was part of the Lewis and Clark Expedition."

"Did he mention the earthquake?"

"An earthquake? Here?"

"No. Above Saint Louis. At New Madrid. It destroyed everything our family owned. My sister settled in Saint Louis and I went into the army. Theodosia never married. She couldn't cook and couldn't find a man who would. She boiled everything, even steak. She just boiled all the water out and added more water until there was no taste left. She can bake, mind you. Pies, cakes, and cookies that melt in your mouth, and she decorates every morsel with lots of color."

"Color means there's an artist in her."

"Must be, because she found work at the Millefiori Paperweight factory. Theodosia is secretary, but she practically runs the place, and she loves her work. She's so proud of her work, she had me watch their glassblowers make thin glass canes using different colors of Murano glass that go inside the paperweights, because she chooses all the designs."

"See, she's an artist. It happens I know something about the Millefiori process. I'm an artist and colors are my passion. Millefiori patterns go back to the time of ancient Rome and Alexandria."

"Didn't know that. I spent six months with her before I left Abbey there, and I thought she had told or shown me everything about how those fancy paperweights were made. Theodosia hated to see me leave. I did a little cooking, but we ate out a lot. Plenty of Mexican café's and German Beer Gardens there. Enough so I learned my little sister was a beer drinker. In public, too. Saint Louis has natural caves along the waterfront where beer can be cooled and stored, so they have a lot of beers, and almost everyone drinks it, because I saw other women drinking with their men folk. I was just glad Theodosia didn't pull out a sack of Bull Durham and begin rolling a cigarette."

"Sounds like she's my kind of girl."

"Well, when I left California, I had done pretty well working my gold mining claim, and its sale along with my army savings allowed me leisure time, but I was ready to move on. Theodosia had placed Abbey in The Lenox School for Young Ladies at Valley Park, and the University of Saint Louis was there for her if she decided on higher learning later on. I had to work at something to keep that inner restlessness of mine from driving me batty, so it was time to find another occupation, and I moved on and began looking. Understand. There was plenty of work in Saint Louis, and it was a second home to me. Saint Louis is in the middle of the States where railroads and riverboats cross, so there was plenty of work, but my world has never been indoors. I went south. South meant cattle and outdoors. I thought I could work cows, maybe even start a small ranch, so I bought a ticket on one of the riverboats that always jammed the banks of the Mississippi, Delta Queen, bound for New Orleans and on to Galveston, and that's what allowed fate to intersect my life to Bill Foley's."

Crystal clear daylight began beaming through the room's curtains, a welcome after yesterday's rain, and Ivy, anxious about her patient, moved to Young Bill when he stirred and felt his forehead.

"I know I'm taking too long," Sam said. "I'll cut it short."

"No. Don't. Every word is interesting. I can tell when he has fever by touching his forehead. It was warm last night. It's cooler now. I'm beginning to think he will be okay. Go on Sam, please."

"Well, after my luggage had been stored in my stateroom, I went back on deck to pass time until the Delta Queen cast off. My eyes began wondering, and I saw a sea of humanity loading and unloading a harbor jammed full of commercial riverboats, and I noticed an oddity. Sandwiched between Germans with blonde hair, Irishmen with dark hair, and plenty of Negros, was a stevedore with bright auburn hair that was showing from beneath his cap. The oddity was when I got off the Delta Queen in Galveston a stevedore with the bright auburn hair approached me. Would two different men have the same unusual auburn hair? I saw it as an omen of fate, because I knew it had to be the same man. Bill Foley landed in Galveston before me because my Delta Queen ran aground near Natchez and Bill Foley's vessel passed it during the night. Had that event not happened would we have ever met? It was just another question without an answer that I myself asked many times.

"In Galveston, Bill Foley came right up to me and offered to buy me a drink if I would listen to a ranching proposition, and ranching was why I'd wondered south, so we went into Irish Rose's Waterfront Saloon. After we sat down, with a whiskey before Bill and a beer before me, he told me he had three hundred dollars. It didn't come easy, he said. His jobs did not pay well. In Ireland, he had been a potato farmer and dairyman with no other skills. He asked me to match his three hundred if his ranching plan appealed to me. He could tell by my clothes that I was worth more than three hundred dollars, but he never asked me for a penny more. We would be equal partners. Three hundred apiece was for supplies for two years while we established our herd. With his plan, the land would be free, and we could gather enough wild free roaming longhorn cows with our sweat to make up a herd. It was plain to me he was strong enough, stevedoring will do that, and I had a working mine where a man built a sluice box and hammered rock to sift through it, so I was no stranger to hard work either.

"As best I remember, this is what he told me about his life. Bill Foley owed his landlord, and he evicted them because he had the power of law to do it. That power began with the King of England and filtered down through each class of noblemen until in fell on Bill Foley. Every man on the class ladder had a birthright, and Bill had none, so he hated the birthright system until it came time for him to use it. When he and his family were evicted from Ireland, the ship that brought them from England was not allowed to land at Montreal, because with a million Irishmen being shipped out of Ireland same as Bill, the Saint Lawrence waterway was clogged, and his ship was forced to continue into the interior of Canada before it was allowed to dock, so he and his family were left stranded near Toronto in the deepest snow of winter, and his family died there."

"Oh, how sad. The poor man."

Young Bill groaned, and Ivy stroked his hand, and he was peaceful. "He's done that off and on all night, but I don't think he feels anything. Go on, Sam. Fit that together for me."

"I'll need more history. Bill Foley made his way into the States at a small village in Michigan, Port Huron, then on to Detroit where he found waterfront work. From there, stevedore jobs took him down the Mississippi to Saint Louis, and in ten years he had finally saved three hundred dollars, and he had a plan. The plan was gathered by listening to

French trappers in Canada and in Saint Louis. The French had the best of a very lucrative Indian fur trade until England developed Sheffield steel. French Canadian trappers got seriously rich, and made Saint Louis seriously rich, trading cheap beads and mirrors for beaver pelts and buffalo robes that brought serious money.

"Bill Foley was a good listener, and he learned from those idle old trappers that Indian braves are vain about their appearance. Braves kill the buffalo, bear, deer, antelope, and trap beaver, but the women do the work of skinning, rending, and sewing the hides. Using robes and rugs squaws made, braves traded for beads so their women could sew them on their moccasins and vests and glorify themselves as big warriors. The thing that jumped out at him was Indian braves loved mirrors. The reason, so they could remove their facial hair. Those fierce Indian braves were more like white women folks with their beautifying."

"That's hard to believe, Sam Ordway," Ivy said. "Surely you wouldn't tease a girl at a time like this, would you?"

"Nope. It's gospel true. I didn't believe it at first. Indian men of all the tribes cannot tolerate facial hair. On the hunt, braves make the kill then squaws do the butchering and skinning then work the hides into robes, buckskin clothes, and tepees. Squaws, not braves, take to the battlefield to recover the wounded and dead. Braves do nothing except make weapons and preen like peacocks. Indian men not only pluck their facial hair, they pluck their chest hair and eyebrows.

"I tell you for a fact, French trappers became wealthy, and Saint Louis became the fur capitol of the world because of the Indian male vanity for mirrors and clam shells that they cupped together to pluck hair, and mirrors are what Bill Foley was going to trade for land."

"That's really hard for me to believe. With all their atrocities, it's hard to imagine them primping like girls. It all sounds like a fantasy. You two must have got away with it, because here you are sitting here with me twenty years later."

"It's true, and we did. We were lucky."

"Go on, Sam. You have me suspended inside your life."

"Bill Foley told me that day the only water he wanted to see from now on is water with land around it. Land means wealth and power, and it was his intent to have both. Then he outlined his mirror scheme, and I felt it was the kind of plan that was insane enough to work, so I matched his three hundred, and we became partners.

"Ivy, honey, this is the point to remember: Dave Winslow was invited later, as a limited partner, because he owned an extra horse, but no money. One of his horses was a paint; not a color any white man would want but a special color to Indians. The paint was a beautiful animal with a coat of splashed black spots against white and with all four legs white below the hocks. It was the kind of horse an Indian would love, and that made the animal valuable for Bill Foley's scheme.

"I'm gonna skip a little here and there," Sam said, "but the three of us worked our way into Texas Indian Territory, but not before we picked out two more horses, one a pinto with splashed markings, like the paint except this stallion was splashed brown instead of black, and a third horse, a slick coated solid black mustang stallion. The black cost me and Bill one hundred dollars each. The price was fancy, but the animal was necessary. He proved to be worth it. My mind's out of breath. Truth is; I wish I had another cup of coffee."

"Sam Ordway, I will not let you stop now. Get on with it."

Chapter Forty-Six

"I insisted on going to Del Rio before we got in too deep. What Bill Foley learned about Indians was all I had to go on, and I wanted to be a little more certain Bill was on to something, so I insisted we stop at Camp San Felipe. The Army had been finding out about Indians for twenty years, and I knew the Army. I was in need of advice, so I asked army regulars and Indian scouts for it. We were going into Comanche territory, and they described Comanche braves as the best horsemen on the continent. Swift Antelope, a Navajo scout, Navajo's being a Comanche's natural enemy, said a Comanche brave lived for two things; war and hunting. He made his own arrows and lances, and the weapons were absolutely straight and true. He showed no mercy and expected none. His reward was glory. Work, as such, was not a thing he understood. He was exactly as Bill Foley had been led to believe; Comanche warriors were vain. Squaws did everything.

"The next question to be answered was how and where to make the barter. Bosque is the Spanish word for woods or wooded area. A Bosque is a special place where trees take root because it is where water dwells, and water is scarce on the plains. Humans and animals, like trees, need water to survive, and a Bosque makes a favored winter resting place for an Indian tribe.

"Stalking Coyote suggested a large Bosque on the San Saba River, while Swift Antelope pinpointed another big Bosque on a bend of the Frio River. I chose the Bosque on the Frio, not favoring the Frio exactly, I was against the San Saba area; it was in the heart of Comanche Territory, and we needed land that was only bordering Comanche territory. It was a good choice, and timing was early enough in the year for us to scout the area for miles around then pick the place best suited for cattle and ranching, then we waited for contact.

"It is a common misconception that Indians are deathly afraid of night. The truth is they strike at their advantage whatever the time. Indians do move at night, sometimes traveling all night, in order to attack at false dawn, that time of half-light when the dull copper color of his body blends with shadows. They appear from nowhere as silent as the shadows that surround them. A deer hunter knows the experience. Deer appear as if by magic. Suddenly they're in front of you, and your eyes blink, because your mind tells you your eyes have been deceived.

"For three days, the three of us waited. It was important to have plenty of open space for the meeting. Many a white man has been massacred for his horse or horses, and we had three of the most beautiful Indian horses any brave or chief would want. Open space would prevent us being set upon unexpectedly. Open space would also give the Indians comfort from any white man's trap.

"The morning of the fourth day, three mounted Indians appeared out of nowhere with about fifty more atop a knoll about five hundred yards from Bill Foley's position which was centered between fortified rock positions manned by Dave Winslow and me. Bill Foley was roughly a hundred yards in front so as to make a triangle with our two fortified positions. He raised a white flag then spiked it and spread the mirrors on the ground. They looked like a thousand glittering daylight stars when the sun hit them. After the mirrors were sparkling, Bill rode back and, one at a time, took the horses out front and staked them next to the mirrors for easy viewing and let them crop grass. Three of the most coveted ponies an Indian would want, and they were in plain sight inviting Indian visitors. Bill Foley counted on the horses for bait; the mirrors for the cake."

"Sam Ordway, if I didn't know you better, I would say you were crazy to do such a thing."

"I've thought on it, and crazy fits some, but what we really were is desperate. Bill Foley was desperate for money and power. Dave Winslow was desperate for Claire Prescott, and I was desperate to leave Chan Li's memory, because I was still alive and needed to begin living again."

"I understand, Sam. Please go on."

"Well, when Bill saw the Indians, he knew they were there to take the bait, so he placed his Winchester over his head and walked out to where the horses were cropping grass, and he laid the weapon on the ground and stepped back then waited.

"Dave and me stood up and walked a step or two from behind our rock fortifications and lowered our Winchesters to the ground just as Bill had. With everyone and everything in plain sight, the Indians came forward slowly. Caution is their nature. We guessed the Indians had probably been watching us for a day or two, maybe even the whole time we were making preparations, for no Indian tribe moves without sending out scouts.

"Bill Foley walked toward the slowly approaching Indians, and Dave and I watched both parties stop when they were within speaking distance. Bill Foley had no knowledge of any Indian language, so he raised his right hand with the peace sign then lowered it. From beneath his shirt, he removed two squares of leather. Both squares were made from cowhide. The squares were cut exactly the same, differing only with the image of the picture of the animal branded on each square. The square Bill presented to the Indian leader had the image of a buffalo, its hump showing plainly. The images were crude, burned into the leather using straight lines to form the likeness of the creature intended, and the square Bill showed the Indian chief and took back for himself was of a longhorn cow, the long horns plain enough so the chief could tell the difference between the two creatures. Next, Bill Foley motioned, to his right with a wide wave of his hand pointing to the leather square the Indian leader was holding indicating all the land on that side was for buffalo. With his left hand, he waved in the opposite direction then waved his leather square indicating cows would be on that side, and he pointed in the direction of the mirrors and the three horses, and with another wave of his hand indicated they were to go to the chief, but the land on Bill Foley's side was to be his, and he pointed to himself and waved at us."

"Were you surprised they didn't try to kill the three of you and take everything?"

"Not much. Indians don't like dyin' any more than Whites. We had enough ammunition to make a lot of squaw widows. Then, there's curiosity. They had to be curious about what we were about. When they found out what we wanted was a small space they didn't care much about against the infinity they had to hunt on, and they were to get what they considered riches, we figured they'd give in, and they did, because the chief nodded his understanding of the agreement. He took the black stallion, and mounted the animal and began riding away leading his and the other animals. The braves packed the mirrors in the sheep skin war bag Bill Foley had made to carry them in. Bill Foley kept his cowhide square, and the chief kept the cowhide square with the buffalo drawing on it."

"So, it wasn't luck; it was superior intelligence?"

"Hell no. It was mostly luck and a lot of downright stupidity."

"You did get what you went for, but go on with the Winslow's part. I want to understand Wyatt."

"Now is where Dave Winslow comes in. As I said before, we three, Wyatt's daddy, Old Bill, and me, came to this land as partners, more or less, with Old Bill the strongest partner. As years passed, we transformed the herd from mean and scraggly Longhorns into animals fit for human consumption. After a few years, the Indian menace faded, and people in the North needed meat, and we worked hard and supplied it, and Old Bill got wealthy. One day, he sat Dave and me down and told us he was prepared to set us up in a ranch of our own that we could choose as much land as we wanted, and he'd stock it for us. That didn't come as a surprise. It had been an unspoken promise all along. Dave Winslow had different plans. Dave had a young wife and they had a family started, and with ranch work slower in winter, we managed to build a starter cabin. Over the next few years while we were improving the herd, we improved Dave's home. It was a nice place when Old Bill made the offer. We expected Dave to carve off a nice piece of land around it. He didn't."

"Why?" Ivy asked. Her tone a bit shocked.

Before Sam could answer, Young Bill began stirring again, and Ivy was beside him like a quick cat. He moaned and his eyes opened and closed, so she placed a wash cloth over his mouth for moisture and said, "Don't try to talk, Bill. You're going to be okay. Go back to sleep," and he did.

Placing her hand on his forehead and finding it cool, she said to Sam, "Not much fever. He's only as warm as he has been."

"Good sign," Sam offered.

"Doctor Wedgewood will come in here any minute," Ivy said. "Finish what you began. Tell me what birthright had to do with the Winslow's."

"Just this: Dave Winslow refused everything. He got religion from one of the Wesley brother's Exhorters."

"Oh. I'm afraid I don't know what an Exhorter is."

"You're too young. They were before your time. The Wesley brothers, John, the founder of the Methodist Church, and Charles his brother who wrote hymns, they say he wrote five or six thousand, came over from England to preach. They were powerful evangelists and Methodist churches sprang up wherever they went. When they went back to England, they left circuit riders who were called Exhorters. They were looked on as disciples, the same as the disciples of Jesus Christ. An Exhorter circuit rider came along before there was a Foley, and he went from camp to camp and cabin to cabin preaching wherever could get a group to listen. Dave was converted. What he asked from Old Bill was a church. That set Old Bill back some. Catholic was his religion, and he begged Dave to take land and cattle. Dave refused. He said he would take only his cabin and the land around it. It would not be right for him to preach and he and his family live above others. Old Bill relented. Dave was his friend, and Old Bill owed a debt, and Old Bill was strong on paying and collecting debts, and Old Bill agreed to build a church for Dave, and he did.

"Old Bill's next surprise came when he asked me where I wanted my ranch. By that time in my life I had had enough of wrestling steers and breaking wild mustangs. I asked Bill to build a town, and I would keep order. I had thought on it, and I gave him sound financial reasons why he should do it; a mercantile store so he didn't have to send a wagon to Bellville or San Antonio every month for supplies, and a bank to hold money from his cattle transactions. During the war, we sent cattle to Mexico. The King Ranch did it first. Richard King and Mifflin Kenedy sent them upriver on the Rio Grande, and the Dons over there sold them to the North, the South, and in Europe, and they paid us in silver Peso's. Zacatecas, Mexico, has rich silver mines. Before the war a Mexican silver Peso was traded equal for U.S. dollars, and anyone in Texas would take it before the dollar, because it was solid silver, and we had acquired lots of silver Peso's. Bill saw the need for a bank right off, and that made it easy for all the other little businesses. I also told him it was time Young Bill had a school. That's how Foley came into being."

"That's absolutely fascinating. Wait; back up a minute. I can't find the birthright link. I see that you and Dave got what you asked for, but it was not a birthright; it was your payment for work and risks taken. Say in words what I should know about Wyatt Winslow's birthright."

"I can't get any plainer than this: Rich men who became powerful hacked out kingdoms then they invented birthrights so they could hand down money and power to their heirs. I hate the system. Doc Wedgewood loves it even though it locked him out and he had to come here. Old Bill Foley bowed to it, but he wants to continue the system so Young Bill can be as powerful as him. Wyatt Winslow was too young to know his father bargained away his ranch birthright for a church. He was the youngest and left for the War of Secession before he had whiskers. Both the boys were taken with the pomp and jubilee kind of excitement that was happening. I remember three wagons coming from San Antonio. They were covered with flags. The first wagon had a band and a recruiter. The second wagon had young men dressed in confederate uniforms who had just signed up and several young girls dressed in pretty dresses waving flags. The Winslow boys could not resist. They were not alone. Even a few of the Mexican vaqueros volunteered. I don't think Wyatt gave his inheritance a thought until he was in mortal pain then needing something other than himself to blame. Wyatt Winslow surely had been thinking the Foley's swindled the Winslow's. Not knowing any better, when he came away from the blessed War of Secession without glory and without an arm and a useless body, he probably felt God had swindled him, too.

"Young Bill and Chastity dallied because they saw each other every Sunday at The Winslow Methodist Church. Here's how that happened: The Catholics have early Masses. The Methodists don't have a preaching service until eleven. Old Bill, Abbey, and Young Bill, came to town every week and stayed in the Town House so they could attend early Sunday morning Mass.

"About here you need to know about Dave Winslow. His voice was beautiful. His speaking voice was low, soft, bass like. His singing voice was just as powerful. It was low, too, but it carried like the wind. It pleased every ear that heard it. That included cows. Dave Winslow could calm a restless herd by singing. He's done it with thunder and lightning in the distance. I heard him. So has Old Bill. While Dave Winslow was alive, his Methodist Church brought farmers to Foley from miles away. He had regular members coming from Bellville every Sunday. That's a long ride for a family. They had to start long before daylight and travel hard, but they came. Some folks came from San Antonio. They had to spend the night at the hotel. Back then, the hotel was full every week-end. Sarah McAllister's boarding house was full, too. What I'm getting at is Old Bill, Abbey, Young Bill, and me, would travel out there after the Foley's finished early morning Mass. We went to hear Dave Winslow sing hymns. We never went inside, Old Bill being staunch Catholic, but we listened outdoors and loved it. After Young Bill became a young man, he and I would ride our animals instead of him riding with his mom and dad in their surrey, and that's the times he and Chastity found each other and Chastity finally got pregnant. After Dave died, his Methodist Church began slowly dying, and Old Bill closed it. He went back to his rule. The only religion allowed in Foley was Catholic."

Chapter Forty-Seven

The O'Hara Law firm read Old Bill Foley's Last Will & Testament when Young Bill was strong enough to sit at their massive mahogany conference table that seated twelve people. Only the two lawyers, Abbey, Young Bill, and Sam were present in the big room.

Nothing special was in the document. Abbey and Young Bill inherited everything equally with Young Bill given power to operate the ranch and all the enterprises. Abbey could intervene only if the operation failed to yield a suitable profit. Sam wanted nothing, and that's what he got.

Abbey hugged his neck as they were leaving and the lawyers were filing past. Young Bill waited behind her. The three of them were alone in the conference room.

"Have you decided when you will marry Bill Waterman?" Sam asked.

"No, Dad. I need time. When I feel like I can be a wife, I'll let him know. I'm going back to the ranch for awhile. How long, I don't really know. I may leave just to get away by myself. I'm emotionally drained. It has been a trying time."

"It has."

Taking her son's hand to leave, Abbey had another thought that caused her to turn back to Sam, "You're going to stay, aren't you?"

"Don't know. Things are changing."

"No, Dad. They have changed. Wherever you go, tell me. I want you to give me away again. Will you?"

"You know I will, Abbey. I still love you. I didn't stop when you chose another man. It seemed a natural thing to do at your age, after I looked back at things."

Young Bill, pale skin showing next to tanned skin at places like his eyes and mouth, had hesitated waiting for his chance, now he said, "Mom, is it true? Are you going to marry him?"

"My answer is yes, I think so. I'm sorry I became attracted to him before your father died. I was afraid to tell you thinking you wouldn't understand, but your father had been down for two years. Mister Waterman did not make his intentions known until recently when he presented me with a ring, and I accepted. Your father suddenly awakened, and we hastily dropped everything. That's where we stand. I'm going away for a time to sort out my feelings. I'll wait until you marry Ivy. When will that be?"

"As soon as she becomes a confirmed Catholic; she's at work on that now."

"I'll be at the ranch. I'm in no hurry."

"I am. She's holding our baby. I want it to have a properly married mother."

"Well, she's in love with you, so she should make a good wife. If I marry Mister Waterman, we will live on his ranch or make Boston our home. You and Ivy can move out to our ranch. The house will be yours. The Will didn't change anything. You're still in charge of everything."

Sam turned and looked back at the long conference table as they were leaving. Abbey had just remarked the Will had not changed anything, and he asked himself, if Old Bill Foley had lived until the following Monday, what would Abbey, Young Bill, and the town of Foley think about Molly Gibbs being Old Bill's daughter and Young Bill's sister?

Sam Ordway was in a pickle, and he was trying to wiggle out of the pickle juice without bringing up Molly Gibbs, yet when Old Bill defined the relationship that fathered the child, Sam was at a total loss to understand why he did what he did. What was it Old Bill had said that day. That he bedded the woman because he had the power to do it. That didn't make sense. But it had made sense to Old Bill. That didn't make it right. Should he, Sam Ordway, tell Old Bill's secret? Did Molly Gibbs have a right to know? Old Bill had confessed to Sam, so only Sam knew, and it would be his word that would start the upheaval.

"Better to let it be for a better time," Sam mumbled halfheartedly.

Pondering about Molly's wealth that had so quickly appeared then quickly disappeared, Sam walked to the jail.

Sitting behind his desk, he soothed his conscience some when he remembered Molly Gibbs was no longer poor as a church mouse; she had fifty acres, a cabin, some chickens, and forty or more cattle. One day Tom Silverhorn would find her. They would make a fine couple, not anything against Cass, he was never going to be an adult, and Tom Silverhorn had been born that-a-way.

With his mind at loose ends with all its moral struggles, Sam remembered he forgot to get the jail's mail when he left the O'Hara Law Firm's office, and he walked back across the street to The Emporium where he found only one piece of mail waiting. It was a letter, and from the handwriting, he knew it came from Claire, so he opened it.

> Dear Sam:
> I miss you. Please sit down and read the rest of this letter privately.

That was it for the first page, but there was another page beneath it. Confused at such a strange beginning, he walked back to the jail. Wanting to solve the mystery quickly, he sat down behind his desk and unfolded the other page. It read:

> I have been in Saint Louis three days, and I'm lonely already. I enjoy the city, Chastity, and my grandchild. That's not the problem. I miss you, Sam. For a long time now, it has been my secret hope that you will ask me to marry you. Since you have not come forward, I am lonely enough, yes and desperate enough, to ask you. Sam Ordway, will you marry me? Gentle things you've said and done since Dave's death show me you care. I think, because you are older than me, that you may be standoffish thinking you cannot perform bridegroom duties properly. If it is beyond you, and you will have me as a companion, I am so willing. A woman like me can find pleasure in giving pleasure to a man she loves in whatever way that may be, and, Sam, I've loved you for a long time.
> Pride goeth before a fall. To write this letter has sapped all of my feminine pride. If you want me, Sam, you must come get me. I have that much pride left, so don't bother to answer this letter. Come get me. If you do that, I will live with you anywhere on earth.

Sam held the pages for the longest looking beyond them. After a time, he looked down and reflected that Claire had not signed the letter. Leaving it unsigned meant she had made the first move. The next move was his.

Chapter Forty-Eight

Sam finished breakfast for Jimbo and himself then took the young man to the schoolhouse and went from there to the jail to find Ivy Vanderbilt sitting in a chair waiting for him. What, he wandered, did she want?

"Sam," she began, "My stage didn't show up last Saturday. When Bill regained his senses, he sent one of his men to San Antonio to pick it up. It came back yesterday. Claude, my driver, had disappeared on a drinking spree. That circumstance has made an opportunity for me to get something done. Can you handle a team well enough to drive a stage?"

"Sure. But I'm not looking for a job. I plan on leaving this one."

"You do?"

"I do."

"That's another reason for you to consider this job. What I have in mind may work out for you. How would you like to have a vacation paid for by me?"

"Depends. What's on your mind?"

"Bill and I talked this over before I came to see you. Bill says you've been to New Orleans. He says you are familiar with Basin Street."

"I am. I visited places on that Street when I was younger."

"Gertrude Spivey's?"

"Nope. I know the place. Not far from Emma Johnson's Mansion."

"Close enough. You can do what I want done."

"And that would be?"

"Sam, I am not a Cattle Baron's wife."

Sam smiled. Then the smile became a big grin. In a way, he was proud she had come at him this way. From the beginning he felt she was a fine woman. She is going to keep spice in Young Bill's life, and he said, "Young Bill told you what I said?"

"He did. But I never owned a brothel. Well, almost. Good fortune and circumstances let me side-step that obligation. Now that we have a complete understanding, this is what I have in mind. I want to pay Gertrude Spivey one thousand dollars, and I want a receipt, and I want a lawman to pay her. She paid one thousand dollars for me, and I ran off. She sends the Pinkerton's after people like me who did what I did. It's worth a thousand dollars to have the Pinkerton's quit. If she sees your star and gets the money, she'll back off, so it's important to me for a lawman to do it. The star will frighten her; lawmen make her nervous. I'll pay your expenses and whatever fee you deem proper. I'll even give you the stage and team. Will you do it?"

"I might have a need for a stagecoach."

"You do? Good. You'll do it?"

"Yep. How soon do you want it done?"

"The sooner the better, but I don't have a set schedule. You'll have to take Margarite with you. She wants to go back home."

"That's strange and not so strange. No need to talk in circles. I know Basin Street is a street of fancy whorehouses. My guess is, as pretty as you are, and the money you're worth, you'd have to be connected there. I guess you were probably a feature for Gertie, but I can't exactly place where Margarite would fit in. Was she just the housekeeper?"

"Yes and no. She inspected the men clients for cleanliness and examined the girls to tell them the days when they might get pregnant. She was not perfect, but, like a good stockman who could judge when a heifer would come into heat, she knew that thing about girls. She also kept the place spotless. I have a sincere fondness for her. She was very kind to me. She's homesick. She misses Simon. Simon is her brother. Will you take her home?"

"I will, but it will be a one-way trip. I'm not coming back. Not anytime soon, leastwise."

"Are you sure about your plans?"

"I am."

"Then, I want to buy your house and everything in it just as it sits the day you leave."

"Ivy, with your money and Bill's, what do you want with my little place on Cedar Street?"

"Will you sell?"

"Not unless you tell me what crazy scheme you have moving in between the common senses in your head."

"You old scoundrel. Let me keep it a secret. I'll tell you if you come back."

"Nope. No deal. What's on your mind?"

"I want to make it into a museum."

"A museum? A museum for what?"

"A museum for the town of Foley. I'll have a bronze plaque made telling how you asked for a town when you could have asked for riches. Bill told me you have souvenirs of your Dad's part in the Lewis & Clark Expedition and letters from him to your mother he wrote her when he was away. I think those things and your personal belongings will make an interesting place for visitors. I'm not willing to become famous anymore, but I would also like to exhibit my paintings. I'll show local landscapes and local people."

"I don't know about that. You say you don't want to be famous. Well, I don't want to be either."

"I want to name it the Sam Ordway Museum. Please, Sam, please."

"People will think I'm uppity."

"What do you care? You're not coming back, remember?"

"Maybe. I might come back. You gonna paint Mexicans?"

"I am. And Methodists, Baptists, Catholics, and even a drunk or two. Bill's going to sit for me. I wish you would, too."

"Not a chance."

"You'll force me to paint you from memory. People will love you and me more if I don't do that."

"I surrender. It's yours. Now that I think on it, it will be a good thing. I'd be proud to leave my father's journal and his letters to my mother. My things don't matter, but those historical items should interest folks."

"You'll come back for our wedding, won't you?"

"Why? You're not coming to mine."

"Oh, Sam. You're getting married? Of course. You're going after your bride. It's Claire. Right?"

"I am, and it is."

"Come back, Sam. You'll see your museum and our new baby. Come back, Sam, and bring your bride."

Chapter Forty-Nine

Ivy Vanderbilt's stagecoach pulled up in front of #33 Basin Street shortly after ten in the morning on a hot and humid September 3rd, and Sam Ordway stepped down leaving the reins in the hands of young Jimbo Winslow. Such a large vehicle parked out front made it necessary for a smaller surrey being pulled by a fancy trotting horse slow down to pass.

"Jimbo," Sam said looking up at him, "You can tell your mother you visited New Orleans. Do not tell her the name of this street. On your honor."

"On my honor, Uncle Sam."

"I'll be a few minutes. Check the brake handle and make sure it's tight. Hold the team."

"Yessir."

Sam turned to the stagecoach door and opened it. When Margarite Doss stepped down, Sam placed manacles on her wrists, and they walked to the mansion's front door which was already beginning to open with large Simon Doss, dressed in his butler's suit, waiting. The clatter of the stagecoach and the passing surrey had caught his attention.

Anxiety came to his face when he saw a lawman wearing a large white Stetson hat with a six-pointed star prominently displayed on his leather vest striding up the walk toward him, and Sam watched his expression change to anguish when he saw his sister in handcuffs.

"I'm here to see Gertrude Spivey," Sam said when he approached him. "Tell her she need not run and hide. I am returning one of her employees."

Huge Simon could not resist placing his gargantuan arms around Margarite. When he did, she whispered in his ear, "I'm not in trouble, Simon. Everything will be okay."

The expression on Simon's face relaxed, and he had them follow him down the hall to the rear of the mansion where, in the sunroom, Gertrude Spivey sat finishing her breakfast by enjoying a last cup of Café Du Monde Coffee. The sight of an uninvited lawman with a star on his vest changed the contentment on her face. When her eyes found Margarite Doss in back of Sam, the change in her expression was more dramatic, almost panic Sam judged, for he saw the coffee cup tremble, and she quickly sat it down. It was not her voice that asked what was happening, it was her eyes; they darted back and forth finally fixing on Sam who said, "Madame, I have business with you. First, I would enjoy a cup of your coffee. Is there any left?"

Too unnerved to do it, she said, "Simon, pour Mister . . ."

"Careful, Gertrude. You know better. I'm not Mister here, I'm Marshal Sam Ordway, an officer of the law. We'll talk after I have coffee."

Simon poured, and Sam accepted it making a point of reaching out for it with a steady hand that Gertrude Spivey could plainly see.

"Cream and sugar, please, Simon," Sam said.

"Not very Marshal like. A lawman should take it black."

"Careful, Gertrude. I may not do you the favor I came here to do."

"Favor? You're bringing back my runaway slave to extort money from me. That's no favor."

"Gertrude, that's foolish talk. Slavery is over. You're making my coffee get cold."

"Drink, Marshal. Hurry about it. My nerves can't stand waiting to find out about your *favor*."

Sam, after adding cream and sugar, began sipping the hot chicory coffee obviously enjoying the strong taste, and he said, "Just like home. Have a cup Margarite and tell me if Kerry O'Shea does it as good."

"Dammit, Marshal. Drink faster. Simon, pour your sister a cup. Margarite, how have you been? I've missed you."

While Simon poured, Sam unfastened Margarite's cuffs. With free hands, she accepted the coffee, tasted it, and replied to Sam, "Kerry does it just as good."

Turning to Gertrude Spivey, Margarite said, "I've missed you, too, Miss Gertrude."

"You should never have left."

"I don't regret leaving. We had fun. Freedom tastes real good. I'll stay with you, if I'm free to go and come when and where I please after my work is finished."

"What's it going to cost me to get you back? I may not want you if it's too much for you to pay back."

"You haven't changed when it comes to money, Miss Gertrude. There's no charge for me, is there Marshal?"

"Yep. Her fine has been paid by her benefactor."

"Probably that white slut she ran off with."

"Careful, Gertrude. She's free now, but she was attempting to open a house where women entertain men for money. It's illegal in Texas. We don't even have a name for it."

"Ha. It's a whorehouse there same as it is here."

"And it's illegal here, too," Sam retorted.

"Alright, Marshal. Get to it. How much bribe money are you after?"

Sam placed his empty coffee cup on the table and faced Gertrude Spivey unflinchingly eye to eye, "To set the facts straight, Gertrude, I'm here to pay you."

"Dammit, Marshal, stop pussyfooting. What the hell are you up to?"

Sam reached inside his vest and brought out an official legal document. It had been drawn up by the O'Hara Law Firm. It was complete with a legally notarized stamp. After opening the document, Sam unbuttoned his shirt one button above his belt, reached in and pulled out one thousand dollars from his money belt which he placed on the table in front of the Brothel Madame along with the official document.

"Read it. Sign it, and the money is yours," he said.

"I'll be damned. It's that white slut. I knew she'd make out wherever she went. She was too pretty, that one, not to make out."

"It says you will telegraph the Pinkerton's informing them you no longer want Ivy Vanderbilt found, and you will not be responsible for any other expenses involved in her case."

"It's not enough. One thousand is what I paid for her. It don't cover the Pinkerton expense."

"That was your business decision. It was a bad one. That makes it your expense. You're lucky to get your investment back."

"You drive a hard bargain, Marshal."

"Not me. Ivy."

"I'll sign. I can use the money. My business has taken a plummet since she ran away. I wish she'd come back. I'd make her a partner."

"No chance. Remember to send that telegram. I have this document which I will take to the Pinkerton office in Saint Louis to verify you have withdrawn from the case. I won't get to their offices for a month. You'll be paying for all that extra time."

"Of course I'll do it. I gave my word. I'll keep it. I find it strange it takes you that long to get to Saint Louis. You've heard of trains, haven't you?"

"Sure. But, I'm traveling by stagecoach, and I have something more important to do than hunt for the Pinkerton office when I get there."

"I see. I was hoping to interest you in spending a night or two with one of my girls. I'll cut you a deal."

"Sorry, Gertrude. There was a time I would have accepted and enjoyed your offer."

"Nothing would stop a man from having a tussle with a girl on Basin Street except another woman. How about it, Marshal. Another woman?"

"Yep. A fine lady."

"She must be if you're passing up what New Orleans has to offer."

"Gertrude, you can help me. I need a gift. Ivy told me you are a woman who dresses well. I'm driving a stagecoach. A coach and slippers make up a fairy tale. Tell me the name of a nice Shoppe where I might find a pair of silver slippers. I'm no Prince, and there are no glass slippers, and life is no Fairy Tale, but I thought a pair of silver slippers might please her."

"Something like that coming from a nice man would please me. I have a pair of white satin slippers that I bought for Ivy I'll give them to you for her. They're very pretty."

"The size would be a bit too small. Tell me the name of the Shoppe and I'll get her a pair one size larger."

"Don't do that. I wear one size larger. I always bought Ivy and me the same clothes but properly sized. I have a pair I'll give. I know they'll make her happy. They have low heels. They're dancing slippers. Do you dance, Marshal?"

"I do."

"Your lady dancing in my slippers. Oh My. What will life think of next? I'll enjoy the thought, Marshal."

Chapter Fifty

Sam, as he was climbing up on the stagecoach to take the reins, addressed Jimbo, "I'll drive through the narrow streets of the French Quarter. When we're a suitable distance out of town, I'll let you drive awhile. We'll swap off that way until we get to Saint Louis and see your mother."

And my bride, Sam thought.

And Sam liked his next thought well enough to say it out loud.

He said: "I'm not on a fool's errand. Old Bill told me he did bridegroom duties until he was eighty. I'm only seventy."

Jimbo Winslow heard, but he was young enough it made no impression.